INTERNATIONAL

SCANDAL

SCANDAL

A Novel by
SHUSAKU ENDO

Translated from the Japanese by
Van C. Gessel

VINTAGE INTERNATIONAL
Vintage Books
A Division of Random House, Inc.
New York

FIRST VINTAGE INTERNATIONAL EDITION,
OCTOBER 1989

Library of Congress Cataloging-in-Publication Data
Endō, Shūsaku, 1923–
   [Sukyandaru. English]
   Scandal: a novel by Shusaku Endo; translated from
the Japanese by Van C. Gessel. — 1st Vintage
International ed.
   p.   cm.
   Translation of: Sukyandaru.
   ISBN 0-679-72355-2: $8.95
   I. Title.
PL849.N4S8813   1989   89-40149
895.6'35—dc20   CIP

Manufactured in the United States of America

10 9 8 7 6 5 4 3 2 1

SCANDAL

CHAPTER ONE

THE OLD CHAIR seemed to need oiling: when the doctor finished examining the charts and swiveled toward his patient, it gave out a squeak. Suguro's ears had grown accustomed to that sound over the course of his visits to this hospital. After the chair shrilled, the doctor always began his pep talk in deliberate tones, and today was no exception.

"The GOT level is forty-three, and the GPT is fifty-eight. That's, well, a bit above normal this time, so you need to take it easy. That time when you overdid things, these numbers exceeded four hundred, didn't they?"

"Yes."

"If you develop cirrhosis, there's a danger it might turn into cancer. Once again, I'm warning you not to overdo it."

Relief swept over Suguro like a gust of warm steam. In the month since his previous exam, his work had put considerable strain on his body, and he had been worried about today's results. But as he thanked the doctor, Suguro thought, *Now I can attend the awards ceremony without any worries.*

For some reason, a serene composure always came over Suguro when he saw the Imperial Palace towering silently in the rain. Of the many Tokyo landscapes, he was particularly fond of this one. The hired car skirted around the palace moat as it headed toward the banquet hall.

That evening, Suguro was to receive a literary prize for a novel on which he had worked for three years. He had collected many awards during his career as a novelist. Now that he had passed the age of sixty-five, he could not quite repress the feeling that tonight's honor was a bit overdue. Still, the accolades showered upon the novel massaged his sense of pride. There was more to it than pride, though. The harmony he had finally been able to achieve with this recent work, both in his life and in his writings, was deeply satisfying. Suguro leaned against the armrest of the car and studied the raindrops trickling down the window.

The car stopped and a porter opened the door. His uniform smelled damp. Beyond the automatic door at the entrance, a young representative of the publishing house that was sponsoring this evening's gathering stood waiting to welcome Suguro.

"Congratulations! This is a very happy occasion for me, too." Kurimoto had supervised the editing of Suguro's novel, and he had provided additional help by gathering source material and making scrupulous arrangements for the research trips that Suguro had taken.

"I owe it all to you."

"Let's not overdo it. But this award means a great deal, since it's for the novel that really closes the circle on everything you've written up till now. Shall we go into the lobby? The selection-committee judges have already arrived."

The ceremony began precisely at the hour engraved on the invitation. The seats for the prizewinner and the judges were on a raised platform, to either side of a tall microphone. Before them, about a hundred guests were seated. The opening remarks of the president of the publishing company were followed by a speech from Kanō, one of the members of the selection committee.

Suguro and Kanō had been friends for over thirty years. They had made their literary debuts almost simultaneously. As young writers, their relationship had been characterized by a mutual apprehension about one another's creative efforts. Sometimes they repelled each other, sometimes they resounded in harmony. Around the age of forty, they had a clear sense of how different they were as writers and went their separate ways.

Kanō, reciting his impressions of Suguro's novel as he looked out over the invited audience, stood with his right shoulder hunched. Both he and Suguro had suffered from tuberculosis as young men, and both had undergone restorative surgery. Whenever weariness overcame them, the shoulder that had borne the brunt of the operation invariably jutted upward. Kanō's advanced age was compacted into the slope of his shoulder. Like Suguro, who now had liver problems, Kanō had suffered from a weak heart for many years, and he kept a vial of nitroglycerin in his pocket.

"Suguro was raised here in Japan as a Christian. In one sense, that was a blessing for him, I think, while in another it was a curse."

3

Kanō, known for his glib delivery, began his speech with phrases intended to draw the interest and curiosity of his listeners toward the central motifs in Suguro's writing.

"Suguro's curse lies in the fact that he must depict his God, a slippery being for us Japanese, as though He could be grasped within a Japanese setting. That is why in the early days no one danced to his pipe. From the very beginning, Suguro agonized over how to convey what he wanted to say—the story of his God—to the many Japanese who had no ears to hear. I first got to know him over thirty years ago, when the war was still on. In those days, he always had a glum look on his face."

Thirty-odd years ago—Suguro pictured in his mind the second floor of a little bar called Fukusuke near Meguro Station. The room was always filled with the musty odor of worn tatami mats. One summer evening, a sun-bleached bamboo blind hung aslant against the window, and in the street someone was blowing a bugle. Five or six young men were leaning against the walls of the room, hugging their knees as they ruthlessly dissected Suguro. A calendar on one wall featured the proud pose of a young woman wearing a bathing suit and sunglasses. The sunglasses were a fad, which the girls of the time had copied from the women who gave their bodies to the Occupation Forces. One of the group criticizing Suguro was Kanō, a thin young man with prominent cheekbones.

"Somehow I don't believe in what you write, Suguro." A man named Shiba poked into his ear with his little finger as he spoke. "You don't yet have a firm grasp on who you really are. You're still writing just from your head. It doesn't feel like the real thing."

Suguro could not refute Shiba's assertions.

"Some parts of your stories are, well, you just haven't bit

into them with your own teeth. There's nothing wrong with talking about God, but it's all very suspect when it seems as if you're trotting out some Westerner's ideas."

Shiba turned up his eyes and peered at Suguro as he spoke. He seemed to be measuring the depth of the wounds his words were inflicting on Suguro.

"Listen, fiction and essays are two different things. Have you ever thought about whether an image can really carry the burden of the themes you're trying to present? I'm very skeptical myself."

The urge to vindicate himself rose as far as Suguro's throat, but to give voice to it would only widen the intractable rift between Suguro and his friends.

None of you has any idea how difficult it is for a Christian to write fiction in Japan. With a grimace Suguro swallowed these words along with the few gulps of beer left in his glass. At the same time, a part of himself could not deny Shiba's claim that his work was suspect. He felt as though he were always concealing something in a distant corner of his heart.

"In those days Suguro was like a persecuted child in our group. We went as far as insisting that he abandon his Christianity. For us young men after the war, religion was what Freud described as a magnification of the father image derived from an Oedipal complex, the opiate of Marx's doctrine, an irrational superstitiousness. And Christians were hypocrites who had gone against their Japanese origins—in short, we couldn't understand why Suguro wouldn't cast off the troublesome foreign God. Besides, he hadn't been converted of his own free will. He had merely been baptized as a child at the behest of his late mother. So his faith seemed to us nothing more than force of habit. As you know, Suguro later published several historical novels about the early Christians in Japan, describing the pathetic believers who were forced into apostasy by brutish officers. I've often thought that Suguro had me in mind when he created those cruel officers."

The audience laughed. Suguro smiled wryly, noting how polished his friend's speech was. The eyes of every guest in the tiny hall were drawn toward Kanō.

"At such times, he would always exculpate himself by claiming that a man whom God has claimed can never escape His grasp. Of course none of us fell for that gibberish. But Suguro has firmly substantiated that claim in thirty years or more as a novelist. He has adopted as the central theme of his writing how to bring his religion into harmony with the Japanese climate. That desperate battle has been waged in the stories he has written over the years. And his present novel represents the fruits of his victory."

Kanō built a rhythm in his speech, first by making his audience laugh, and then by drawing them tightly into his net. That rhythm elicited an immediate response in the faces of many of the women seated in the packed hall. Kanō was sensitive to such responses and seemed to be constantly evaluating the effectiveness of his speech by stealing glances at those faces.

"But Suguro's distinction as a writer lies in the fact that he has never sacrificed his literature for the sake of his religion. He has never relegated his art to the role of servant to a faith that someone like myself could never accept. In other words, Suguro as a novelist has thrust his hands into aspects of life that his Church undoubtedly abhors—the evil, loathsome, filthy acts of men. That is why his literature has never become subservient to his faith."

Kanō knew just how to stroke Suguro's ego. He was quite right in saying that such problems had caused Suguro anguish at one point in time.

Suguro remembered the words of an old foreign priest

who had earned his trust: "Why you don't write stories that are nicer, more beautiful?"

Suguro had known that priest from his childhood. Before the war, the priest had been a ragpicker in the slums of Osaka, and at the same time had cared for the suffering and looked after orphans. The Japanese who knew him considered the priest a foreign counterpart of Ryōkan, the benevolent medieval Buddhist monk. Whenever Suguro spoke face to face with him, the priest's wine-colored eyes and childlike smile melted his stubborn heart. Each time he laid eyes on the priest, Suguro was reminded of the biblical passage "Blessed are the meek."

One day the priest, with a look that suggested some deep sorrow in his heart, muttered to Suguro, "I read your novel over the New Year. It is full of difficult words, but I read it just the same. May I ask you a question?"

"Yes."

"Why you don't write stories that are nicer, more beautiful?"

His remark and the look of profound sorrow on his face continued to jab Suguro in the heart when he sat in his tiny study scribbling away with a pencil.

Still, he was never able to write a single more beautiful, nicer novel. His pen somehow persisted in depicting the black, dark, ugly realms within his characters. As a novelist, he could not bring himself to skirt over or ignore any of the components of a human being.

And yet he sensed that as he described the murky hearts of his characters, his own mind, too, became cloudy. In order to sketch a repellent heart, his own heart had to become loathsome. To reproduce jealousy, he was forced to demean himself, submerge himself in envy. The more he wrote, the more did he become aware of the kind of stench that reeked from deep inside each person. In one period of his life, while he wrote of that stench, he was constantly reminded of the face of the priest and of those words of his: "Why you don't write stories that are nicer, more beautiful?"

In time, Suguro began to feel that he had found his own personal answer to this question. He had the notion that a true religion should be able to respond to the dark melodies, the faulty and hideous sounds that echo from the hearts of men. As he continued to write, that notion turned into something close to assurance, rescuing him from his uneasiness.

"The uniqueness of Suguro's literature lies in his discovery of a new meaning and value for what religion refers to as sin. Sadly, being without religion myself, I haven't the slightest idea what sin is. . . ." Kanō paused there, allowing for a sardonic interval of silence. Enticed by the silence, several members of the audience began to laugh.

"After a period of groping his way through the darkness, during which time he gleefully depicted the sins of mankind, Suguro began to assert that a yearning for rebirth lies concealed within each act of sin. Within every sin, he suggests, lurks the desire of men to find a way of escaping from the suffocating lives we lead today. I think that's what is original in Suguro's literature. And in his latest novel, these unique concepts are portrayed with considerable maturity."

Kanō's voice took on a subdued tone, as though he were remembering something from the distant past. "It's over thirty years since I first met Suguro. I suppose that for the past decade or so, he has felt very much like the poet Bashō when he wrote:

> *None to accompany me on this path:*
> *Nightfall in autumn.*

"When one of us novelists passes the age of fifty, we may be impressed by what our old friends write, but we are no longer influenced by their work. All that is left for us is to continue digging, one stroke of the hoe at a time, deepening the hole that is our literature until the day we die. I think Suguro must share my feelings in this regard."

With his audience listening intently, Kanō was concluding his speech.

Kurimoto stood behind the rows of chairs. It was his task to direct late arrivals to their seats, but he was also trying to catch a glimpse of Suguro as he was handed the award. After the ceremony, Suguro wanted to thank this young man for all the work he had done behind the scenes while the novel was being written.

A woman from the editorial staff of another publishing firm was standing next to Kurimoto. Suguro did not know her name, but when he visited Kurimoto's office he often ran into her at the entrance. She was small in stature, but he remembered her well because of the air of charm she revealed on her plump, dimpled face. Behind Kurimoto and this woman he saw another face.

Suguro blinked. It was, indisputably, his own face. It wore an expression that could be taken either as a grin or a sneer.

He blinked several more times. There was no one standing behind the two editors.

The reception got under way.

In various parts of the room, circles had formed around popular writers and illustrators. When Suguro closed his eyes, the high-pitched, laughing voices and din blended with the countless footsteps scuffling across the hard floor, all of which sounded like flour being ground in a mortar. Other guests had clustered in front of the tables offering sushi and noodles; conspicuous among them were the white faces of the hostesses who had come to serve.

"Thank you for a very nice speech." Suguro tapped the hunched right shoulder of Kanō, who was amusing a group of three or four editors with his patter.

"Ah, do you think it was all right?" To cover his embarrassment, Kanō quickly changed the subject. "You look like you've lost weight. Are you OK?"

"I'm fine. But at our age, physical problems of all kinds come as no surprise."

"That's what we were just talking about here—how my memory has become noticeably worse recently. I can't recall a thing about a book I've just finished reading. Sometimes, at parties like this, I can't for the life of me remember the names of people I'm talking with."

"I'm just the same."

"They say your eyes are the first to go, then your teeth, then something else. With me, it's eyes, then memory, then teeth. That's not even including my heart, which has always been bad."

"What about the other faculties?" a young editor asked.

" 'Other faculties?' Diminished, of late. How about you, Suguro?" Kanō's eyes flashed mischievously. "Of course you're a Christian, and you have one of those model wives. But didn't you play around at all until you were too old? Or maybe you are up to something you haven't told us about?"

"Now why would I go jabbering secrets to people that I haven't even told my wife?"

Unlike when he was younger, Suguro now knew how to respond to the harmless taunts of his circle.

After lingering in one group for a while, he moved away to greet some other people. Two of the elder statesmen of the literary establishment, Segi and Iwashita, were chatting together.

"Suguro, this new novel is the best you've written," the critic, Iwashita, his face flushed and a glass of wine in his hand, cloyingly complimented Suguro. Since he was Suguro's senior in the literary world as well as a graduate of the same university, Iwashita was always looking for ways to take Suguro under his wing. "Don't you agree?" Iwashita tried to elicit a similar endorsement from Segi Michio, also a critic.

"I do have reservations," the plump Segi stated, forcing a smile, "but this is a day for congratulations, so I'll keep my opinions to myself."

"Don't mind him. Segi's always brutal."

"It's a critic's job to be brutal."

These verbal exchanges were the special province of the literary world. For over thirty years, Suguro had heard more of these exchanges at parties, bars, and round-table discussions than he could hope to count. But as he went through the motions of sipping at the glass of diluted liquor that a waitress had brought him, Suguro wondered what aspect of his novel Segi might single out for attack, and felt he knew what it would be.

But there's nothing I can do about it, even if they are critical, he protested to himself, while outwardly still smiling. *I've brought my life and my writing into harmony in this novel. There's no way I can upset that harmony, no matter what anyone says.* With satisfaction, he remembered Kurimoto saying that in this work he had closed the circle on everything he had written. When someone came to pay his respects to the two critics, Suguro took advantage of the interruption and walked away to join another group.

"Sensei!" A woman Suguro had never seen before, who was perhaps twenty-seven or twenty-eight, tugged familiarly at his jacket. A splotch of lipstick was displayed on her front teeth as she grinned at him. In her right hand she clutched a lighted cigarette, in her left a glass of liquor.

"Sensei, have you forgotten me?"

Suguro batted his eyes. As Kanō had said, he was at an age when he often forgot the names and faces of people he had met only once or twice.

"How horrible of you." Again she spoke with familiarity and laughed. "We met at Shinjuku. I was drawing portraits on the street corner . . ."

"Where?"

"On Sakura Street. You do some very naughty things on that street, Sensei."

"You're confusing me with someone else. That wasn't me."

"Don't play the innocent. You said you'd come to see the exhibition of our pictures. Remember—you had my friend do your portrait. And after that . . ."

She was probably drunk. Still clutching Suguro's jacket, she gave a meaningful wink. The blotch of lipstick on her teeth marked her as a kindred spirit with the fledgling designers and aspiring actresses who lolled around the streets of Shinjuku and Roppongi.

"I think you've mistaken me for somebody else."

"Oh, I understand. You don't want anybody to know you were having a party with us in the middle of the night. Because you're a Christian. Of course, we must keep a distinction between appearance and reality."

Suguro jerked his jacket from the hand of the clinging woman and tried to walk toward another group of people. A newspaper photographer had just aimed his camera at Suguro, who instinctively forced a smile onto his taut face.

"Oh, what a lovely pose!" she said, leering from the side. "Was that appearance or reality, Sensei?"

The surrounding guests turned toward them. It was obvious that they were staring at Suguro. He deliberately shrugged his shoulders as if to say, "I don't know what's going on here," but he had to force himself to keep smiling.

Kurimoto broke in and physically escorted the woman away. When he returned, he said, "I'm very sorry. I've no idea who brought her here. I put her in the elevator and sent her on her way."

"I didn't know what to do. She was awfully insistent. . . ." Suguro was concerned that Kurimoto might actually be suspicious of him. "She said she had met me late one night in Sakura Street in Shinjuku."

"Yes, she was quite shrill."

"Where is Sakura Street?"

"It's at Kabuki-chō. . . ." Kurimoto hesitated for a moment. "The street's lined with peep shows and porno shops."

"She claimed I was playing around there."

"She said the same thing out in the hall. I snapped back at her pretty severely—told her you would never go to such a place."

Suguro nodded in relief. Kurimoto was a somber sort of man who would probably go around issuing stern denials to everyone at the reception who had heard the conversation— denials that there was any truth to her story.

The rain had stopped, but several puddles dotted the roadway. Vacant taxis sped by one after another, splashing water in their wake. The woman raised her hand to hail a cab but seemed to change her mind and set out walking in the direction of Tokyo Station. A sudden gust of wind filled the black cape she was wearing. Kobari, who was trailing her, was reminded of a bat spreading its wings.

Near the entrance to the subway, he spoke to her. "They gave you a bad time back there, didn't they?"

She stopped walking, and her body stiffened. "Who are you?"

"Sorry. I'm a correspondent for a weekly magazine. Of course, the journal I work for isn't as genteel as the publishers that sponsored the reception tonight. But that's what gives us our spark." He proceeded with a line of questioning he had assimilated as part of his job. "You were lying back there, weren't you? Claiming that Mr. Suguro would fool around at some shady spot in Shinjuku. I didn't believe a word of it."

"You can call it a lie if you want. There's no point in asking me about it if you think I made it all up."

"If it's true, then tell me about it. I'll make it worth your while."

"I don't like dirty tricks. You'll turn it into an article for your magazine, won't you?"

"Oh no," Kobari quickly protested. "I have no intention of writing it up. I just have a personal interest in whether Mr. Suguro would really go to a place like that."

"There's no reason for me to lie. To begin with, it was Mr. Suguro who invited me to come to the reception."

"Really? He invited you to the reception? Now, I just want to make sure, but it definitely was Mr. Suguro?"

"Of course it was."

"Where on Sakura Street did you meet him?"

"In front of a shop called Sweet Honey. He was just coming out of it."

"Are you really an artist?"

"Is there something wrong with being an artist?"

"Do you have exhibitions?"

"Why would you ask something like that?"

"I could feature you as a rising new talent in our magazine."

He thrust a business card at her. She accepted it, but there was still a touch of anger in her voice when she replied, "I'm having an exhibition near Takeshita Street at Harajuku. On the twenty-seventh."

"Perfect. Now, tell me everything you know about Suguro."

Kobari gave her a syrupy look and placed a hand on her shoulder. She brushed it away and scurried down the subway stairs, her cape fluttering.

"Wait! Damn it. At least send me an announcement of the exhibition," Kobari called down the stairs, but she was nowhere to be seen.

So, it's true, is it? He felt as though the vague impressions he had felt each time he looked at a photograph of Suguro in a newspaper or magazine had finally been substantiated.

Of late he had had nothing to do with literature, but in his college days Kobari had ardently hoped to become a novelist himself. But even then he had been unable to abide the odor of religiosity that hovered over Suguro's books. The bastard really spreads it thick, he had thought.

As a student, Kobari had been inspired by dialectical materialism, and he was ill at ease with those like Suguro who deluded the masses through their belief in the opiate of religion. Memories from his childhood were also entangled in these feelings. As a boy, he had gone several times to the neighborhood Protestant church to take English lessons. The bespectacled, flat-chested woman evangelist had taken a dislike to Kobari and often heaped sarcasm and insult on him. She did that because Kobari had stayed only for the English lessons and hurried back home when the minister came in to preach. But later in his life, he thought of that woman evangelist every time he heard the word "religion."

He went down the subway stairs, but there was no sign of the woman either near the ticket machines or on the platform of the Hibiya-line train. But Kobari was too absorbed in the pleasurable feelings that welled in his chest to care. The task of dragging in the mud a writer who turned out such pompous stories was an assignment well worth the writing for this reporter. A senior journalist, he recalled, was the one who had driven Prime Minister Tanaka from power, and as he waited for the train he repeated, almost hummed to himself over and over, the name of the shop the woman had mentioned: "Sweet Honey, Sweet Honey."

The train was crammed with the weary stench of life. Kobari hung on to a strap in front of a young woman whose legs were spread open sloppily and a middle-aged man who was inscribing red circles on a racing form. Once again Kobari thought of the reception. He had gate-crashed the party in search of material for a story and had chanced to be standing right next to Suguro when the woman had caught hold of his jacket. He had identified an alarm on Suguro's face that was more than simple embarrassment. It was evidence that the woman's words were not a lie.

Fraud!

Perhaps he had hit upon the source of his distrust for Suguro's novels. A man who sneaked glances at naked women in peep shows and fondled hostesses at petting parlors was, with those same hands, committing to paper lofty phrases of high moral content.

The suit that the woman had tugged at looked to be woven

of expensive material. When he compared that with his own clothing, enmity welled up once more inside Kobari. He turned his eyes to the darkness that lay beyond the subway windows. Back in his apartment, he sat down beside the disheveled, sleeping figure of the woman he lived with and drank the last few swigs of a bottle of whiskey.

Two or three days later, Kobari paid a visit to a part of Kabuki-chō in Shinjuku that was very familiar to him—the area lined with peep shows and Turkish baths. It required little effort to locate Sweet Honey. Kobari found it in a building known as the Porno Emporium, where separate floors were allocated to the showing of films, to shops that peddled magazines, and to Turkish baths. When Kobari stepped into the elevator, it was still early evening, and the emporium had not yet attracted many customers. Still, the elevator reeked of the rancid stench of men. He showed the man at the reception desk a photograph of Suguro that he had cut out of a literary anthology and asked, "Does this man come here often?"

The clerk shook his head and waffled, "We have a lot of clients. You can't expect me to remember every single one."

Even flesh traders seem to feel an obligation not to divulge the secrets of their clientele unless the inquiry comes from the police. In fact, when he questioned two or three other merchants in the building, Kobari got the same answer and was flashed the same vacant smile.

These men were not alone in giving Kobari a contemptuous look. When he related the incident at the reception desk to an old school chum who had worked with him on a literary journal at the university, his friend's face paled with distaste. "You really don't believe what she said, do you?"

Confident that this friend would side with him, Kobari could not mask his disappointment when he responded, "What's that supposed to mean?"

"You've finally turned into a sordid wretch, haven't you?" spat his friend. "Do you get some kind of kick out of dreaming up a groundless scandal and trying to drag down a writer like Suguro? I realize, of course, that that's the fashion in journalism these days."

Kobari was piqued, but the thought that he alone could unload a bombshell that would startle the reading public sent tingles of indescribable pleasure shooting down his spine.

Whenever he had an appointment or went out drinking with his fellow journalists, Kobari tried to arrange to meet them along the Golden Avenue in Shinjuku. On his way home, he would stroll through Kabuki-chō. No matter how many times he ambled along those streets, however, he never caught sight of Suguro or the woman artist.

He half felt like giving it all up. But very late one night, when he was buying a ticket from an automatic machine at Shinjuku Station, he happened to glance up, at which moment he caught his breath. The profile of a man who looked very much like Suguro was walking toward the taxi stand, accompanied by a woman wearing glasses. Leaving his change in the machine, Kobari dashed after them, but the pair had already stepped into a taxi. He hailed the next taxi and instructed the driver to follow the departing vehicle.

Through the rear window of the taxi ahead, Kobari saw

the woman rest her head on the man's right shoulder. The taxi drove along the Kōshū Highway and headed toward Yoyogi.

Eventually, Kobari's driver said uncomfortably, "They seem to be heading for the love-hotel district. Shall I keep following them?"

"Yes. Stop a little beyond where they do."

At Yoyogi, the first taxi stopped outside a mansion with an imposing gate. Kobari's cab slipped unobtrusively past and parked seventy or eighty meters ahead. By that time, the man and woman had disappeared. Kobari went to look at the mansion. A nameplate read YOYOGI SWAN HOTEL. A row of Himalayan cedars stretched blackly from the gate as far as the carriage entrance. Kobari inquired at the front desk, but he was curtly turned away, the desk attendant denying that any guests had checked in.

Suguro made a daily pilgrimage from his home to the office he rented near Harajuku, since he could not do any writing in the hotels and inns where many of his writer-friends worked. He was unable to collect his thoughts unless he was seated at the familiar desk in the tiny room filled with the smells of his own body.

There were other requisites. From long years of experience, he knew that the room needed to be small and dark and that it had to maintain the proper humidity. The office had three rooms in addition to the kitchen and bathroom. He used the largest room to receive visitors. There he met people from publishing houses and newspapers. The medium-sized room became his bedroom when he worked late into the night. The vital room, where he did his writing, had apparently been used as a storeroom by the foreign family who had rented the apartment before him. It received very little sunlight, and because of the thick curtain that hung over the window, he had to turn on his desk lamp even at midday. But since these conditions perfectly suited the demands of his subconscious, he had converted the room into his study.

Last year a photographer had come to take pictures of his office for a magazine feature entitled "An Author's Study." When Suguro explained his reasons for choosing this room for his work, the photographer had promptly declared, "This room is very much like a mother's womb. You must have a strong desire to return to the womb." He had gone on to explain that the yearning to return to the womb was a furtive urge to revert to the state before life had stirred within the mother's uterus—to go back to a state of sleep within the amniotic fluid. To describe it another way, it was not so much a yearning for life as a desire for death, for eternal rest.

Each morning when he unlocked the door to his office, Suguro went into that tiny room and sat down in the same chair he had used for many years. He would first glance at the photograph of his late mother that hung on the wall. Then he would look fondly at his desk lamp, at the clock that ticked with precise regularity, and at his Chinese penholder. The expression on his mother's face in the photograph changed from day to day. One day she would look very happy, another day she would look glum. Suguro felt that the marks she had left on his life ran deep. He had been baptized because of his mother's influence.

In any case, the novels he had produced over the past decade—*The Voice of Silence, In the Wilderness,* and *The Emissary*—had been completed by the accumulation of his daily labors, much in the way an ant transports its food one granule at a time.

No doubt it was the same for other writers, but for Suguro the process of creating any given work of fiction was comparable to entering an alien land without a map. Being a cautious sort of person, he never considered setting out on that journey until all his travel preparations were complete, from the careful selection of his themes to determining the time he would need to gather his material. Still, there were many times when he had no idea where he was being led, and all he could discern through the faint light were the blurred outlines of his point of departure. The road ahead was veiled in dense darkness. For the space of fifteen years, he had undertaken many of these stressful journeys, making his way forward with groping hands, and all within the confines of this tiny room.

With the awards ceremony behind him, Suguro tasted the same bitterness of the literary journey in his study. To plan a new short story, he drew the curtain and sat hunched like a watchmaker over his desk, dimly lit by the lamp. But even though he made some notes, the usual inspiration did not come.

Normally he would spend over half a day at this replica of manual labor, hearing nothing but the sounds of his pencil scratching across the surface of the paper, and he enjoyed the effort despite its attendant pain. But of late, that joy lay dormant in his breast.

Setting his pencil down, he tried to dispel the anxieties that impaired his work. The face and words of the drunken woman who had accosted him at the reception clung to him like an ink stain on his middle finger.

"We met at Shinjuku. You do some very naughty things, Sensei. . . . Oh, I understand. You don't want anybody to know you were having a party with us in the middle of the night."

An air of intimacy and the stench of alcohol had clung to

each of the words spewed out from between her lipstick-splotched teeth. It was absurd for him to be so immobilized by the remarks of a drunken woman.

He rotated his head sharply five or six times and reread part of his manuscript. He always scrawled his first drafts in tiny characters on the back of the manuscript paper, corrected them in colored pencil or pen, and then hired a secretary to make a clean copy of the final version.

> Perhaps because of his advanced age, recently he had slept very lightly, having several dreams in the space of one night. All of the dreams were distinct; when he had finished with one, he immediately awakened. Once he was awake, he would stare into the darkness for a while, thinking only of the death that would eventually overtake him. He had turned sixty-five this year.

He took a red ballpoint pen from its holder and changed "All of the dreams were" to "Each one of the dreams was." As he made the correction, he sensed that old age would be the principal motif of this story.

The telephone rang. He picked up the receiver, irritated at the interruption, and heard the familiar, staid voice identify its owner.

"This is Kurimoto. I wanted to know how the short story is coming."

"I've managed to get about halfway through it."

"What's the title?"

"I'm thinking of calling it 'His Declining Years.' "

Kurimoto said nothing for a moment. Then: "I'm sorry about what happened. Yes, I mean the drunk woman. It was chaotic at the reception desk, so I still haven't been able to find out who brought her there."

"I'm sure you haven't. I mean, I've never seen the woman

before in my life." Suguro made his point emphatically and waited for Kurimoto's reaction.

"Actually, a postcard addressed to you has come care of us. It appears to be from her. The name on the card is Ishiguro Hina. Apparently she wasn't lying when she said she was a street artist. It's an invitation to an exhibition."

"What makes you think it's the same woman?"

"On the back . . . ," Kurimoto stumbled, "she's written, 'Liar. You're a liar, Sensei.' . . . What do you want me to do with the card?"

Suguro started to say it was of no use to him, but then he hesitated. He did not want to see the postcard, but at the same time he did not wish to leave something of that nature in Kurimoto's hands.

"I can't think. Well, why don't you send it along." He gave a casual laugh, hoping that the young editor would not sense his agitation.

After he had hung up, he felt more unsettled than before. *She's relentless.*

He remembered the persistence with which she had clung to his sleeve at the party, and he intuitively sensed danger in shelving the matter in case it developed into a major controversy. To dispel his anxiety, he blinked his eyes several times; it was a habit with him.

Two days later, the postcard that Kurimoto had forwarded was included in the mail delivered to his office. Ishiguro Hina, a name that sounded like that of an artiste, had been printed on the invitation with a paintbrush. He was surprised to discover that her exhibition was to be held on Takeshita Street, not far from his office. Just as Kurimoto had said, scribbled on the back of the card with a ball-point pen were the words *Liar. You're a liar, Sensei.* Suguro averted his eyes, as though he had seen something of ill

23

omen, then tore up the invitation and threw it into the waste-basket.

> Recently I had a dream in which I met Akutagawa Ryū-nosuke. He was wearing a rumpled summer kimono, and sat with his arms folded and his eyes downcast. He did not utter a word, but suddenly he stood up, parted the bamboo curtain behind him, and went into the next room. I knew that the neighboring room was the world of the dead. But soon the curtain opened again and Akutagawa came back into the room where I sat.

Suguro wrote the words as he hunched over his desk, then read them aloud softly to test the tone of the passage. This section was not fictive, but an experience he had actually had some two months before. He remembered that when he awoke in the middle of the night from that dream, his wife had been sleeping peacefully at his side.

Of course he had not told his wife about the dream. Ever since his son, Tatsunosuke, who worked for a trading company, had moved to America with his wife, Masako, Suguro had made a point of not mentioning anything that would cause his wife the slightest worry. Since their marriage, in fact, he had, unlike other novelists, presented himself to the world as an upright husband and father—not because he was a Christian, but from the knowledge that the typical novelist's pose as a scoundrel did not suit his nature. Whatever he might write about in his fiction, Suguro had decided that in his daily life, and in the face he presented to the world, he wanted to be an ordinary citizen. So in his relationship with his wife, he rarely did anything that would upset the balance they had established in their lives.

Twice a week, his wife came to clean his office. On these occasions, he put on his family-man face, a look different from the one he wore when he was writing. For Suguro, the donning of a different face did not entail artifice of any kind, nor did it connote playacting or hypocrisy.

His wife, who suffered from arthritis, developed aches in her knees and in the joints of her hands during the rainy season and in the autumn. This was the result of the debilitating effort of taking care of her husband thirty years earlier, during the course of his long stay in the hospital and three thoracic operations. On cold days, he felt deeply indebted to her as he watched her push the vacuum cleaner. If he suggested they hire some help, she always laughed and shook her head.

In the seasons when her limbs did not ache, they would sometimes have lunch together and then go out for a walk. They always took the same route: they walked down the slope at the front of his office, passed through Yoyogi Park, and went along Omote Sandō before returning to the office. They would sit together on a bench in the park, watching the young people play badminton. Even if they said nothing to each other, after more than thirty years of marriage there was a poised tranquillity between them that Suguro could feel almost palpably as she sat beside him. When the pages of his manuscript lay before him, he was a novelist who peered into the depths of his soul, and he disgorged what he found there. But as a husband he was careful not to expose himself beyond the essential boundaries. That was his way of showing compassion to his wife, who had been raised in a Christian home and educated at a convent school.

On the weekend after Suguro had destroyed the invitation to the art exhibition, his wife had been unable to come to his office because of a mishap to one of her relatives, so Suguro spent both Saturday and Sunday at the office, making corrections to his story. On those afternoons, from behind the drawn curtain he could hear the merry voices of many people, faint in the distance.

At the time the afternoon sun began to wane, he left the office and climbed down the slender, sloping path. As always, his stroll took him toward Yoyogi Park. Recently, the roads to the park had been jammed with groups of young men and women—famous now in Tokyo and styled the "Bamboo Shoot" generation from the name of the Harajuku boutique where punk fashion originated—as well as those who had come to gawk at them. They formed rings here and there and danced bizarre dances to music blaring from cassette players. Both sexes wore long pink and white robes like Korean native garb, and even the young men wore rouge on their cheeks. The nature of the groups varied from circle to circle, each dancing in step to a different leader. Joining the throng of spectators, Suguro watched the dancing beside a foreigner who was filming it with an eight-millimeter camera. When he had been the same age as these young people, Japan was fighting in China in the prologue to an even larger war. It was a reflex action for his generation to recall such events. He could not arrest the memory even if he tried.

When he stepped back from the crowd, Suguro accidentally trampled on the foot of a young woman who was standing behind him.

"Oh, sorry!"

The girl crinkled her eyes good-naturedly and flashed him a sweet smile. But her face soon wrinkled in pain, and she lifted her right foot.

Out of concern, Suguro asked, "Are you hurt? Take your shoe off and let's have a look."

"I'm all right." She tried to force a smile.

"Sit on the bench over here. Take a look at your toes."

She sat down as she was told and removed the tennis shoe,

which was muddy at the toe, along with her sock. She looked rather embarrassed as she did so.

"They're fine."

"Your foot looks a little red to me. Why don't we go to a pharmacy?"

"I don't need anything."

"Well, at least let me buy you a drink or something." He pointed to the row of stalls rimming the park, which sold everything from hot dogs to vegetable pancakes. "What would you like?"

"I said I was fine . . ."

"I'd be more than happy to buy you something."

"Well, maybe a cola."

When he came back with a cola in a paper cup, she was shaking her foot back and forth.

"Mister, does this place interest you?"

"You young people have a lot of energy."

"A lot of older men like you come here. Men interested in young girls."

"Really? There can't be very many like that."

"Sure there are. They talk to us when we're walking down Omote Sandō. Middle-aged men, even men as old as you . . ."

"They talk to you—about what?"

She flashed him another smile, this time perhaps because it was difficult for her to say anything in reply.

"Are there girls who say yes?"

"Of course there are. But middle-school girls will only go as far as B. Then they ask for money."

"B?"

"Don't you know what A, B, and C are?" With the same lack of guile she might have used to recite the names of the latest pop singers, she explained that A was kissing, B was petting, and C was the final step.

She had chubby cheeks. Suguro was filled with envy for

the long life that still stretched out before her, in contrast to him.

"How old are you, mister?"

"I'm an old man."

"But you don't look that old."

"Do you go as far as B?"

"Me? . . . I certainly don't."

"Do girls of your age really need pocket money that badly?"

"Sure we do." Her eyes narrowed in another amiable smile. "My family doesn't have any money. They don't even give me an allowance."

"Your father works, doesn't he?"

"He was run over by a motorcycle four years ago, at Miyamasuzaka. So my mom is selling insurance now. I feel too sorry for her to ask her for money."

"But do you really need that much?"

"Even someone like me has colleagues to get together with. And then . . . I like to buy things for my little brother."

Suguro grinned when she used the grown-up word "colleagues."

"Are you in high school?"

"Middle school."

Humph, still in middle school with a body like that, Suguro thought, glancing again at her ripening breasts and at her thighs, poured into her faded jeans. The girls of his youth, whatever their breasts might have been like, did not have the full thighs of this girl.

"Where do you live?"

"Why do you want to know a thing like that?"

"Don't misunderstand me. I just thought maybe I could find you a part-time job if you need some money."

"What kind of job?" She was smiling affably once again. "They don't allow middle-school students to work. I worked at McDonald's with a friend of mine. We lied and told them we were in high school, but they found us out right away and we were fired."

"In any case, you shouldn't mimic the bad girls. Ignore those approaches from men."

When Suguro started sermonizing, she looked down and began digging at the dirt with the toe of her shoe. "I guess I ought to be going."

As Suguro got up from the bench, he noticed how bedraggled her tennis shoes were. "Just a minute." He pulled his wallet from his pocket. She watched carefully as he put his hand inside it, but when he drew out a five-thousand-yen note and offered it to her, she stepped back apprehensively.

"If you'll promise not to do anything improper, I'll give you this money. Buy some new shoes or something. And I'll try to think of a job you could do. If you're interested, call me here."

He wrote his telephone number on a piece of paper, then walked away without glancing back. He was disgusted with himself for impulsively giving money away in a moment of sentimentality.

At home that evening, as his wife sat knitting, he told her about the girl.

"If she's in middle school, she could clean my office, don't you think?"

"I suppose she could, but I don't know. Are you really serious about employing her?"

"Yes. I promised I'd find her a job. And it would help you out, too." He hated to see his wife massaging her joints and pushing the vacuum cleaner in the winter.

"I don't mind doing the cleaning myself."

"I know that, but . . ."

Usually he never discussed household affairs with her, but this time he stubbornly asserted himself. It would mean killing two birds with one stone. His wife would no longer have to grapple with the vacuum cleaner during the cold and rainy seasons, and the girl wouldn't have to succumb to propositioning.

The girl's name was Morita Mitsu, and when she had come two or three times to clean the office, Suguro's wife, who had been skeptical at first, appeared satisfied.

"She's a very nice girl. From what you said, I wondered what kind of girl she'd be, but she really is an innocent child."

Suguro nodded in relief. "She has a good heart. When I first saw that smile of hers, I wondered if she wasn't a little weak in the head."

"She says she has two younger brothers and a younger sister. When I gave her a piece of cake, she wouldn't eat it herself. She wanted to give it to them. It was so touching. Apparently the surgery her father had after that accident was a failure, and his insides are in terrible shape." His wife had already extracted a wealth of information from Mitsu about her family.

As Suguro's wife said, Mitsu was even less sophisticated than Suguro had imagined. That first Saturday afternoon, she had come by his office after school, and under his wife's direction she pushed the vacuum cleaner around and scrubbed the sinks. With her precocious physique, she was able to take over from Suguro's arthritic wife. She carried cardboard boxes stuffed with magazines down the stairs to the janitor's room, and she even helped with the shopping. After two weeks, she had mastered the routine, and even without Suguro's wife present she managed the cleaning of the reception room and bathroom, singing pop songs as she went.

During a break from his work, Suguro sat down on the sofa and watched as Mitsu cleaned away.

"What's that song?"

He did not even know the names of the young singers who were in vogue, but from Mitsu he learned of such popular performers as Kyon-Kyon and the Shibugaki-tai.

"Sensei, I thought you knew everything, but you really don't know anything at all, do you?" She stopped pushing the vacuum cleaner and teased Suguro, who still confused such trendy singers as Toshi-chan and Mattchi no matter how many times he saw them on television.

"I'm totally ignorant of the world you live in."

"Sensei, would you like me to teach you some middle-school language? What do you think 'getting grounds' means?"

"I don't have the faintest idea."

"That's what you call sneaking into a coffee shop on your way home from school. How about being 'happified'?"

"Beats me."

"You say that when something good happens to you, when you're happy. It's embarrassing to come right out and say you're happy when you're happy. You call your mother 'Eek'! To 'upper' means to shoplift. 'NHK' "—the acronym for the national broadcasting network—"is now applied to a Naughty Horny Kid. To 'haze out' means to cut a class at school, and a 'fishy dish' refers to a girl who pretends to be innocent in sexual matters."

Suguro, fascinated by the phrases that sprang from her mouth one after another, made a note of them all.

When Mitsu set to work, her face flushed and beads of perspiration formed on her cheeks, chin, and throat. The sight of those lightly glistening young drops made Suguro feel almost dizzy, as though he had come close to a flower of overpowering fragrance. In her moist cheeks and throat he sensed something that he himself had lost.

"I can't believe how efficient she's getting," Suguro's wife said one day.

He nodded. "Now aren't you glad I hired her?"

"I wonder if we should take her to church?"

"She'd just be bored. You can forget that idea. Once she gets a little more used to the work, though, the two of us ought to take that trip to Nagasaki we've been talking about."

For some time, Suguro had wanted to take his wife to Nagasaki once the weather turned warmer. Nagasaki and its environs had appeared in several of his novels, but his wife had never been there. She, too, had been looking forward to the trip.

The same night he had had that conversation with his wife, Suguro had a dream. He was looking at his own face in the bathroom mirror at his office. He was surprised by how old he looked. Wrinkles and pockets of flesh circled his eyes, and around his chin were clusters of tiny white spots that looked as if they had been applied with the tip of a toothpick. When he looked closer, he saw that they were whiskers. He had become so old . . . and death was getting closer. He awoke feeling restless.

From the next bed he could hear the soft, regular breathing of his sleeping wife. That breathing always reminded him of the sound of the clock in his study. The ticking of that clock provided him with an indescribable feeling of peace as he hunched over his work. Similarly, the sound of his wife's nocturnal breathing summoned up images of the peaceful composure they had maintained in their marriage. In those breaths, he could smell the untarnished world she had carried with her from her youth. It was the breathing of a woman reared amidst the unassailable love of her parents and siblings, a woman who had never harbored the slightest doubts about what went on in her husband's mind or in his career. That assurance sometimes prompted him to envy and aroused a loathing that he had never so much as thought to express. At such times, his wife's world seemed to smell of soap bubbles.

After he awoke, he fell asleep again and had another dream. Once more there was the mirror in the bathroom (he couldn't understand why mirrors were always showing up in his dreams lately), but this time Mitsu was standing in front of it, dressed only in a freshly washed pair of flowered panties. She was grinning into the mirror, unaware that he was watching her. Between her slightly parted lips he could see her teeth and a slender thread of saliva: the image was a bit too voluptuous for a young girl. Then it seemed she knew Suguro was hiding behind the door and that she was smiling that way on purpose. She called back to him, "Your wife'll be angry."

He woke up. He could still see that grinning face. His wife slept peacefully.

In the darkness, Suguro was ashamed of his profane dream. At the same time, because it was a dream, he did not feel responsible for it. There was no need to feel embarrassment or guilt over a dream. But he realized that he would probably remember the dream every time Mitsu showed up to clean the office, which gave him an odd feeling.

In his diary, he noted obliquely, "Had a bad dream," and recorded nothing further, inwardly fearing that after his death some whimsical publisher might commit his diary to print.

CHAPTER
TWO

SUGURO WAS DISCUSSING his forthcoming work with Kurimoto, who was dressed like a banker in a smart necktie. Even when there were no work plans to discuss, Kurimoto, who neither drank nor smoked, would invariably pay a call on Suguro. He seemed to consider this an editor's duty, and each time Suguro saw that upright face he thought how much better it would have been for Kurimoto to have become a high-school teacher.

Suddenly a vacuum cleaner started up in the next room.

"Is your wife here?" Evidently Kurimoto was startled by the sound, having thought that he and Suguro were alone in the office.

"It's not my wife. That's a middle-school girl we've employed."

"Middle school?"

Suguro related the particulars by which Mitsu had started working for him, speaking in a low voice even though there was no likelihood Mitsu could hear them from the next room above the vacuum cleaner.

"She's much more tenderhearted than she looks. She says there are men at Harajuku who seduce her classmates."

Kurimoto said nothing for a few moments. Then abruptly he asked, "What did you do with that postcard?"

"Postcard?"

"The one I forwarded. . . . You know, *that* postcard."

"Oh—I threw it away, of course." Suguro had assumed that Kurimoto had forgotten the entire incident, and he was caught off guard when his editor asked about it with a solemn face. "There was no reason for me to go to her exhibition."

"As a matter of fact, I went." Kurimoto peered into Suguro's eyes. "I thought I ought to find out what kind of woman she is. In case she tried to make any further trouble for you."

"And?"

"They actually did run an exhibition. Right near Takeshita Street."

Kurimoto seemed to have visited the gallery in an effort to protect the reputation of the author with whom he worked, but to Suguro it was an unwelcome favor. He wanted to put the incident at the reception out of his mind as quickly as possible and had no wish for it to be brought up again.

"Was she there?"

"No. A woman with glasses was keeping an eye on the gallery. She said she was an artist, too."

"What kind of pictures were they?"

"A lot of sound and fury. They all played to the audience. There was one of a fetus in the womb—in fact all of them were on the grotesque, eerie side. Sort of top-heavy, un-digested."

"So I would imagine." Suguro nodded, finding Kuri-moto's descriptions easy to imagine. "I could have guessed as much from the kind of woman who painted them."

"There was a portrait of you."

"Of me?"

"She mentioned it at the reception, remember? That you had her and her friends sketch you at Shinjuku."

"That's ridiculous. I never did anything of the sort."

"I'm just repeating what she said. I think they must have turned the sketch into an oil painting."

Suguro said nothing and blinked his eyes several times. Mitsu must have finished cleaning the next room; the vacuum cleaner had been switched off.

"Did it . . . look like me?" Suguro asked softly.

"On the surface, yes. And forgive me for saying so, but it was a vulgar face."

"Vulgar?"

"The face resembled you, certainly, but it wasn't you at all. That's to be expected, naturally . . ."

"Then do you think maybe someone is impersonating me?"

"I think so. The painting was titled, *The Face of Mr. S.*"

"So they've taken the first letter of my name, too?"

"I wouldn't worry about it," Kurimoto said, trying to console him. "No one is going to believe it's you. I was going to make a strong protest, but the woman wasn't there, so I left without saying anything."

After Kurimoto left, Suguro remained buried in the sofa, staring out of the window. The dark gray afternoon sky split open, and a pale sun emerged.

Mitsu came from the bathroom and gazed at Suguro with concern. "Are you feeling all right, Sensei?" She was, as

Suguro's wife had said, sensitive to the misfortunes of others. That quality was sifted together with her geniality and her slow-wittedness.

"I'm fine." He put on the mask intended for household consumption and smiled back at Mitsu. It was the face his wife trusted and, at the same time, the face his readers believed in. "I'm going out." He got up from the sofa and asked a favor of Mitsu: "My wife will be here soon. Would you mind staying until she arrives?"

"Of course."

He followed Kurimoto's directions; it was the first time he had been on Takeshita Street. He had heard that this was the street in Harajuku most often swarming with young people, and the report appeared true: the strollers along the street included middle-school girls in long skirts that brushed against their toes, men as old as Suguro, young women shouldering bags that looked for all the world like mendicants' satchels, and young men with their hair bleached a cream color.

As Kurimoto had instructed him, he walked along a narrow road called Brahms Lane and came to a sign that read ART NOUVEAU GALLERY. On the first floor was a boutique selling cheap trinkets; the gallery was on the second floor.

He climbed the stairs, which smelled like cement. At the reception desk, a woman sat with crossed legs, reading a magazine. She gave a low gasp of surprise, evidently recognizing Suguro. Still clutching the magazine, she followed him inquisitively with her eyes as he walked around the deserted gallery.

Over twenty paintings ringed the four walls in a single row, like a continuous band of cellophane. A glance at three or four and Suguro had concluded that a talent barely indistinguishable from that of an amateur had been camouflaged with eccentric motifs. Both the realistic and abstract paintings were blatant imitations of European and American avant-garde works: two women coiled together; venomous snakes and moths with their wings spread wide; a drawing of a boy with a bulging head; an infant gazing up with fear from within the womb, the child's eyes opened wide in terror. As he scanned these works, which were distinguished only by their drab ostentation, Suguro was searching for one partic-ular painting.

The portrait that Kurimoto had identified as *The Face of Mr. S* was hanging near the corner of the room. Conscious of the woman's eyes on his back, Suguro tried to feign dis-interest as he approached the picture. It was a drawing of himself. In it he was staring straight ahead with a sneering smile on his face, as though he had washed up from a realm of gloomy colors. While the face was certainly his, there was something in the expression, not exactly the vulgarity that Kurimoto had described, but something lewd and ex-cessive.

As he averted his eyes in a mixture of anger and embar-rassment, Suguro remembered that he had seen this face be-fore. That's right—it was the face that had been peering at him from behind Kurimoto and the woman editor at the awards ceremony. In dismay, he stood frozen before the portrait. He knew of one other face that resembled this one. He had seen it when he visited the medieval cathedral in the French town of Bourges. He had climbed the spiral staircase behind the priest who had been his guide and gone out on a windswept balcony in the belfry. From the balcony, a pro-fusion of human and bestial faces glowered down upon the broad fields below. One of the stone faces, like that of a madwoman, had displayed the same sneering smile as in this painting. "What kind of face is that?" Suguro had asked, but the French priest had merely shrugged his shoulders.

Realizing that the receptionist was still watching him, Suguro approached her.

"Is a Miss Ishiguro here?" He did his best to suppress any emotion as he made the inquiry.

The woman quickly stubbed out her cigarette. "I'm expecting her shortly."

"Is she the one who painted that portrait?"

"No, that was Miss Itoi."

"There can be problems when an artist does a portrait without asking permission." When he challenged her, the receptionist grimaced as though she had been slapped. "Unless she's had the approval of her subject . . ."

"She said she had obtained permission."

"Who did?"

"Miss Itoi. The artist. I understood that you had her and Miss Ishiguro sketch you at Shinjuku."

She looked away. Suguro was about to contradict her when he sensed a shadow moving behind him, and the receptionist's eyes suddenly sparkled.

"Madame Naruse. I've been expecting you."

When Suguro turned round, a matronly woman wearing an elegant, wide-collared jacket and a scarf nodded slightly and entered.

Suguro left the gallery. The receptionist's affectedly jocular laughter echoed behind him. Outside, the sun was somewhat more veiled than before. At his age, such changes in the firmament filled Suguro with weariness. He pushed through the doorway of a coffee shop opposite the gallery. He found a seat next to the window, but the scene before his eyes was still that of the portrait. The image was more vivid than when he had seen it in reality. It depicted the face of a man whose ugliness flowed not from his visage but from his soul.

He didn't know what to think. For a moment he was gripped with fear and put a hand on his sweat-sprinkled forehead.

He calmed his nerves and tried to draw some inferences from the experience. Perhaps the portrait was not a depiction of the coarse sneer he had seen, but had in fact captured the unexpected smile or affable grin of the model. And possibly he had taken that straightforward smile as lewd and excessive because his subconscious still harbored graphic memories of the apparition he had seen at the awards ceremony. If that were the case, he had merely added his own interpretation to Kurimoto's offhanded labeling of the expression as a "vulgar face."

With that thought, he retrieved a small measure of relief. Once he was able to regard a trivial portrait as trivial, the sneer lost the power to cause him mental confusion—in the same sort of way he had managed to restore a sense of order to his life and his mind by writing the words "Had a bad dream" in his diary the morning after he had experienced that dream involving Mitsu.

When he raised his head and gazed idly out of the window, the woman he had seen in the gallery had come out of the building and was heading toward the coffee shop, evidently also in quest of a few moments of respite. After locating a vacant seat, she put her handbag and a book on a chair beside Suguro and removed her jacket. She had a broad forehead and large, strong-willed eyes, which are rare among Japanese women.

She took a sip of the espresso that was put down in front of her and lowered her eyes. She seemed to be deep in thought, for when she raised her head and noticed Suguro, she nodded to him in surprise. She had not realized until then that the man she had sat directly beside was Suguro.

"Hello again," she ventured.

For lack of anything else to say, or rather to break the ice, Suguro asked, "Did you see the picture called *The Face of Mr. S*?"

There was no way she could have overlooked it.

"Yes."

"Does it look like me?"

She tilted her head slightly and smiled uneasily. Her hair was lightly flecked with silver, but she appeared to be a bit younger than his wife.

"What sort of painters have they collected for that exhibition?"

"It's a group of young women. They purport to be seeking beauty in ugliness. An aesthetics of deformity, of all things."

"So is that why they chose my face? I suppose my face *is* ugly, but it's galling to have it drawn by them. And it's annoying that they made it as horrid as that," he said good-humoredly.

"I don't think it's all that horrid. It seems like a face with a good deal of humanity in it."

His wife spoke in this kind of voice and with these kinds of phrases when she was trying to placate him. It must be a characteristic of women of their age.

"How did you come to know these artists?"

"One member of the group was a patient for a short time in the hospital where I work. . . . That was my first introduction to them."

"I wasn't impressed with any of their work. Does someone like you find it interesting to mix with women who draw such weird pictures?"

"Why do you ask?" She smiled at him. "I could be very much like such women."

Suguro's curiosity was aroused by this woman who resembled his wife.

"You said you work at a hospital. Are you a doctor?"

"Oh no. I'm just a volunteer. I'm sorry—my name is Naruse."

"Mine is Suguro."

"Oh, I'm very familiar with your name and your writing."

The conversation broke off there, and both returned to their separate cups of coffee. Suguro's eye caught the title of the book she had placed beside her handbag. It was the work of a critic who had a wide following among young people.

"So you even read books like that?"

"I enjoy reading," she said defensively. "I don't understand much, but I can't keep my hands off a new book when it comes out."

"The author of that book is quite critical of me, I think. Says I'm afraid of sex. . . ." He gave a deliberately wry grin. She said nothing, and from her disconcerted expression Suguro concluded that she had read the critique. "You read that part, didn't you?" He had become serious.

"Yes."

"Every writer has his own field of operations. The themes I've pursued haven't included sex . . . but that doesn't mean I've avoided the topic. I think I've dealt with it to some extent."

"Yes, I remember you once wrote that the psychology of sex resembles the frame of mind in which one yearns for God." She nodded gently. "I can't remember which book you wrote that in."

"It was a collection of essays about five years ago."

He was flattered that this woman was so familiar with his

work that she was even well acquainted with his essays. From her manner of speech she seemed to know a great deal about many things. Perhaps she was engaged in some kind of intellectual work.

"From reading my books, do you . . . agree with that critic?"

"I don't know much about difficult questions like that. But I have sensed, maybe because you're a Christian, that you always associate sex with sin."

I'm no pubescent schoolgirl, he protested, but he realized that somewhere deep down the Christian influence that had been with him since his youth had led him to make a distinction between healthy and unhealthy sex. Healthy sex was . . . he thought of his wife's face, and knew that a scent of duty had wafted constantly over their conjugal relations. Yet he had found considerable satisfaction in that relationship, and his wife had never uttered a word of complaint. He couldn't begin to imagine his wife expressing displeasure over such matters.

"Well, if you'll forgive me for asking, what are your views on sex?"

It was a thoroughly impertinent question to ask a woman nearly as old as his wife, let alone someone he had just met for the first time. But he felt a need for a bit of perverse retaliation.

"It frightens me, to be perfectly frank." She smiled.

"Why? If I'm talking like a Christian, you're talking like a virgin."

"No, that's not what I mean. I feel as though our erotic behavior expresses our profoundest secrets, the ones we ourselves aren't aware of."

"The secrets we ourselves aren't aware of?"

"Yes."

When Suguro heard those words, his memory suddenly

replayed the dream he had seen that one particular night. When he had stolen a furtive glance at Mitsu standing half-nude in the bathroom . . .

He quickly averted his eyes. This was an unusual encounter. Until a few moments ago, it would have been inconceivable for him to have had such an open, frank conversation with a woman he had never met before, a conversation the likes of which he had never had with his own wife.

"Have you ever written anything yourself ?"

"Oh no, certainly not. A long time ago I did try writing a few imitative verses, but that's all."

As he looked out of the window, he caught sight of a young man standing in the street. He wore a blue windbreaker with white sleeves, and he was peering into the coffee shop. Very likely, as he passed by he had recognized the man sitting by the window as the writer Suguro, and had stopped out of curiosity to look at him.

When he had asked someone where he might find an art gallery near Takeshita Street—the location that the drunken woman had mentioned at the reception—he was told he would find the building by making a right turn off this narrow alleyway. The sky was virtually blocked out by a row of yellow-colored buildings, and the street was lined with lamps fashioned after the gaslights of former days. Even Kobari knew that an attempt had been made here to reproduce the back streets of Montmartre.

A man stepped out of one building and paused in the street. Kobari gasped. It was Suguro, the very man Kobari was seeking. The writer glanced behind him, as though he were waiting for someone, then went into a coffee shop on the opposite side of the street.

Kobari gazed into the coffee shop from behind a telephone

pole. Fortunately, Suguro did not appear to have noticed him, but sat at a table near the window and gave his order to a waiter. Then he slumped wearily back into his chair and became submerged in thought. Kobari recognized the pose as the one Suguro had struck on television recently. His way of sitting always made him look jaded. When Suguro appeared on the screen, Kobari's lover stretched her arm out and changed the channel.

Shortly, an older woman wearing a chic beige jacket and a scarf came out of the same building Suguro had left; as though by prearrangement, she, too, went into the coffee shop. They seemed to know one another, because they sat in adjacent seats and were soon engaged in earnest conversation.

The woman did not seem to be Suguro's wife. This was not the face of Suguro's wife that had appeared in a photograph at the front of a literary anthology. In the course of their conversation, Suguro glanced out of the window only once, but he seemed to be unaware that he was being watched. He merely uncrossed his legs.

Eventually the two stood up together. Kobari hid behind the telephone pole and then followed them as they walked together down Takeshita Street. Then, unexpectedly, they nodded slightly to one another and went their separate ways. Suguro walked off toward the train station, while the woman headed in the opposite direction, toward the Palais France on the main road.

Kobari hesitated for a moment, trying to decide which of the two to pursue, then opted for the woman. Threading her way between the young men and women rubbing shoulders and glancing offhandedly into shop windows, she walked confident and erect down the street. She impressed Kobari as a woman of strong character. She crossed the pedestrian walk at the wide intersection and entered a back street in Omote Sandō.

There was a chance she might grow suspicious if he trailed her down the nearly deserted alley, but he resolved to stay with her and maintained a distance of about thirty meters. As he followed her, he realized the absurdity of what he was doing. It would be one thing to follow Suguro, but it seemed pointless for him to go out of his way to stay on the trail of a woman merely because she had had a chat with Suguro in a coffee shop.

Why was he going to these lengths to pry away the writer's mask? The sense that his actions were despicable rested comfortably beside the pleasure he knew he would feel at peeling off Suguro's mask. Suguro's smiling face as he sat on the rostrum at the awards ceremony. The waves of applause when he received the award and made his acceptance speech. Kobari could still remember it vividly. A writer who spent his entire life constructing one single macrocosm and then shut himself off safely within its boundaries. That smugly self-satisfied look. From within the sturdy, safe walls of his world, he scattered the oh-so-noble words he had written. Kobari wanted to agitate that face. In his school days, he had participated in demonstrations to topple the Establishment; in his desire to join in the student movement, a sense of justice had blended with the urge to shake those who were secure loose from their moorings.

They passed through a residential district and came out into a side street lined with elegant clothiers and antique shops. One shop contained nothing but ship's fittings. From the way the woman walked unwaveringly along this street, Kobari concluded that she was familiar with the neighborhood. When she came to a six-story hospital, she stepped up to the door.

Fed up, Kobari considered turning back. The woman was standing at the entrance to the hospital, chatting with a middle-aged nurse who wore a cap ornamented with two black lines. The nurse bared her buckteeth and smiled in a way that fully exposed her kindheartedness. Presently, the woman left the hospital and headed toward the main thoroughfare in Omote Sandō.

Kobari thought she might take the subway, but instead she stopped in front of a pet shop and peered through the display window at the various breeds of puppies that wagged their tails or dozed in tiny doghouses. Kobari likewise stopped in front of a clothing store several shops down and pretended to stare into the window, but his curiosity and his desire to follow the woman had utterly dissipated. It seemed unlikely that this pet-loving lady would prove to be a key figure in his quest for Suguro's true face.

But five, then ten minutes passed, and still the woman did not move. Kobari eventually realized that she was studying the puppies not because she was a dog fancier, but because she was supposed to be meeting someone there. Thankfully, the woman seemed to have no idea that she was being watched. From time to time she would glance toward the subway entrance, evidently waiting for someone to appear.

A plump-cheeked woman in round glasses, the kind of old maid who can be found in the ranks of any institution, came climbing up the subway stairs. Kobari was crestfallen as he watched the two women toy with the dog chains and collars at the doorway while they talked.

The woman Kobari had been following bought a green dog collar, after which she and the woman in glasses hailed a taxi.

Kobari no longer had any desire to follow them. He knew nothing would come of it. He quickly returned to the gallery.

*   *   *

"We'll take a ten-minute break, after which we'll discuss the two stories that are still in the running." The chief editor who chaired this selection committee was seated at the center of the table. Once he had announced the brief intermission, the waitresses who had been seated quietly in one corner of the room noisily rose to their feet.

The Garakutagawa Prize, about which they were meeting, was merely a newcomer's prize, but it was considered significant enough by the public for the winner to be announced on television. The award was given twice a year, and the selection committee met each time at the same restaurant in Tsukiji, along with the committee that presented the Naomoto Prize for popular fiction. Suguro, who had become a judge along with Kanō just three years earlier, was still considered a neophyte on the committee.

"I imagine Nozawa will propose that we offer no award this year," whispered Kanō to Suguro, who was seated on his left.

"I'd be in favor of no award. Both of these stories seem contrived to me."

"I don't think there's anything wrong with their being contrived."

Suguro could not agree. In addition, he thought that Kanō's scathing attacks on each of the other nominated works that evening had been rather vicious. As he listened to the merciless verbal whiplashes that came forth from Kanō's mouth, Suguro was reminded of the faces of his comrades from many years before, seated in the tiny bar at Meguro and unsparingly damning his own writings as "suspect." That next year, Kanō had made his debut in the literary world with the receipt of this same Garakutagawa Prize, and the following year Suguro, too, had received the award. Almost thirty-five years had slipped by since then, and many of their contemporaries from those days were no longer writing fiction.

Kanō snarled at Suguro's dissension and took a gulp of his beer. Then, with a look of displeasure still on his face, he said, "The standards for the Garakutagawa Prize have slipped in the last three or four years, haven't they?"

"They certainly have." This time Suguro nodded. "I agree with you there."

"I wonder if the prestigiousness of the award will crumble if we don't introduce some rigid standards very soon. The way sex is described in these finalists' stories is nothing less than pornographic, as far as I'm concerned. There's no true eroticism in them. Don't you agree, Yoshikawa?" Kanō called across the table to Yoshikawa, who was putting drops into his eyes. Yoshikawa was their senior on the committee, and a writer acknowledged by all to be a master of the short story.

"Now, now—there's nothing to get steamed up about." Yoshikawa smiled in the hope of deflecting some of the anger that Kanō was now venting loudly. "But you're quite right—they haven't really caught the essence of eroticism."

Like a far-distant echo, that comment summoned forth a remarkably similar statement from the edge of Suguro's memory. "You avoid writing about the profoundest depths of the sexual relationship." Accompanying that memory was an image of Madame Naruse's face looking back at him with those large, audacious eyes.

"Then, Suguro, are you going to vote for this one?" Kanō was asking. "You gave it high marks earlier."

"No, I'm going to vote for 'A Place to See Rainbows.' "

"That's a piece of fluff!" Then Kanō peered at Suguro as

though he had just remembered something. "I need to talk to you when this is over."

"Can't we talk now?"

"I have to talk to you alone." He looked away.

The meeting resumed. As in the first round of discussions, each judge rated the nominated stories as "Good," "Fair," or "Poor" and explained his reasoning. Then the votes were tabulated. Unlike the first round, however, in this round "A Place to See Rainbows" received a majority vote. Yoshikawa did his best to mollify a disgruntled Kanō.

"Well, I'll put up with it this time," Kanō spat over his shoulder. "But it leaves a rotten taste in my mouth."

Since newspaper reporters were waiting for the results, Yoshikawa and the chief editor left the banquet room together.

"After dinner let's take a car together," Kanō mumbled to Suguro.

Suguro smiled and replied, "You're being very secretive for some reason."

"It's not something I want anybody else to hear."

Kanō lapsed into an unpleasant silence that Suguro could not fathom.

When the hired car carrying the two men started up, Kanō thought for a moment before directing the driver. "To the lobby of the Imperial Hotel, please."

Kanō would not even mention what he wanted to discuss until they were seated in the hotel lobby. Somewhat irritable when they finally sat down, Suguro asked tightly, "Well, what's this all about?"

Kanō glanced around the lobby to make sure that no one was listening. When he spoke, he still looked angry. "Actually, there's . . . there's a strange rumor about you making the rounds."

"What kind of strange rumor?"

"Supposedly, you're a frequent visitor to the peep shows around Kabuki-chō."

For a long while, Suguro stared at this man who was his friend.

"And? Do you believe the rumor?"

"Me? It's not my problem," Kanō said disdainfully. "I just wanted you to know that the rumor is circulating. And because you're always so circumspect."

"Circumspect? Go ahead and call me cowardly if you want."

"Anyway, wouldn't your readers feel betrayed if they heard a rumor like that? It wouldn't matter if it was about me, but you're a Christian and all. You'd be in a hell of a mess if the Church or the fathers found out, wouldn't you? And worse than that . . ."

"My wife, you mean?"

"Yeah."

"My wife believes what I tell her, no matter what anyone else says," Suguro said confidently. "But who did you hear this from?"

The lobby was almost deserted. A uniformed bellboy went outside to welcome the passengers of a large bus that had just arrived from the airport.

"A magazine reporter named Kobari. I'd never met him before, but he phoned me about two weeks ago. Said he wanted to ask me about you in confidence. He claimed he'd met a woman artist who told him what you were up to."

"Ah." Suguro smiled grimly, coming to grips with the train of events at last. "So that's it. At that awards ceremony a while ago, a drunken woman elbowed her way in and started babbling that nonsense at the top of her voice. If that's it, I know all about it. Kurimoto at Dōkansha Press knows about it, too." He yawned deliberately. "I'm sorry to have worried you about nothing. It's all completely groundless. So forget it."

Suguro assumed that this remark would set Kanō's mind at rest, but his friend maintained a sullen silence.

"Why don't we call it a day?" Suguro urged.

"I get so tired after these committee meetings," said Kanō. "Sometimes at night I get a pain in my heart."

"You be careful. Your heart is none too strong."

"Suguro . . . Where were you the night before last?"

"Night before last?" Suguro cocked his head. "I was at home reading the nominated stories. Why do you ask?"

"You didn't go to Shinjuku?"

"No."

Kanō looked away and muttered, "I saw you the night before last. On the platform at Shinjuku Station."

"On the platform? Don't be ridiculous. I was at home all evening. My wife can vouch for that."

Kanō glanced up at Suguro in silence. Then, as though he were muttering to himself: "About eleven-thirty I was on the train with Mitomo from Dōkansha Press. I'd given him a manuscript at a bar on Golden Avenue, and then we had a drink together. We were heading back in the same direction, so we both got on the packed train. I happened to look out of the window while I was talking to him, and on the uptown train platform . . . I saw you sitting on a bench with a woman in glasses."

"You saw me?"

"Yes. It was you."

"Are you sure it wasn't someone who looks like me?"

"No, it was you." Kanō was emphatic. "I know it was you. Mitomo was surprised, too."

"I was at home. How many times do I have to tell you before you'll believe me?"

"I believe you. But I also saw you on that platform. Then the uptown train came in and you disappeared."

"That's absurd. There aren't two of me, you know." Suguro had to work at a smile. "It must be a look-alike. This impostor is pretending to be me. He's using my name and tramping around Shinjuku. Call my wife and ask her. Ask her where I was the night before last."

"I don't have to call her. I'm sure you were at home. But I also know what I saw."

"What sort of woman was she?"

"She was wearing one of those long, brown scarves coiled around and around her neck, the way all the young women wear them today. She had boots on. And glasses."

"I don't know any woman like that."

"In any case, if the rumor gets around, you're the one who'll suffer. If you're going to act, you'd better act quickly."

Suguro sensed that it was hopeless to try any more to change Kanō's mind. He knew from long experience that Kanō could never be swayed from his opinions once he had pronounced them. With his lips, he affirmed his trust for Suguro, but his expression almost audibly proclaimed his doubts.

If that was the case with his old friend Kanō, matters would be even worse with outsiders. And according to Kanō, a reporter, nosing the stench of a corpse from far off like a hyena, had already begun to investigate Suguro.

"I understand." Suguro nodded, struggling to control a tangle of emotions—apprehension, confusion, anger.

Suguro waited at the edge of the road for Kurimoto to return. Beyond a row of motorcycles, a young man emerged from the doorway of a porno shop. Through the opening, Suguro could see the neckless outline of a flesh-colored doll poised among others on a shelf. It was Fukurokujū, the God of Longevity, wearing a lecherous smile. The shop had no patrons: surely they must all be bored with the shop's selection of sex appliances and the cellophane-covered magazines featuring photographs of nude women with one knee drawn up to conceal their pubic regions.

On the opposite side of the street was a plaza with movie theaters. A painting of a naked young woman wrapped in a leopard-skin coat adorned the marquee of one of them.

If his memory served him right, many years back there had been a hushed, secretive atmosphere in this part of town even in the light of day. Several love-hotels had their entrances concealed behind hedges of withering bamboo. Garbage cans lined the road, and unexpectedly a stray cat would come darting out between them. It had been a dank, arcane neighborhood. But because so much time had passed, his memories were not unequivocal.

That atmosphere had now completely changed. The streets they had traversed to get here were now crowded with office workers returning home, and school-age boys and girls swarmed the neighborhood even though it wasn't a Sunday. From all directions he could hear the clang of pinballs in the *pachinko* machines and the cries of barkers echoing alongside the dust-muffled noise from the bells of movie theaters announcing the beginning of their features. The forced effort to create an artificial atmosphere of pleasure echoed in the cheerless jangle of the *pachinko* balls. The faces of the pedestrians also seemed dead to stimulation, responding to neither sound nor color.

Suguro suddenly remembered what Madame Naruse had said: "Our erotic behavior expresses our profoundest secrets, the ones we ourselves aren't aware of."

Erotic experiences express what is buried deepest within each individual—but in these quarters eroticism was treated too lightly, too cheaply. A chilly putrefaction clung to everything, the way the vomit of last night's drunks clung to the streets, the walls, and the telephone poles. Eroticism here had nothing to convey; the carnality that was pandered to here was not the eroticism that Madame Naruse had described.

A disgruntled-looking Kurimoto returned. "Nothing but kinky shops everywhere. I found out where Sakura Street is."

Kurimoto was a young man, but he had graduated in religious studies and his sole hobby was playing the classical hand drum. Apparently this was the first time he had walked these streets, and his forehead was bathed in sweat.

"Let's go there," Suguro responded. "We may run into my impostor." He put special emphasis on the word "impostor," but Kurimoto said nothing.

When they came to the road that joined Yasukuni Street with Hanazono Street, the volume of noise swelled even though the sun had not set. Sandwich men and barkers were posted in front of every shop, handing out flyers or calling to the passersby. There was no need to read the flyers, for a deluge of signs along the right side of the street announced: PEEP SHOW and PRIVATE MASSAGE. Other stores boasted such unique messages on their marquees as FASHION MASSAGE, PRIVATE ATELIER, or SPECIAL BOXING and SPECIAL PRO WRESTLING.

"What do they do in those places?" Suguro asked under his breath.

"You watch while naked women wrestle," Kurimoto answered with a frown. It was difficult to determine whether the frown was aimed at the show or at Suguro.

He had felt Kurimoto grow somewhat distant at about the time Kanō had taken him aside for a talk. Because of his own seriousness, Kurimoto was quick to believe what others told him. And since he worked at the same publishing house as Mitomo, who had been on the train at Shinjuku with Kanō, there was no doubt that Kurimoto had heard the rumors. One such experience could be written off, but when Kurimoto heard about the incident that had even surprised Kanō, he would certainly begin to have doubts of his own. This was evident in the fact that he tried to avoid the subject whenever he called at Suguro's office.

When they reached the center of Sakura Street, a sandwich man dressed like the Little Tramp ambled up familiarly and smiled, showing a missing tooth.

"Haven't seen you in a while, Sensei!"

His sandwich board read: PORNO PALACE—PALACE OF PLEASURES. He was short and sallow-cheeked, a man as scrawny as the coattails he dragged behind him.

"Have you been over to the parlor, Sensei?"

Suguro was timidly silent for a moment, then tugged gently at Kurimoto's sleeve as a signal and said hoarsely, "Parlor? Which parlor?"

"What're you talking about? Namiko's, of course."

"Not yet."

The sandwich man still grinned guilelessly. "If you're looking for Namiko, she's at the ramen restaurant."

"Which ramen restaurant?"

"What're you talking about? The one right over there, of course." He pointed his chin toward a store across the way.

"Ah." Suguro took a thousand-yen bill from his wallet and handed it to the sandwich man.

"Always good to do business with you. You'll make Nami cry if you don't come around more often."

Suguro fled from the man and defended himself to Kurimoto by saying, "He must look just like me, this impostor. Even that fellow couldn't tell us apart."

The young editor made no reply.

It was still early, and beneath the fluorescent lights in the ramen restaurant only four or five customers were slurping noodles. It required no effort to pick out from the group a woman of twenty-seven or twenty-eight with a pallid complexion and rough skin. When she looked up from her magazine, she stared at Suguro in surprise.

"What are you doing here so early?" she cooed, drawing out the ends of her words.

"You're Namiko?" Suguro asked softly, not wanting anyone else to hear.

"You're such a horrible tease. Namiko's already gone back to the shop. You know I'm Hanae." A shimmer of doubt passed across her eyes. "Waaaait a minute. You're Suguro Sensei, aren't you . . . ?"

"Yes, I am, but . . ."

"Why did you think I was Namiko?"

"Let's go and get some sushi."

"Sushi? But I've already ordered here."

"I'll pay for it."

She picked up the handbag beside her, which looked like an imitation Gucci.

They went into a nearby sushi restaurant and sat down. Hanae silently studied the faces of Suguro and Kurimoto and then said, "Is something wrong?"

"No, not really."

"You really are Suguro Sensei, aren't you?"

He did not reply.

"Are you someone else? No, it couldn't be. You look just like him. Are you somebody else?"

"I really am Suguro. The fellow you've been meeting is somebody else."

"Your twin?"

"He's not related to me. And I haven't met him yet, either."

"That's creepy." Hanae stared at Suguro with a look of genuine fear. "I don't want any sushi. I'm leaving."

Kurimoto stopped her from getting up. "Wait. We're not going to cause you any trouble."

Suguro chimed in, "I'd like to hear a little about this man."

"Do you work for a magazine, you two?"

"No. But it's true that I am the novelist Suguro. That other man is an impostor."

"What do you want to know?"

"He's put me in a tight spot. You can understand that, can't you? A man who looks just like me comes around here, claiming to be me and blabbering all kinds of nonsense."

Hanae seemed to have lowered her guard a bit. Kurimoto had the presence of mind to put in a quick order for saké.

"Then everything he said was nonsense? But he looks just like you. The spitting image." She kept staring at Suguro with nervous eyes.

"Do you see him often?"

"He came to the parlor."

"What parlor?"

"Where we work. Where we play babies."

"Play babies?"

"You haven't heard about it? It's been in the magazines and on TV." Hanae seemed proud of the fact that their work had been featured on television. "Our clients dress up like babies—are you sure you haven't seen pictures anywhere, where they dress up in diapers and suck on pacifiers?"

"The children do?"

59

"No, no! They're all full-grown adults. They play with rattles and baby toys."

"Why?"

"I don't know why. A lot of men wish they could be babies again. That's what one of our clients said, anyway. That's the kind of client who comes to our parlor."

"What sort of men patronize your place?"

"A lot of famous men. Doctors and assemblymen—gentlemen like that."

When she mentioned the assemblymen, Hanae crinkled up her nose and had a laugh at their expense. Perhaps she had suddenly thought of some of her clients who were members of the Diet, and remembered them decked out in diapers and sucking on pacifiers. She chuckled again as she lit a cigarette.

Kurimoto grimaced in disgust and turned his head away. Perhaps he had visualized an old man identical to Suguro dolled up in such an absurd manner, and the thought had been more than he could bear. His revulsion was silently transmitted to Suguro, who felt wretched and embarrassed.

Suguro finally broke the silence. "Then you're saying that my impostor . . . did those kinds of things at your shop?"

"You mean Suguro Sensei?"

"He isn't me!" There was unwitting anger in his voice.

"Him? He came a lot. Nami was his partner. She said he was a little annoying."

"Annoying in what way?"

"He was always complaining . . . saying that they didn't have disposable diapers when he was a child, or they didn't have this kind of toy in the old days."

"Then he really turned into an infant?"

"Yeah, most of our clients do. . . . That really gets them going." She went so far as to lower her eyes and demonstrate a look of ecstasy—the look of a child sleeping peacefully in its mother's arms.

Suguro thought of his own study. A musty room kept dark even in the daytime. A room where he could realize his desire to return to the womb in a blanket of security. What manner of difference could there be between that sense of security and the desires of these men to become infants? Deep in the hearts of men lay a blackness they themselves knew nothing about.

"They're perverts," Kurimoto muttered from the periphery of the conversation. "Clients like that."

"Men are all the same. Even famous men turn into babies at our parlor."

"How much do they pay, these clients of yours?"

"Thirty thousand yen for two hours."

With nimble fingers, she lit another cigarette with a cheap lighter.

"Thirty thousand?"

"We're on the cheap side. At Roppongi they get fifty."

"What else do you know about this man?"

"Not much. I went to a hotel with him once. But . . . Nami's the one who went with him most of the time."

"What else?" Suguro pressed her, eager to have sufficient evidence to persuade Kurimoto that he and this man were separate individuals.

Unexpectedly, Hanae repeated, "You're sure you aren't our client?"

"I've told you I'm not."

"If you're really someone else, then I'll tell you. . . . That man, the one who looks like you, does some weird things."

"Weird, how?"

She smiled knowingly. "First we went to a discothèque. . . . He said he liked to smell the perspiration on our necks when Nami and I danced. . . . Then we went to a hotel, and after I took a bath, he stroked my shoulders and my breasts . . . and then he licked me, just on the neck and shoulders, like he'd gone crazy. It made me sick. I mean, I'd just taken a bath, and to have an old man slobber all over you. An old man's saliva is really nauseating." She realized Suguro had not said a word. "I shouldn't have told you about this."

"It doesn't matter." He wanted Kurimoto to agree. "It wasn't me, after all."

"But it's really spooky how much you look like him. You sent a chill through me when you said you were somebody else. One other thing—by the mirror in the bathroom, he tried to strangle me."

"Strangle . . ." Suguro was alarmed. "You mean he tried to kill you?"

"He said afterward that he wasn't trying to kill me. But his eyes terrified me. They were all bloodshot. Nami said he did the same thing to her."

"What the hell's he up to?" Kurimoto shook his head several times in disbelief. "He must be half crazy."

"Doesn't it bother you to have to work with clients like that?"

"Of course it bothers me. That's why I quit the place. . . . But Nami laughed and said he was just pretending. If you let him pretend, he'll give you lots of money. But writers do strange things, don't they?" Hanae smiled a labyrinthine smile. "I wonder what he writes. I haven't read any of it."

Suguro could endure no more and broke his silence. "I appreciate your time." He pulled two bills out of his wallet. "This isn't very much."

"Thank you." Her tone suddenly turned businesslike. "Are you leaving?"

"Yes."

"Why don't you stop by the parlor? Nami's there, and I'm sure she'd wait on you. Hey, why don't you ask Nami in person about this guy? Yeah, you ought to do that."

"No. I've heard enough for today."

Stern-faced, Suguro walked with his eyes focused straight ahead, oblivious to the blinking neon lights and the cries of the barkers. When he reached the broad avenue, as though that were some sort of sign, he turned to Kurimoto and said, "Now do you believe there's someone out there impersonating me?"

"Yes." Kurimoto nodded, swept up by the force of the question.

"It's enough if you believe me."

"Yes."

"If Mitomo at your company or anybody else starts spreading outlandish rumors about me, would you tell them about this man?"

"Of course. But why are you making such a big issue out of it?"

"Because I thought even you had started to suspect me."

Kurimoto took a breath and said, "Sensei, you've got to get your hands on this man."

A young woman approaching from the opposite direction riveted her eyes on Suguro's face, then pulled on the sleeve of the young man with her and whispered, "That's the novelist Suguro."

Suguro heard the whisper. Kurimoto, who also heard it, repeated softly, "Sensei, for your readers' sake, too, you've got to get your hands on this man."

CHAPTER
THREE

KOBARI ROAMED Sakura Street as Suguro had done. His reportorial sense of smell told him that he would be sniffing out something in the near future. He was confident of his ability to unearth some clue that would help him corner Suguro.

As he darted around on his assignments, if he was anywhere near Shinjuku he always checked out Sakura Street. It took no more than ten minutes to traverse the short, narrow road. Each time he walked its length, the thought "maybe this time" crossed his mind. But that "maybe this time" seemed as though it would never become a reality. Whenever he returned home without a lead, he felt exhausted and miserable, and he was reminded of Suguro's self-satisfied face as he sat at the awards ceremony.

"Maybe this time" finally came.

A wintry rain had begun to fall around dusk, prodding Kobari to consider abandoning his quest that day, but he changed his mind and ambled down the short slope from Shinjuku Station.

Among the many people beneath umbrellas walking toward him, he glimpsed a face he knew he had seen somewhere before. He could not immediately recall who it was, but just as the person passed him, he remembered. It was the woman who had emerged from the subway at Harajuku to rendezvous with the other woman Kobari had followed because she seemed to know Suguro. This woman was short and wore round-rimmed glasses; a drab woman seen from any angle, but undoubtedly the woman he had seen at Harajuku.

He glanced behind him. Holding her umbrella at a slight angle, the plump woman was shuffling up the hill. The legs that peeked out beneath her skirt were also hefty.

He walked swiftly past her and continued on with seeming indifference, then whirled back again. As the woman slowly started past him, he called out with a laugh, "Hey. Are you by chance a friend of Suguro Sensei?"

He had no idea why these words had popped out of his mouth. If she denied knowing Suguro, he would have to deal with the situation from there.

"You are a friend of Suguro Sensei, aren't you?"

"Well, I wouldn't say we're friends," she replied with uncommon familiarity. "I've had a few drinks with him."

He knew that "maybe this time" was now. Unlike the woman painter he had grilled after the reception, this woman did not seem guarded. There was even a smile in the eyes behind the round glasses.

"Oh yes? Then you're the one," he said. "The one Sensei told me about." From there the cogwheels began to turn smoothly, like those on a brand-new machine.

"Are you a friend of Sensei? How did you know that I knew him?"

"He said you wore glasses and had a round face." Kobari was bluffing, but she displayed no sign of suspicion. "You're an artist, aren't you? Why don't we go somewhere for tea?"

"Tea?" She giggled. "You're a tea drinker, huh?"

"Saké's fine, too, if you like."

"I'll have a drink with you. But I'll manage with just black tea."

On this street, the lines that men threw out to women and the ways in which women accepted their invitations were all of this variety. When they sat down in the café bar, before he had even ordered, Kobari asked, "So . . . are you the one Sensei allowed to draw his portrait?"

"Yes sir." She smiled trustingly from behind her glasses. "That's me."

"And there was another woman with you at the time, wasn't there?"

"You mean Hina? She was there."

"That's what Sensei told me. He said he was very drunk by then."

"Really? He said that? I didn't think he was all that drunk."

"Well, anyway, he let you sketch him, right?"

"It wasn't like he came right out and asked me to. I just kind of sketched him while we were talking at the hotel. I had my sketchbook with me, since Hina and I were out on Sakura Street that night trying to make some money by doing portraits."

The word *hotel* did not slip unnoticed past Kobari. *So Suguro had gone with these women to a hotel.*

"What did Sensei do at the hotel?"

"He talked a lot at first. He's a writer, after all. And he's so perceptive."

"Why do you say that?"

"He could tell just from looking at me that I'm a masochist. Do you mind if I have some saké?"

She made her announcement offhandedly, as though she were reporting a fondness for lace ruffles. Kobari took a fresh look at her, but she still had the same congenial, bespectacled face, with no trace of the morbid, masochistic tendencies she had admitted.

"I didn't catch your name. Mine's Kobari."

"I'm Itoi Motoko. I'm just *delighted* to meet you," she said jokingly, sounding like a TV personality. "I'm an up-and-coming female artist. To put bread on the table, I draw pictures on street corners."

"So . . . he really could detect that you're a masochist?"

"He did. He said that's why he invited us to the hotel. He wanted to watch Hina and me make love."

"And . . ." Kobari swallowed hard. "Did you?"

"Sure. It's no big deal. It's just a question of preference. And he was very good about paying us."

"So all he did was watch?"

"Of course not. The second time around he joined us."

"He stripped naked . . . ?"

"Do you know anybody who makes love with their clothes on?" She snickered. "Do you keep your clothes on when you sleep with a woman? If you do, you've got some kind of complex."

"So Suguro got into the nude. . . . But an old man's body must seem awfully ugly to you."

"That's true. Not like young people. He has these spots in places, and his skin's all dry, and his stomach pokes out. . . . And he smells."

"He stinks, does he?"

"Well, it's not really a stink, but the smell of an old man. Like the smell of a crematorium. Or when you light incense. But his ugly body really turned me on."

When she spoke, the eyes behind her glasses narrowed into slender lines of thread. She was able to say the most startling things with total serenity through smiling lips.

"Why?" Kobari asked in disbelief.

"I don't know why. When I was in high school I dreamed I was made love to by an ugly man. But when I woke up from the dream, I didn't feel disgusted at all. In fact, the idea excited me. It felt exquisite when Sensei held me down and covered me with his saliva and then choked me at the end. . . . It was so marvelous I felt I could die happy right then. All because his body is so ugly."

"I can't relate to that way of thinking."

"I'm sorry for you. Do you only use the missionary position when you go to bed with a woman? Sex is awfully deep, sir. All kinds of sensations come bubbling up from the bottommost part of your body. It's like a strange new music."

As Kobari listened, he was struck by the woman's depravity. To his mind, a pervert was on a par with a madman or a criminal, someone with a dark, detestable side that needed to be hidden from others. Inexplicably, a Christian writer had become part of that world and had engaged in degenerate acts with such women.

"Sensei agrees with me. We were talking after the three of us had done it, and I asked him why he thought I was turned on by ugliness. He said there was an irrational mystery buried in the hearts of men. Reason says people should feel pleasure in beautiful things, but in fact we can find beauty in ugliness and be intoxicated by it. That's what Sensei said. Don't you think he's right?"

He balked. "That must be a sensation only a few people share."

"But even you have that basic instinct. There's joy in depravity for all people, according to Suguro Sensei. That's how fathomless the human heart is. Hina and I completely agreed with him. We told him how up-to-the-minute that sensation was, and how well we understood what he was talking about. That's because we're painters. The well-known artists only believe in the old clichéd kinds of beauty. But for a long time now, Hina and I have been trying to portray the beauty that lies in objects that everyone else considers foul and hideous. We completely agreed with him. You would have understood if you'd come to our exhibition. We've just had it, but it's over now."

"I saw it. Sensei's portrait . . . "

"Oh? I was trying to capture Sensei as I saw him that night."

Motoko shifted her sweaty body toward Kobari as though she had known him for some time. He found it hard to believe that this outgoing woman, so hefty beside her svelte friend Hina, was a real masochist. With her round, stolid face and glasses, she seemed, in Kobari's experience, like the kind of woman who stifled you once you had her in bed, with her clammy skin and sluggish responses.

The old chair seemed to need oiling. When the doctor finished examining the charts and swiveled toward his patient, it squeaked. Suguro's ears had grown accustomed to that sound over the course of his visits to this hospital. After the chair made its noise, the doctor always commenced his lecture in deliberate tones, and today was no exception.

"The GOT level is eighty-two, and the GPT is one hundred

and six. That's considerably higher than the last time you were here. Have you been working yourself to the point of exhaustion? Even emotional stress is going to take its toll on you. As I've told you, in this condition there's a much greater risk of this developing into cirrhosis."

"I see."

Naturally, when he returned home Suguro reported significantly lower test figures to his wife. Although they had both reached an age when they were hovering on the brink of death, he found he could not bear to make her taste loneliness and anxiety.

> The pines celebrate a thousand years of verdant longevity;
> Though decked with moss their colors never fade.
> The chaste young bamboo shoots
> Have yet to know the weight of the snows.
> The plum that journeys to the unknown region
>   of Tsukushi
> Was spawned in days past in the harbor of Naniwa. . . .

On stage, Takehara Han had begun to dance the *Felicity of the Pines*. Suguro was left breathless by the serene voice of Tomiyama Seikin, the husky chanter, and by the dancing of O-han, who never missed a step though she was now past eighty. There was not a superfluous moment in the entire dance. The stage of the National Theater was too large for a folk dance, and the lights were irritatingly bright, but when O-han rose to her feet the space no longer seemed gaping. The empty spaces snapped taut around her.

He was glad he had come out with his wife tonight. She had been deeply moved by a performance of O-han's *Snow* on television and had mentioned how much she wanted to get tickets to the dancer's performance. Suguro had privately enlisted the help of a friend who worked for a newspaper and had obtained two tickets. As they sat side by side watching *Felicity of the Pines*, he considered what a fine old married couple they had turned out to be.

The two of them would go on living serenely together, and they would die serenely. As far as his writing was concerned, all he needed to do was probe more deeply into the grooves he had already dug. No overdoing it. Avoiding adventures.

> *Live forever, they pray and dance.*
> *The auspicious cranes flock together and*
> *   cavort.*

O-han's movements came to a full stop. She held the flawless, stone-still pose for several moments. The curtain fell and a lighted sign announced a fifteen-minute intermission. People rose to their feet; a woman seated in front of them, who had the air of a restaurateur, greeted several individuals around her in the audience.

"Right after intermission is the *Snow* number you've been wanting to see," he whispered to his wife.

"Yes, I know. It has really been wonderful so far."

"Shall we go out in the lobby?"

They went out into the congested lobby and sat down.

"There's something I want to talk to you about." His wife put her silver-colored handbag on her lap and turned toward him with a serious expression.

"What is it?"

"It's hard to talk about this here, but I've been thinking about firing Mitsu."

"Firing her?"

"I knew you wouldn't like the idea, so I haven't said anything until now. . . . But she's stolen money on two different occasions. The first time, some envelopes with money for the gas and water bills disappeared from the table at your office. Then yesterday I found a registered envelope from the television station lying on the floor in the hall. The money inside was gone."

Suguro pictured Mitsu's face and was silent for a moment. "But what makes you think it's her?"

"When I asked her, she said she took it."

"She admitted it? Just like that?"

"Yes. She said that the mother of one of her best friends had left home. The father, who throws all his money away at the bike races, was in the hospital on top of everything else, and the girl had to take care of her brothers and sisters."

"So Mitsu felt sorry for her friend and took the money to give to her?"

"Yes."

"That's the kind of girl she is. She's just as tenderhearted as you said."

His wife sighed. "But we can't have her stealing. I had a good talk with her after the first time, but then she went and did the same thing again. I can't feel at ease with her any more, and I'd like to get the whole thing settled."

"I see. . . . " Suguro paused. "Do whatever you want. After all, we didn't hire her because we had to."

Suguro recalled his dream. His wife did not know that Mitsu had appeared nude in his dream. There was of course no reason for him to tell her about it. But had she sensed some vague, instinctive danger in bringing Mitsu into her husband's office? Because he had never regarded her as the sort of woman to engender such feelings, he looked her hard in the face.

But she said calmly, "Yesterday I went to the hospital where Mitsu's friend's father is staying."

"Why?"

"I was worried about what would happen to him after we fired Mitsu. The hospital is near the subway exit in Omote Sandō, and it seems the man has cancer. I left a little something with the nurse and asked her to give it to the man's children. . . . The nurse knew all about Mitsu. She said on days when the patient's daughter couldn't come, Mitsu came in her place and looked after him. That's what made her take the money."

The first bell rang, and several of the patrons who had gathered in groups to chat began making their way back into the auditorium. Many in the audience seemed to be women dressed in professional geisha attire and businessmen with a fondness for classical Japanese music. Someone noticed Suguro and bowed to him from the distance, but for the life of him Suguro couldn't remember the man's name. It made him feel all the more keenly how forgetful he had become. So Mitsu would no longer be coming to his office. That was all right. Each time he saw her pushing the vacuum cleaner and singing, he was depressed by his memories of that dream.

"There were several volunteers working at the hospital. They divide up the responsibilities and come to help out. When I went, there was a truly elegant lady working there as a volunteer. The nurses told me she was a widow and that her husband had been a college professor."

He stood up, only half-listening to what his wife was saying. They walked shoulder to shoulder toward the door of the auditorium.

"This Mrs. Naruse works there twice a week as a volunteer. You know that I've been thinking about doing volunteer work for a while now. Well, I learned all sorts of interesting things from the nurse."

"What did you just say? That woman's name?"

"Mrs. Naruse. Is something wrong?"

"No, it's nothing. I thought it was someone else." He covered his tracks and again peered into his wife's face.

It couldn't be the same woman.

The woman at the coffee shop had introduced herself as Mrs. Naruse. He also had the impression that she had mentioned her volunteer work, but he couldn't be certain. At his age, he no longer had distinct memories of events that had happened even recently.

"I wonder if I ought to study to become a volunteer. What do you think?"

"You can do anything as long as it doesn't affect your arthritis. You don't have a son to look after any more."

"Will you be in your office tomorrow?"

"I've got an autograph session at Kinokuniya Bookstore in Shinjuku. Tomorrow afternoon."

When Suguro and Kurimoto arrived at the bookstore in Shinjuku the following afternoon, a line of autograph-seekers had already formed. The line included young students as well as middle-aged women and older men. Suguro flashed a warm, friendly smile in their direction as he stood in front of the table for the signing.

These are my readers. The ones who read my books and lend me their support.

Sometimes, as he sat at his tiny desk, he would try to imagine what sorts of people would read his stories. With dread, he wondered how distorted each work, permeated with the odor of his own life and formed like kneaded clay from his own hands, would end up by the time it reached his readers. This very minute, those readers were lined up before his eyes.

"We'd like to have you come forward now in numerical order to get your autograph," a store employee was saying into a portable microphone. "Please place your number slips on top of the book and then hand it to the clerk here."

Slowly, Suguro removed the cap from the black calligraphy pen, smiled at the first young man who held a book out to him, and wrote his name.

"My n-n-name, too. . . ." Out of nervousness, perhaps, he stuttered. The bookstore assistant started to refuse the request, but Suguro added the young man's name. He felt it was the least gesture of gratitude he could offer someone willing to read his work.

After about fifty signatures, his wrist began to tire. The tip of the calligraphy pen had worn down, and it was difficult to write with it. He wiped his hands with a cold towel and removed the cap from a new pen.

There was an assortment of readers. Along with the middle-aged women who thanked him courteously as they walked away, there was one old man who snatched his autographed book away with a sullen look. His grandson had asked him to get the signature, but he was in a huff over having to wait in line so long, the assistant confided to Suguro. One man seemed to be a used-book dealer. He took a stack of ten of Suguro's books out of a cloth bag and asked the author to sign them all.

Suguro took a short break after signing a hundred books. A new line began to form during that interval.

Kurimoto was negotiating with the bookstore assistant. "There are too many people. Let's bring it to a halt after a hundred and twenty."

"It's all right, I don't mind." Suguro waved his hand. "I'll sign another thirty or so."

As he looked at the front of the line of readers, Suguro

saw a familiar article of clothing. It was a blue windbreaker with white sleeves. The man who wore it brusquely demanded, "Write my name in there, too."

The assistant intervened. "We really don't have the time for that, I'm afraid."

"I saw some other people get their names put in. Please write 'For Kobari Yoshio.' You write the *bari* with the character for needle, and the *Yoshi* means righteousness."

Sensing the man's eyes on him, Suguro wrote out the four characters that made up the name of Kobari Yoshio. Just as he finished writing, it came to him in a flash. Kobari was the name of the journalist whom Kanō had mentioned in the hotel lobby after the committee meeting.

But he could not be certain this man was the journalist merely because of his name. As he opened the next reader's book to sign, he followed the man with his eyes. The man disappeared down the stairs. At that moment Suguro had the feeling he had seen the young man somewhere before, but he had no idea where.

Maybe I'm wrong.

He tried to force himself to relax, but it was hopeless. Before long, Suguro had convinced himself that the man had come with the intention of feeling him out. *But there's nothing to be worried about,* he told himself as he massaged his right forearm.

When he had finished signing autographs and stood up, his legs felt unsteady. His arms were tired and his shoulders painfully stiff. He thought of the look on his doctor's face as he turned in that squeaky chair and suspected that his test results would be precarious again today.

"I'd like to get some rest," he told Kurimoto.

"Of course, but . . . there's a fellow waiting over there who says he *has* to thank you for something."

77

Suguro looked in the direction Kurimoto was pointing. The autograph session was over, the store was preparing to close, and the floor was almost deserted. Each of the bookshelves seemed to be facing toward him, oppressively. Beyond them, standing ceremoniously stiff, was a young man with thick glasses.

He gave a clumsy Pinocchio-like bow and said in a strained voice, "Ever since I was in school, I've been a great fan. I've read almost nothing except your books."

"Really?"

"I work at a school for handicapped children. I didn't like it at first, but I'm very happy there now. I have your books to thank for that."

Suguro listened to the onerous words with a smile on his face. The young man, oblivious to Suguro's embarrassment, pushed his glasses up his nose and took a photograph album from under his arm.

"Would you look at these? They're pictures of Kōmyō Academy."

"Kōmyō Academy?"

"That's the school for handicapped children where I work."

Four or five photographs were pasted onto each page of the cheap album. One picture was of the young man dressed in sports clothes, bowling with his students at a fitness event. In another he was pushing a wheelchair for a paraplegic child. Yet another showed him at a cultural festival, his leg poised in midair as he held hands with a child dressed up as a rabbit.

"On nights when I'm on duty, after I tuck the children into bed, I very often read one of your novels."

Suguro could say nothing in reply.

"It may be impertinent of me to say so, but at those times I feel eyes of some sort behind me. Gentle eyes keeping watch over the children."

Suguro looked away. The convictions of this young man, who professed to be inspired by Suguro's fiction and to derive joy from his present line of work, weighed heavily on Suguro's heart. But even with his eyes averted, he maintained his plastic smile—the same smile that he kept in reserve for his family and for any readers he might pass on the street.

"That's a very nice thought, but a novel doesn't have the power to change a reader's heart," he mumbled in an attempt to buoy up his own emotions. "At least my novels don't . . ."

"Oh yes. Yes, they do." The young man seemed to take Suguro's refutation as modesty. Again he slid his glasses up his nose. "If they didn't, I wouldn't have . . . decided to be baptized."

"Baptized?"

"Yes. I'm going to be baptized next month."

Suguro felt no elation of any kind. So his books had given direction to the life of one individual. To Suguro, the very idea was unbelievable. He felt like a hypocrite and stared at the ground. He had not written a single story with the intent of instructing others. He had not become a novelist with the goal of promulgating Christianity.

"Would you shake my hand?" There was grime under the nail of the young man's index finger. Suguro feebly clutched the sweaty hand.

When he looked up, someone was watching them from the doorway behind the young man. It was the arrogant fellow who had demanded the autograph earlier. The man looked on as these two shook hands, an expression of derision evident on his face.

The cogwheels rotating at the very core of his heart suddenly went berserk. The reason for the malfunction was clear.

Something had intruded itself into Suguro's life on the night of the awards ceremony, and the internal machinery that had run in smooth synchronization up until then abruptly ran amok.

In his only refuge—his tiny study—Suguro lay his head down on his desk and lectured himself over and over again. *It's nothing. You're exaggerating the whole thing.*

That was surely the case. Other writers had had impostors annoy them, and they would regard his problem in the same light. All he had to do was ignore it like the others had, and the problem would vanish.

The thought should have been reassuring, but his mood did not improve.

Images floated before his eyes. The face identical to his own that he had seen at the awards ceremony. Superimposed on that was the portrait hanging in the gallery. The base, loathsome, sneering smile was the same in both images.

Sometimes when his wife was not there, he would go into the bathroom at his office and stare at his face in the mirror. A fatigue-worn face. Yellow-splotched eyes. A spray of white hair in his sideburns. The face of a sixty-five-year-old man. He was sixty-five and still full of doubts. He was restless and as skittish as a mouse.

He stuck his tongue out at the mirror and remembered a scene from a German film he had seen in his middle-school days. It was about an aging—sixty-five, in fact—stage actor who fell in love with a young woman and ended up jilted and scarred by the experience. In the film, the old man had scornfully stuck his tongue out at himself in the dressing-room mirror.

This is who you are. This is your face. Just how different is it from the face in the portrait? A voice deep inside him posed the question. It was directed at a man concerned solely with his public image, constantly aware of the eyes of his readers. The question was intended, it seemed, to nudge him in one direction or another.

Late in the middle of that night, he woke up to the ringing of the telephone.

Who could that be? At this time of night?

His wife, too, had been awakened. "Would you like me to answer it?"

"No, I'll get it." He left the bedroom and turned on the hallway light. He brought the receiver to his ear, and in a voice that even he recognized as angry said, "Hello. Hello?"

The caller did not respond.

Whoever it was seemed to be listening to his reaction. Eventually the line went dead. Suguro had the feeling it was not a mere crank call, and for a while he stood motionless in the darkness, scarcely even breathing.

On Saturday evening, his wife came to clean the office.

"I'm going to do some shopping in Omote Sandō," he told her. "I'm running out of 3B pencils, and I'll probably end up sleeping here tonight. I'm not making much headway with my work."

"Oh?"

She was dusting a flower vase and showed no signs of doubting her husband. She knew that Suguro used only 3B pencils to write the drafts of his stories.

"I don't mind your staying the night," she said. "But tomorrow is Sunday."

"It is, isn't it."

"You really should go to church once in a while." She smiled as though she were teasing a child. When Suguro saw that look, his memory suddenly flashed back to a short story by a foreign writer. It was a masterful work describing the relationship between a middle-aged man and his wife. The wife was the epitome of a compassionate, model spouse and did everything for her husband without complaint. She was fastidious at cleaning the house, always cleaned the sheets, and was an excellent cook. Though he was grateful for such a wife, he wearied of her for reasons he could not explain. Thus he began an affair with a woman he had met at a bar. When he visited the woman's chaotic apartment with the cries of children seeping through the walls, he somehow felt a sense of tranquillity he had never experienced with his wife.

"Yes, I know. And I'll be eating out."

"Call me tonight, OK?"

Suguro was ashamed to have thought of that particular story as he spoke to his wife. He left the office and took a shortcut to Omote Sandō. He was only halfway up the steep slope when he ran out of breath. Old age had not confined itself to his liver; it gnawed insidiously at every part of his body. If he got fewer hours of sleep than usual, the next day he had no energy, and when he went for long walks he felt sharp pains in the core of his knees. At such times, he sensed death slowly approaching.

In the brief period during which he had neglected this route, a new store displaying foreign-made shoes and a record shop had opened in Aoyama Street. After buying his pencils, he walked along the street. The lampposts were already beginning to flicker on, and the leaves had fallen from the trees planted along the promenade. Before long, he passed in front of the hospital that his wife had mentioned to him. It was facing directly onto Aoyama Street, and through a window he could see a young woman in a white gown gazing languidly down at the street.

The waiting room was deserted. In front of the pharmacy,

an elderly patient huddled and puffed on a cigarette as though he were cold. Suguro asked a passing nurse for directions to the pediatric ward.

"Are you here to see a patient? I'm afraid visits in the pediatric ward are limited to family members."

"No, I'm looking for one of the volunteers who works there."

"What's the name?"

"Mrs. Naruse."

After a pause, the nurse raised her arm as though she were handing him a letter of reprieve and pointed to the elevators, directing him to the fourth floor. As he waited for the elevator, Suguro wondered why he had come to see Madame Naruse, and again he thought of the foreign story. He had met her only once, so what had stirred his interest in this woman? He had become aware of his desire to see her only after he had bought the pencils. Was it because he felt he could talk to her about things he could never discuss with his wife?

A young doctor was in the elevator that had ascended from the basement. When it stopped on the fourth floor, both Suguro and the doctor stepped out into the hallway.

White silhouettes fluttered like seaweed behind the frosted glass at the nurses' station. From his own long experience in the hospital, Suguro knew that this was a relatively quiet hour of the day for the hospital staff.

"Where would I find a volunteer named Mrs. Naruse?"

He heard the nurses talking to each other.

"Mrs. Naruse? Is she in today?"

"I think she's in the physiotherapy room," one of them said.

He walked down the corridor in search of the physiotherapy room. When he passed the restroom, he saw the doctor who had been in the elevator straightening his hair.

"Which way is the physiotherapy room?"

"Right at the end."

The doctor showed no suspicion of Suguro. He even bowed, perhaps recognizing him as a writer who had appeared on television.

As he approached the physiotherapy room, Suguro heard an infant's cry. When he peeked through the door, he saw Madame Naruse, dressed in a blue jogging suit, and a young nurse who looked no older than a high-school girl, helping a child of ten or so to practice walking. Suguro decided he should just watch from a distance and then go home. The child, clutching the parallel bars, struggled to move forward one step at a time, as Madame Naruse instructed. A girl of six or seven came running up to her and clutched her jogging suit.

"Tell me the Boopie story," she said, tugging at the volunteer's sleeve.

The boy in the walker stopped and concurred. "Yes, tell us the Boopie story."

"All right, Shige. I'll tell you if you take two more steps." She took both of the girl's hands in hers and with a smile drew her close.

"What's Boopie?" the nurse asked.

"It's a fairy tale I made up. It's about a big bully of a wolf who has been ostracized by all the other animals in the forest. But there's just one animal, a little rabbit named Boopie, who treats him kindly, and he finally mends his ways."

"That's a nice story. Do you make up a lot of stories like that, Mrs. Naruse?"

"The children asked me so many times to tell them stories that I finally ran out of all the stories I read when I was a child. So I started inventing my own."

"Did you tell the stories to your own children, too?"

"Oh, I don't have any children."

The children tugged insistently at Mrs. Naruse's arm. The nurse reproached them, and Shige began to cry. The volunteer picked him up in her arms to soothe him and started to tell him the story of Boopie. Yes, Suguro thought, now she's in my wife's realm. When she's like this she's identical to my wife. But this same woman, when they had exchanged views about Suguro's fiction, had willingly discussed topics like sex that his own wife would never dream of mentioning.

"The little rabbit, he brought some ice to help fix up the eye that the wolf had hurt."

"What happened to the bad pussycat?" Shige asked from Mrs. Naruse's lap.

"The bad pussycat was lying in wait along the road to ambush the little rabbit."

She looked up and glanced toward the door, and there she noticed Suguro. She broke off her story in surprise and glanced down at her jogging outfit. "Oh, to be seen like this." Her large eyes flashed embarrassment when she smiled.

Suguro waited outside the pharmacy on the first floor while she changed her clothes.

"I'm so sorry." She reappeared wearing the same beige coat she had worn the first time he met her. "Sorry to keep you waiting. You caught me off guard."

Suguro explained that his wife had been to the hospital a few days before and had heard Mrs. Naruse's name mentioned.

"She tells me you're quite famous among the volunteers here."

"Oh, my. . . . It's just that I've been coming here for so long."

"Where do you go from here?"

"Home. Not that I have a husband to look after, of course."

Her tone indicated that she expected an invitation from Suguro. He recalled a Chinese restaurant nearby that specialized in chicken wings. The words of invitation flowed naturally from his mouth.

"Are you sure it's all right? Not going back home? Your wife will be waiting for you, won't she?"

"She's going to have to eat alone tonight anyway. I've got work piled up. She's used to it."

"I feel sorry for her." The sympathy stopped at her lips. In sudden recollection she said, "You'll have to forgive me for the things I said the other day."

The Chinese restaurant was unusually crowded for this early in the evening. The manager, who knew Suguro from his previous visits, directed them to a corner table, where Suguro had dined on two earlier occasions with his wife. Suguro sat down across from Madame Naruse, who was seated in the same chair in which his wife had sat. He felt another twinge of the pain that had stabbed at his chest earlier.

"Do you have a problem with spicy dishes?" he asked in an attempt to dispel the pain.

"No, I like them. This is Szechwan cuisine, isn't it?"

"Yes, so the flavor may be rather strong."

Suguro ordered *Yún bái ròu*, a pork and garlic dish, and *Yú tóu shā gūo*, a pungently seasoned fish head.

"Well, well now," he said humorously, "you really seem to be fond of children."

"I am. What about you?"

"Oh, I suppose I fussed over my son as much as any parent. But he's married and working overseas now, so I haven't seen him in a long while. Why are you doing volunteer work at the hospital?"

She smiled. "Maybe it's because I don't have any children of my own, but I love the feel of a child against my body when I hold one. They're so soft, and they smell so sweet."

"What do you do when you aren't at the hospital?"

"My cousin runs an antique art business at Kyōbashi." Her lip curled. "How dreadful. This is starting to sound like a background investigation. Writers really ask anything and everything, don't they?"

"My apologies. . . . There are a lot of things I suddenly felt like talking about with you."

When the meal was served, Madame Naruse plied her fingers and chopsticks meticulously, and she dined with agreeable gusto. Suguro carefully studied her large eyes and wide forehead as well as the movements of her mouth as she was eating. There was something about her that was utterly unlike his wife. They discussed food as they ate. When he began to tell her about a superb seafood restaurant he had unearthed in Hong Kong, she surprised him by saying she was familiar with it.

"Do you go abroad often, then?"

For some reason she hesitated. "Yes. Once every couple of years. But my trips are peculiar."

"Meaning . . . ?"

"I make a special plan and then set out. But anyway," she said, quickly changing the subject, "the other day I read your story in this month's *Shinryū Magazine*."

"As you pointed out once before, it's another story that avoids the subject of sex."

"I'm sorry. After you left, I really wished I hadn't said anything. It was the first time I'd met you, and to be so rude . . . "

"Not at all. I'm very grateful for what you said. That's what first intrigued me about you. But why is someone like you—someone who does volunteer work at the hospital—so interested in sex?"

"Is there something wrong with that?" She wiped her mouth with her napkin. "For a hospital volunteer to be interested in sex? What's truly strange is for you to think that way. Excuse me for asking, but I get the feeling that you never discuss such things at home, do you?"

"No, my wife and I have hardly ever mentioned the subject. . . . Does that mean you discussed it with your late husband?"

"No." She shook her head soberly. "Of course we didn't. But it was our sexual relationship that created the deep bond between us—or rather, something buried in both our hearts that was manifested in sex. There was a unity between us in that way."

She had finally touched on the topic he most wanted to pursue with her. As a writer, he felt the tactile responsiveness and the thrill one experiences upon hooking a fish.

"I don't really understand what you mean." He feigned ignorance, as the specialty of the house, a scorched rice dish, was brought to the table and he ladled the crusty rice into a small bowl.

"I suppose not."

"Would it be rude of me to ask for more details?"

"Yes, it would be rude." She smiled. "That was something private between my husband and myself alone."

Suguro was captivated by her crisp rebuff. She appeared even more of a mystery, and curiosity tingled inside him.

"It's the kind of story that rouses a writer," he muttered, mostly to himself.

She pretended not to hear, keeping her eyes down and poking at her food with her chopsticks.

"You said before that sex expresses our profoundest secrets."

She smiled and opened her eyes impudently wide. "I'm not going to talk about it, even if you try to beat it out of me."

"You don't understand. I'm not trying to find out the details of your private life. Just answer the harmless questions. Do you honestly believe that sex expresses the secrets that are buried in our hearts?"

"Yes."

"That was the case with you and your husband, wasn't it? Now, I'm not asking about the inner secrets between the two of you. What I want to ask you is . . . you dip the rice into the soup and eat it . . . what I want to ask is, when did the two of you become aware that such secrets existed?"

"I don't know about my husband, but in my case I never suspected until I was married, no, until after I'd been married for a while, that *those* kinds of secrets were hidden inside me."

"You first realized it after you'd been married for a while."

"That's right. After a certain something happened."

"That certain something being . . . ? Don't worry, I'm not asking for details. . . . At some point, you became aware of something inside yourself that you had not been conscious of before. Is that accurate?"

There was no way to shut him up once his curiosity as a novelist had begun to pump like the pistons of an engine. This was always the case with him.

"Yes, I became aware of secrets I had not known about before," Madame Naruse repeated, carefully placing her chopsticks on her plate.

"Secrets you had not known before then." Suguro, too, repeated the words. He tried imagining various possibilities, but her face revealed nothing.

Deftly operating her long chopsticks, she brought the scorched rice, called *Shí jǐn gūo bā*, to her lips. A dry, crunching sound came from her mouth as she bit into the crisp rice. As Suguro stared at the movements of her mouth, he felt a raw carnality there. It was an erotic sensation, reminiscent of a sexual act in a way that had never occurred to him when he had dined with his wife—or any other woman—before. And in the movements of her fingers as she plied her chopsticks and lifted her cup to her mouth, there was a fluidity that made him think of a spider entwining its prey in a web.

"You seem to be enjoying your food." He sighed instinctively.

"Oh? I am very fond of eating."

"One thing about that art exhibit. You said you knew the woman who painted that portrait."

"That's right."

"Did she say anything about . . . about me—I mean, about the man who is impersonating me?"

"A little."

"Such as?"

"Such as having a drink together, and doing the preliminary sketch for your portrait."

"Hold on. That isn't me. It's a portrait of the impostor." Suguro set down his chopsticks and looked at Madame Naruse rather desperately. "Does my face look as repulsive as that to you?"

"Why are you so caught up in this whole thing?" Madame Naruse raised her eyes and studied his face. "If you're repulsive, then I'm a repulsive woman."

Not knowing what she had in mind by a "repulsive woman," Suguro said nothing. Madame Naruse stretched out her hand and took a few of the small shrimps on her plate to eat. He could see her teeth moving behind her gently closed lips. Her expression as she relished her food reminded him of something. That was it—the look of a carnivore as it devours its prey. The matron he had seen surrounded by children at the hospital seemed to have changed into a completely different woman now.

"You seem like someone else altogether." He exhaled once again.

"In what sense?"

"The way you look when you eat. I can't relate it to how you looked at the hospital."

"Well, that's perfectly understandable. No one has just one guise or one expression."

For a moment, Suguro wondered if this was the look that had been on her face when she made love to her husband.

"Then do you have other guises, other personalities?"

"Do you?"

"I suppose I must have. Without them I couldn't write."

"That's just how I am."

A waiter dressed in white escorted a young couple to the table next to theirs. The man looked as though he had come directly from playing tennis on the indoor courts at the nearby gymnasium. He put his racket on a vacant chair.

"What other kinds of personalities do you have?" Suguro asked.

She avoided the question. "Oh, look at the snow."

The young man's hair glistened in spots, as though coated with dew. The snow was beginning to melt.

"Can't I persuade you to tell me?" he persisted. "Under any circumstances?"

"Sometime, maybe. . . . Sometime I'll tell you," she muttered through her smile.

"Oh, look at the snow outside."

The woman mumbled to herself as she opened the window

to take in the stockings she had hung out to dry. Hearing her voice, Kobari quickly hid the photograph under a book. But she went directly into the kitchen, so he took the picture out again.

The woman in glasses had a belt tightly wound around her neck, and her lips were slightly parted. Her tongue peeked through, and the excretions from her mouth blotted her chin like coffee grounds. There was not a trace of agony in her expression. She appeared to be smiling. It looked to be a smile of joy.

The photograph had come into his hands totally by accident that afternoon. He had been visiting a friend who sold particular kinds of freelance photographs to such magazines as *Focus* and *Friday*.

In the apartment house workroom that his friend shared with kindred photographers, numerous strands of film dangled blackly from the windows like pantyhose, and a large desk was piled high with freshly developed prints. While his friend worked in the darkroom, Kobari flipped through the photographs and read the captions scribbled on the back of each with a ball-point pen: *Molested high-school girl and the assailant, who was arrested at Shinjuku Station; Well-known actress reunited with the father she has not seen since childhood.*

As Kobari shuffled through the photographs as if he were sorting trump cards, his hand stiffened and froze.

"Hey!" he called to his friend.

"What?" The door to the darkroom opened, and the photographer, dressed in a lab coat, thrust his head out in irritation.

"What's this a picture of?"

"That?" His friend gaped at the photograph that Kobari was waving in front of him. "That was a party at a special hotel in Roppongi, sponsored by a wife-swapping magazine.

Let's see, at this one there were mainly people with kinky tastes. Parties like this are pretty commonplace in Tokyo these days. I don't know if a publisher will want them, but I thought I'd take them over to *Friday* anyway."

"Did you meet this woman?"

"Which woman? Let me see." In the chilly room, his breath was white as he spoke. As he reached toward Kobari to take the photograph, his lab coat gave off the pungent smell of chemicals.

"Hmm, I really don't remember her at all. There were twelve or thirteen people there, and at first they kind of stood back and hesitated, but before long the place was half-crazy with activity. . . . Oh, now I remember. This woman here, . . . the men of like persuasion really made a big thing of her. They called her Mot-chan."

"Was she wearing glasses?"

"I can't remember. Do you know her?"

"Sort of. What's the name of the hotel where you took these?"

"The Château Rouche, at Roppongi."

Kobari stuck an unlit cigarette in his mouth and looked at another photograph. In this one she was not wearing glasses, but it was definitely the same woman. He recognized the round face and plump body from when he had spoken to her at the café bar on Sakura Street. She and three or four naked men were toasting each other with beer bottles and glasses. Several hazy profiles of men and women looking the other way appeared in the background. Kobari tried to locate Suguro in the group. There were two slender men who might possibly be him, but one of them was the wrong age. The other man looked somewhat like the writer, but Kobari could not be certain. Of greater interest to him was the blurred back of a woman facing away from the camera. Something about her back reminded him of the older woman he had tailed recently.

"You must have had a hell of a time getting into a party like this."

"I've got connections. It's tough for a photographer. You have to set your bait in all kinds of places."

"Could I borrow this photo just for a day?" Kobari asked. "I'll make it up to you."

The Château Rouche, at Roppongi—Kobari knew almost instantly that his friend, who had no facility for languages, had confused it for the Château Rouge. It was an S&M hotel renowned among men and women of that predilection.

Kobari took the photograph and boarded the subway to Roppongi. His friend had verified that the woman in glasses was widely known and called Mot-chan by those of her persuasion. So an inquiry at the Château Rouge might provide more detailed information. And with that information there was a possibility that he could get his hands on the truth about Suguro.

"Disgusting."

Half an hour later, Kobari had lured the woman who managed the Château Rouge into a snack bar across the street. She knit her brows and clutched a menthol cigarette between fingernails painted a wine red.

"It's disgusting the way you guys always have to take pictures when we have these parties. You're reporters, right? This woman doesn't work for me. She first came as a client with a man, then she became a regular, and every now and then we hire her as a part-time helper. That's it."

"What kind of helper?"

"There aren't many women who'll consent to play the

masochist role. They make a lot more money in a day than the sadists, but we have some pretty violent men among our clientele, so nobody else'll do it. . . . But she's a real pro."

"What exactly does she do?"

"I can't explain it in words."

The manager was a long-faced woman of about forty who wore large tinted glasses. A chain was attached to the frames, and it shimmered every time she blew the smoke from her cigarette.

"Then what's a 'real pro' masochist?"

"Well . . . " She exhaled some smoke and mulled over the question. "The heart of the matter is that Motoko really wants to die."

"Has she had some tragedy in her life?"

"Tragedy?"

"Something very painful. That would make her want to die."

The woman stared blankly at Kobari. Then a condescending smile spread across her lips like a ripple on a lake. "You're really innocent, huh. She's a masochist. Masochists are people who like to suffer."

"What kind of men did she come with? I'd like to know."

"We respect the confidentiality of our clients. After all, some of our customers are famous actors, baseball players, and businessmen." She spoke boastfully, as though this list were the pride of her establishment. Then she took a long drink of the rosé wine she had ordered.

"How about writers? I bet you have some famous writers, too."

The expression on her face did not change, but the hand that held her cigarette fluttered.

"Hmm. I wonder."

He pressed her. "I won't make any trouble for you."

"I've got to get back. I can't leave the business unattended."

On the television screen, Suguro appeared somewhat fatter than he really was, and four or five years younger. But when he moved, the shadows and emaciated lines of age erupted clearly on his jaw and neck.

"Mr. Suguro, you're a writer who has spent many years recording human sin," the interviewer was saying.

Initially, Kobari had no idea whether this man with the long face who spoke with measured vivaciousness was a critic or a network announcer.

"But just how would you define sin as it appears in your literature?"

The camera zoomed in for a close-up of Suguro as he blinked his eyes.

"I think there are two aspects of sin." From nervousness, perhaps, his voice seemed clogged with phlegm. "In order to live in our society, every day we suppress a variety of desires and instinctive urges. There is a sector of the heart that stores up those drives." He pointed to his chest. "It is the realm we call the unconscious. . . . These suppressed drives and instincts are not extinguished, but collect within the unconscious, waiting for the opportunity to spurt forth once again. When they spew out in some distorted shape, we often end up committing acts that I have chosen to label sins."

"Mr. Suguro, since we're on television, could you explain this in somewhat simpler terms?" The interviewer tilted his head and smiled ingratiatingly.

Suguro was somewhat put out, but he continued. "Let me

give you an example. Many times in our lives in society our pride is wounded, or we are unable to find suitable outlets to satisfy our desires or our sense of superiority. Would you agree with that?"

"Certainly. That sort of thing happens every day."

"At those times, we can't simply hurl our dissatisfactions into the face of whoever has offended us. And so a rift develops in what had been a perfectly harmonious relationship. In this way, each day we compact our discontent and our resentment into the bottom of our hearts, but they don't just dissolve there. Suppressed passion never dissipates. In reality, these emotions are stored up in our hearts, where they smolder like embers in a hibachi."

"That seems like a very Freudian view."

"You could certainly regard it as Freudian. . . . Those smoldering embers can unexpectedly burst into flame. They can catch fire."

"Quite true. In fact, the heroes in all of your novels seem to be people who are suffocated by the lives they lead. They writhe in agony in that stifling condition until they end up committing sin."

"That's right. My protagonists groan in torment and ultimately wind up committing sin."

He batted his eyes and croaked out the words—minute actions that were a manifestation of Suguro's nervous disposition. But Kobari realized for the first time, as he saw Suguro in close-up, that there was something uneven about the writer's face. One eye was larger than the other. His right eye was bigger than his left eye. To Kobari, the two eyes began to look like a Picasso painting in which the eyes are observing two separate objects. It was as though the caption *Multiple Personalities* had suddenly been superimposed upon Suguro's image on the screen. Come to think of it, Kobari had read in some new "how-to" book that many people with eyes of different size have duplicitous personalities.

"Then are you saying, Mr. Suguro, that in your writing sin is generated not so much from the conscious as from the unconscious mind?" the horse-faced interviewer asked.

After a moment of perplexity, Suguro corrected him. "No. More precisely, I think that sins of every variety are linked in one way or another to the unconscious."

"Then we can consider the unconscious mind to be the womb, the hotbed of sin, would you say? Is that the concept of sin you believe in, Mr. Suguro?"

"I . . ." Suguro blinked. "I'm not a theologian. You'll have to ask an expert about these matters. I've just stumbled toward that idea while writing my stories."

"I see." The interviewer's eyes evinced sincere curiosity for the first time. "As a matter of fact, the other day I posed the same question to the noted Buddhologist, the Reverend Takemoto. It seems that the doctrine of 'Consciousness Only' in Mahayana Buddhism shares the same views you have just expressed, Mr. Suguro."

Suguro nodded but did not speak.

"We have a tape of the Reverend Takemoto's comments, which I'd like us to look at together, Mr. Suguro. Unfortunately the Reverend Takemoto was unable to be with us today. He's on his way to Paris to participate in an international conference of Buddhist philosophers."

A web of oblique red lines darted across the screen, and an energetic man with shaven head appeared, both hands folded neatly in his lap.

The same interviewer, seated to one side, seemed to be trying to induce his subject to comment. "Buddhism, then, has taught for many centuries that it is the unconscious mind that governs the human heart. Is that a fair summation?"

"I suppose that is accurate."

"What is the name given to this realm of the unconscious in Mahayana teachings?"

The Reverend Takemoto spoke deliberately, as though he were reciting a prearranged speech. "Yes. We call it the Manas-Consciousness and the Ālaya-Consciousness. The Manas-Consciousness could be described as something like an egotistical consciousness. This is the region where we put ourselves at the center of every event, where we regard every incident in terms of our personal interests, and where we consider only our own benefit. The Ālaya-Consciousness, on the other hand, is the place where the seeds of desire and carnal appetite that produce all our sufferings swirl about in countless numbers."

"By seeds, you are referring, I believe, to the Sanskrit term *bīja*. These desires and appetites—in Buddhism they are regarded as sins, aren't they?"

"Yes, you could say that."

"And these seeds that are the source of sin are swirling around in our unconscious minds?"

"That is correct. We call them the 'seeds of defilement.' "

Oblique lines again flickered across the screen, and the camera picked up on Suguro in the studio.

"Mr. Suguro, it seems to me that this Buddhist view is very similar to your opinion."

Suguro, somewhat lost, had to agree.

"Have you studied Mahayana Buddhism? You are a Christian, of course . . . "

"No, I haven't studied Buddhism. As I said earlier, I came to this idea in the course of writing my stories."

Kobari could tell from the melancholy shadow that appeared on Suguro's forehead that the writer had grown tired. He reached toward the television set and turned off the tedious, irritating voices of the two men and then stared at Suguro's face as it silently mouthed the words.

Eyes of differing size. Kobari couldn't be sure if this was a mark of double-dealing, but he could detect a somewhat turbid cloud over Suguro's face. He could not find words to describe just what that murkiness signified, but to Kobari the cloudy shadow was the secret part of this writer, which no one had yet uncovered.

"You are . . . a fraud," Kobari called out to the elderly writer, whose mouth still flapped silently. He turned the volume up again.

"Ah, then you are suggesting, Mr. Suguro, that while the unconscious mind is the womb of sin, it is simultaneously the womb of salvation?"

The topic had shifted while the volume had been off.

"Yes, that's my impression. Perhaps *salvation* is too strong of a word, but the sins that men commit are a manifestation of their yearning for rebirth."

"Rebirth?" The interviewer's eyes again flashed with undisguised interest.

Suguro nodded. "It's true that my characters squirm in suffocating circumstances and then commit their sins, but if you think about those sins . . . in the lives of the characters, they turn out to be . . . " As Suguro groped for the right words, he also seemed to be plumbing the interviewer's response. "Their sins, in the final analysis, end up being . . . an expression of their craving for a new way of life."

"Can that be called salvation?" the confused interviewer asked.

"Maybe it can't be styled salvation, but the potential for salvation is contained within the sin."

" 'The potential for salvation is contained within the sin.'

I consider that to be a remarkably unique opinion. Is that a Christian belief?"

"Well . . . " Once again there was an impatient look in Suguro's eyes. "I suppose it isn't. But that's the impression I've had while writing . . . "

"It seems to be another opinion rather similar to that of Buddhism. There is, for instance, the saying 'Good and evil are one and the same,' suggesting there is no distinction between the two."

"Oh? But my sense that the potential for salvation lies within sin isn't derived from Buddhism . . . "

"I see. Now we'd like to hear from the Reverend Takemoto once more. . . . "

The screen images were scrambled again, and Takemoto's pious face appeared.

"So the seeds of desire and lust swirl around in the womb of sin, the Ālaya-Consciousness. But isn't it true that Mahayana Buddhism teaches that the seeds of salvation are also activated within this same Ālaya-Consciousness?"

"Yes." Takemoto stole a glance at the script that was open on the table in front of him, an indication of his timid, uncompromisingly serious personality. "These are called 'seeds of purity.' Just as white blood cells devour bacteria in the body, these seeds slowly envelop the seeds of defilement, which bear the potential of evil desires, and proceed to purify them."

"Ah, then in the Buddhist view the unconscious is both the womb of sin and the matrix of Buddha's salvation?"

"That's generally the idea."

The front door was roughly thrown open, and Kobari's girlfriend, laden with shopping bags, called out to him, "Are you home? It's so cold outside." As she walked past the stained sofa where Kobari was stretched out in front of the television, she continued, "I wonder if it'll start snowing again."

"This doctrine of Mahayana Buddhism also seems to be what you're expressing in your work, Mr. Suguro."

"Which doctrine is that?"

"Are you sure you haven't been influenced by Buddhism, Mr. Suguro?"

"I don't think I have. But perhaps I have inherited some of that influence through the blood of my ancestors. . . . I am, after all, a Japanese writer, not a European or American writer."

"Why on earth are you watching this deadly stuff?" the woman asked in bewilderment as she placed a bag loaded with onions on the sofa.

"Be quiet. I'm working."

Kobari was not listening to the "deadly" conversation. His attention was riveted on the face of the writer caught in close focus—that face with unbalanced eyes and murky shadows. He still looked in his fifties if you concentrated on certain parts of his face, but when he twisted his neck the wrinkles that formed there exposed his old age. Kobari could tell that the writer, unaccustomed to television appearances, was exhausted by this dialogue. He might be able to temporize with his mouth, but it seemed to Kobari that the camera had captured the nebulous shadows within which lay the secrets this man had never displayed to the world.

His telephone was ringing. He heard its shrill clang as he opened the door to his office after returning from a walk. His telephone had rung late at night with no one at the other end. It had happened more than once or twice now. The caller was silent and seemed to be listening at the other end of the line for his response. He finally let the telephone ring unanswered, and the pertinacious noise eventually ceased in resignation.

He glanced at the mailbox, but it was empty. Perhaps the delivery was late today. He went into his study and switched on the desk lamp. The soft light he knew with fondness illuminated his penholder and the desk clock; the hands ticking away the seconds intensified the silence in the room. He rested his chin on his hands, and in the emptiness recalled the expression on Madame Naruse's face as she had savored the scorched rice dish. That look surfaced in his mind several times a day, stirring his curiosity about her. Exactly what sort of woman was she? There was an aspect of her mind, quite separate from her outward appearance, that somehow stimulated the authorial instincts in Suguro. Near the end of their evening at the restaurant, he had jokingly suggested that she write him a letter, but he could not imagine her acceding to such a request.

The telephone rang again. He ignored it, but it jangled persistently for over a minute. Finally, he gave up and lifted the receiver to his ear.

"Is this Suguro Sensei?" an insistent voice asked. "I'm a reporter by the name of Kobari. . . ."

"Kobari?" Suguro paused for a moment. "You contacted Mr. Kanō, didn't you?"

"That's right. I'd like to have a chat with you."

"What do you want? Is it the same old rumor that I'm frequenting disreputable neighborhoods?"

"I can't discuss it over the phone. If we could talk it over face to face, there'd be less chance of misunderstanding on either side."

"What do you mean by 'misunderstanding'?"

"It would be rather embarrassing for you, wouldn't it, if

103

I wrote about you solely on the basis of my own conclusions about the evidence?"

Suguro was ruffled by the intimidating tone of Kobari's voice. "Fine, I'll meet you. But I don't want you coming to my office."

"Then would you mind meeting me in Roppongi? Right now would be fine, if that's convenient."

Get this settled right away, a voice sounded inside Suguro's head. Reining in his agitation, he noted the address for their rendezvous. On his way out, he picked up the two or three letters that had fallen through the mail slot and crammed them into his coat pocket.

His taxi plodded down the bustling night streets, and he got out near the designated snack bar. When he walked through the door, he recognized the man seated with a glass of water in front of him as the one who had hounded him at the signing session.

"I've met you before, haven't I? At the signing session."

The man ignored this salutation and gestured with his chin toward a photograph lying on the table.

"Do you recognize this woman?"

Suguro looked at the photograph and said irritably, "No, I don't."

"Oh? Take a closer look. Are you sure you don't know her?"

"No, I've never seen her before."

"You're positive?" Kobari's eyes were unrelenting, like those of a detective interrogating a suspect.

"Absolutely positive."

"But . . . this woman told me she had had a good romp with you, Sensei. And then she sketched your portrait. She's an artist in the making. She works part time on Sakura Street doing portraits."

"Don't talk nonsense. None of that ever happened to me."

"But this woman is a good friend of a certain lady of your acquaintance."

"A certain lady? Who is that?"

"You met a certain woman at a coffee shop on Takeshita Street, didn't you?"

So that's it. Suguro finally realized that the man he had seen peering into the coffee shop the day he first met Madame Naruse was this reporter.

"And what of it?" Suguro was flustered. "Is there something wrong with that?"

"If that lady and the woman in this picture are close friends . . . I'm not sure you can insist you've never seen her before."

"I beg your pardon." Suguro's face flushed. "I don't intend to stay here and listen to false accusations. You can do what you want with the gossip you've picked up, but I shall have an appropriate response ready if you put any of it in print."

"I must apologize." Kobari meekly retracted, being a man who knew the correct tactics. "But the fact of the matter is that there are some unsavory rumors circulating about you. There was an eccentric woman spouting off a few at your reception, you know."

"I remember. But the rumors have nothing to do with me."

"In that case, you really ought to offer some evidence in one form or another to prove your innocence." Kobari drained his glass of water. When the bartender came to take his order, he brusquely asked for a whiskey and water. "I'm just a nobody of a reporter, but I've been getting information from people who claim they've seen you at a variety of places."

"That's someone impersonating me. He's a damned nuisance."

"Can you say that with complete confidence? If you can, would you be good enough to come with me and meet a woman near here? It won't take very long. You'll understand why once we get there. It'll only take ten minutes. You are confident in your position, aren't you?"

"Of course I'm confident," Suguro shot back at him, but even as he spoke he felt that he had fallen into this man's trap. A wind was gusting out of a back street as they left the snack bar. Kobari had switched to a flattering tone of voice.

"I have several friends who are fans of your work, Sensei." Suguro's face stiffened, and he did not respond.

At first glance, the Château Rouge appeared to be a commonplace three-story building. To avoid being seen by anyone, the patrons arrived in cars, as if they were visiting a motel.

"I don't want to make any trouble for you, so please wait here."

Kobari left Suguro standing in the street and disappeared through the doorway. Suguro buried his chin in the collar of his Burberry. When pedestrians approached, he lowered his eyes and tried to look as detached as a religious ascetic.

Kobari reappeared with a middle-aged woman in tow. With her sunglasses, she looked like the owner of a couturier's shop or boutique, the sort of woman who often strolls the streets of Roppongi, but she was introduced as the manager of this establishment.

She addressed Suguro hospitably. "Please come inside. You must be cold out here. This gentleman keeps asking me over and over again about whether you know Motoko, and whether you've been a guest at our château," she explained with a smile.

"Is that so?" Suguro strained to turn this woman into an ally. "I'd be grateful if you'd give him a clear denial, just as

I have. Apparently he's a magazine reporter, but his job seems to consist of writing filthy exposés. . . . And he wants to turn me into one of his victims. I intend to sue if he fabricates anything about me. If it comes to that, I'll want you to testify, but it may be messy for you."

"That would be a problem. We have some distinguished clients, and it would badly damage the trust we've built up."

"Then you're going to have to come clean," Kobari declared exultantly to the woman.

"Well . . . I'll show you some film. If you'll promise not to write anything."

"Film?"

"Yes. Some film from that party. I'll show you that, and if this gentleman doesn't appear in it, you've got to promise not to write about my parlor."

Kobari assented with his eyes. Suguro had no objections. The manager led them into the vacant building, which was still not open for business. The entire structure smelled of leather. Next to the cluttered office was a tiny reception room furnished with a television set and a badly faded sofa. A porcelain Hakata doll stood atop the television.

"Motoko painted this." The manager motioned toward a painting on the wall. On a canvas splattered with yellowish-brown paint, the artist had drawn swirls like the shell of a snail. The lines of the vortex were done in red.

"I can't stand abstract paintings." Kobari gave the painting only a passing glance.

The manager crouched down, inserted a videotape into the machine, and turned it on. The television screen lit up, and white static lines scurried across it. Suddenly, a large ballroom appeared, with naked men and women in black masks dancing together. Their movements were less like dancing than the slow fluttering of trees in the wind. From the contours of their breasts and stomachs it was evident that some of the women were no longer young. Several of the men were also strikingly fat and ugly.

"Was this filmed here?"

"Of course not. We rented out another place. For our third anniversary party."

Kobari unexpectedly came up with the name of the hotel. "It's a hotel in Yoyogi, isn't it?"

The manager pretended not to hear him. "Right here everyone's still at the jabbing stage," she explained wistfully.

"Jabbing?"

"They're all still strangers, so they feel each other out."

The scene changed. A middle-aged woman lay with her arms and legs splayed while three masked men fondled her from separate directions. The camera never moved while their heads busily roamed her body like dogs feverishly lapping up water. The names of wines he had learned many years ago skirted in and out of Suguro's mind—Médoc, Saint-Emilion, Entre-Deux-Mers. Perhaps it was his age. Unlike earlier times, when he watched the sexual grapplings of others, he was left feeling only chilled and miserable.

"This is a yawn." Kobari had also tired of seeing the same actions repeated over and over again. He pulled out a cigarette but twirled it in his fingers without smoking it. "There's no originality at all. They all do the same damn things. I can't believe they aren't bored to death."

"Motoko was the only one out of all of them who was able to climax," the manager murmured. "Right after this . . ."

"After this?"

"Yes. There's just a little more of this repetitious stuff."

There were in fact several more minutes of the same tedious sexual gropings on the tape. Although the body positions and techniques changed, every movement was ultimately hollow and sordid.

The screen suddenly went dark. A milk-white reflection shimmered on the screen for a few moments, and then abruptly a woman's face appeared, her mouth gaping. Though her eyes were open, her face looked like that of a blind person. Grayish splotches like strands of cotton streaked her hair. Kobari soon recognized her as the woman in the photographs, stripped of her glasses.

The camera panned downward. Someone's hands were wrapped around Motoko's throat and proceeded to tighten. A ring was on one finger; the hands were those of a man.

"What's the white stuff in her hair?" Kobari asked in a rasping voice that betrayed his agitation.

"There are four men tormenting Motoko here. The first one sprinkled wax from a candle on her. . . . Look, you can see wax on her shoulders. There are several globs in her hair. Then she begged for someone to strangle her, so another one of the men began choking her. . . ."

Motoko was looking up at the ceiling, her eyes half shut and her lips slightly parted. Her tongue thrashed back and forth as though her throat were parched. As the man's hands gradually tightened around her neck, it became evident that she was experiencing sensations of rapture and pleasure—the feeling of plummeting down a tunnel toward death. Part of the man's head towered over her.

Proudly, the manager declared, "You see how careful we are to avoid photographing the faces of our clients? Some of the men had taken off their masks at this point."

"The bitch is flapping her mouth like a goldfish. She must be in a lot of pain." Kobari shuddered, a look of loathing full on his face. For him, the world displayed on the video screen could be regarded only as an aberration.

The manager's voice was harsh, as though she had been personally insulted. "You should have heard what she shouted."

"She shouted? What did she shout?"

" 'Kill me!' "

"Oh? Like 'I'm dying, I'm dying,' eh?"

"No, not that. A true masochist, you see, really wants to be killed. They sincerely want to die. Often Motoko would say, 'I'm always afraid of death, but when I reach that point I want to be thrashed and beaten and then just melt away. I want to be hurt and tortured and then just die on the spot. That's how I feel deep down inside. How beautiful it would be if I could die like that.' "

"She's insane, crazy."

"Sane or crazy, people are all the same. Aren't they, Sensei?" The manager unexpectedly solicited Suguro's opinion. She seemed to think that, being a novelist, he would empathize with her feelings and those of the people captured in the videotape.

Suguro said nothing and gaped at the television. The tape had ended, and the screen emitted only a hollow, static whir.

The writer's stiff face did not relax when he left the Château Rouge with Kobari, or even after they had stumbled into the blaring nocturnal clamor on Roppongi Avenue. The neon signs, the processions of automobiles, the winter lights in the string of shops, the streams of pedestrians all seemed somehow shallow and meaningless to Suguro after he had seen that tape.

"Would you like to sit down somewhere?" Kobari suggested, feeling a bit resentful. He was sorry most of all that he had not been able to locate Suguro or the matronly woman among the participants in the video.

110

"No, thanks," Suguro refused indignantly. "After this, I hope you'll stop sniffing around like a bloodhound."

He raised his hand and hailed a taxi, then climbed in without looking back. He sat back and closed his eyes, but that face was still imprinted on his eyelids. The eyes half opened, the lips slightly parted, the tongue darting back and forth like a green caterpillar. Globules of melted candlewax caked her hair. That face . . . yes, it resembled another face he had seen. Years before, when he had climbed the belfry of the cathedral at Bourges, he had seen the faces of madmen on every side of the balcony. His mind suddenly shifted to Motoko's painting that hung in the tiny reception room, the painting of a vortex whirling like the shell of a snail. As he had peered into the vortex, he had felt as though he himself were gradually being sucked into its scarlet center. That was the sensation Motoko had wanted to depict, perhaps the feeling she had experienced when she was beaten and choked by various men. "I want to be thrashed and beaten and then just melt away. I want to be hurt and tortured and then just die on the spot." That was how the manager had described the sensation. These seamy emotions and horrifying desires dwelt inside Motoko, and in the depths of every human heart. But why? Where did they come from?

"Would you like me to take the road in front of Harajuku Station?" The driver's question interrupted his musings.

"Yes, please do."

He felt tired all over. He opened his eyes and gazed out at the dark rows of denuded trees in the outer gardens of the Meiji Shrine. When he reached into his pocket for the taxi fare, his fingers brushed against something solid. It was the three letters he had picked up on his way out of the office. Occupied with thoughts of his meeting with Kobari, he had stuffed them into his pocket and forgotten them. One was a letter from a publisher, the second from a man whose name he did not recognize. The third thick envelope did not have a return address.

"Would you mind turning on the overhead light?" he asked the driver.

When he opened the second letter, he realized that it was from the young man who had asked to shake his hand after the autograph session. The postmark was from the city where the man's school for handicapped children was located.

> Last Sunday I was baptized, as I told you I would be. After the service, when I first tasted the consecrated bread of the host on my tongue, I felt that a variety of different experiences had brought me to this point. The most important of those experiences was my encounter with your books. By reading your novels, I have advanced one step at a time toward this point. . . . I think that God spoke to me through your fiction, Sensei. May the Lord continue to bless you as you write.

A bitter lump welled in Suguro's chest. He felt a prick of conscience, as though he had lied to this young man who had such blind faith in his writings—had lied, in fact, to all his many readers. Don't overestimate me, he wanted to tell them. It's as much as I can do just to deal with my own problems; I can't take on the responsibility for your lives, too. In that room at the Meguro bar, the one with the creaky blind over the window, Kanō and the others had read his first writings and declared them suspect. They had been right. Guilt had clung to his heart over the succeeding three decades and would not loosen its grasp no matter how much time passed.

"Don't overestimate me." Involuntarily he said the words aloud.

"Eh?" The startled driver looked back at him. "What did you say?"

"No. It was nothing."

He blushed and looked at the floor, then quietly tore the letter up. In half. Then in half again. As though he were ripping apart the face of the young man with the clammy hands. . . .

He slit open the envelope of the third letter. The white, watermarked paper was tightly filled with the fluid characters of a woman's hand. Had this woman, like the previous young man, also taken Suguro to be something other than a novelist, as some kind of religious figure who . . .

> After some hesitation, I decided to write this letter to you. . . . That night you treated me to dinner, you said you wanted to know about my other self. . . . Not wanting to get you into any trouble, I haven't written my name on the envelope. But I'm sure you'll know who sent it.

The words flew to his eyes from the paper. It was a letter from Madame Naruse.

CHAPTER
FOUR

When I looked up and saw you standing at the doorway, watching as I played with the children at the hospital, I felt embarrassed, as though someone had looked at me while I was sleeping. Then, when you invited me to dinner, I felt as though I were dreaming. You must have thought me an altogether shameless woman.

After some hesitation, I decided to write this letter to you. It would be meaningless for me to try to embellish or prevaricate as I write about myself and, what's more, I felt it would be rude in the truest sense of the word to attempt something like that in communicating with you. That night you treated me to dinner, you said you wanted to know about my other self. Since I had never talked about that with another person, I could not summon the courage to discuss it with you. But I have come around to thinking that you of all people will understand. That you will not misinterpret what I tell you. Even more important, because you have exhibited such intense interest in this question of separate personalities, that you yourself might have something to hide even as I do.

These are the reasons I am sending you this confidential letter. Not wanting to get you into any trouble, I haven't written my name on the envelope. But I'm sure you'll know who sent it.

In sending you this letter, however, I am placing my trust in you, and since I shall be telling you secrets of my own life and that of my late husband, I would ask, after you have read it, that you dispose of it so that it will not be seen by others.

My husband and I were distant relatives. He was the same age as you, Sensei. You may have heard his name—it was Naruse Toshio, and he was a professor at P University. I know very little about such matters, but it seems that he did some substantial work in the field of modern economics.

In his second year at college—and perhaps you had the same experience—Naruse was drafted into the army as part of a mobilized student unit. He served in China until the end of the war.

While he was at the university, he lived in a dormitory for Christian students near the Shinanomachi railway station. On two or three occasions, I went with my mother (I was still in elementary school) to visit him at the dormitory. Though he was only distantly related to us, my mother had known him very well from his childhood, and she helped him in various ways after he came up from Okayama to attend school in Tokyo.

The superintendent of the dormitory was a Professor Yoshimatsu, who taught in the Philosophy Department at Tokyo University. My husband had considerable respect for him and joined his study group. For a time, he even thought about being baptized because of Professor Yoshimatsu's influence. He later told me that he had been able to find a place in that dormitory, which was reserved for Christian students, because he had special permission from Professor Yoshimatsu.

Once, when we visited the dormitory, my mother lodged a request with him. "Toshi-chan, could you help Mariko with her studies?"

"Of course. If you think I can handle it." He was dressed in a blue kimono with white splashes that day, and he looked at me and smiled with his white teeth. As I'm sure you'll remember, many of the students at that time wore kimonos.

I was still in elementary school, but as I looked at his smile and the whiteness of his teeth, the very picture of health, I thought how nice he was. I realize now that that was the beginning of the bond that formed between me and my husband.

I liked school, so I always looked forward to his visits on Wednesdays. And he enjoyed coming, because after he had gone over my books and my homework with me, he could have a square meal at our house.

He told us all kinds of stories at the dinner table. Even though he was in the Economics Department, he knew a lot about literature. Now that he is gone, I remember with a stinging fondness his version of *Gulliver's Travels* and the tale of Ivan that appears in one of Tolstoy's folk stories.

One day, Toshio asked me out of the blue, "Do you know what it's like inside the human heart?" It was a difficult question for a girl my age to answer.

"There are several rooms inside the human heart. The room at the lowest level is like the storeroom you have here in your home, Mari—it has all kinds of things stored up in it. But late at night, the things you've locked up and forgotten in there begin to move."

I thought of our storeroom. Along with the wooden boxes and the gramophone covered with dust, there were several dolls that my older sister had left behind when she got married. One was a blond-haired girl doll my father had brought back from Germany; her large eyes didn't seem cute to me, they seemed eerie. I could never bring myself to like her, so we put her in the storeroom. I tried to imagine her stirring late at night after we had all gone to sleep.

"Do the dolls in our hearts really start moving in the middle of the night?"

"The dolls in our hearts? Yes, that's right. The dolls in our hearts begin to move and dance. And they show up in the dreams we have at night."

It was a wondrous, dizzying story. I tried to picture that doll with her eyes propped eerily open, remaining motionless inside my heart during the day, but dancing by herself when night fell.

Evidently, Toshio was also studying religion at about that time. After we were married, he laughingly told me that it was because he was studying religion that he had zealously launched into his discourse on the depths of the human heart, even though it was beyond my comprehension. And I had listened to him with such intense concentration— He chuckled . . .

I am imposing on your patience by recording these trivial memories, Sensei, but there is a reason for it. Of course, I have in an excess of sentimentality mulled over my recollections of the past on numerous occasions, but I always come back to the belief that the conversation Toshio had with me that day about the human heart became the starting point for the rest of my life. I don't think that anything that happens in our lives is pointless or wasted. You'll understand shortly why I say that that conversation was the starting point of my life.

About a year after Toshio started tutoring me, the student regiments were organized. Even as a child I had a vague sense that the war was gradually turning against us, and each day I felt depressed. When they starting rounding up even university students like Toshio, I began to wonder if Japan was going to lose, and I asked my mother about it. All she did was sigh and say, "Even the students now."

Sensei, do you remember the send-off ceremonies that were conducted on rainy days in the outer gardens of the Shrine? Those processions in the rain that are often shown on television even now. I've been able to locate Toshio in those films, among the students in their square caps as they march through the puddles of water with shouldered rifles.

He was assigned to a regiment in Chiba. Three months later my mother, my sister, and I visited the barracks along with Toshio's father, who had come up to Tokyo. Toshio was dressed in an ill-fitting soldier's uniform, and his hands were all swollen and chapped from frostbite. With his swollen hands, he greedily devoured the lunch my mother had made and put in a lacquered box for him. When my sister handed him the book of poetry he had requested, elation lit up his face like the sun emerging after a rainstorm. He was starved for the written word.

We were allowed three of these meetings before his regiment was sent off to China. To be honest, a thrill of delight raced through me when I received the first postcard from

119

China, stamped with the seal of the government censor. What brought us such delight was the fact that he had not been sent to the perilous islands of the South Pacific. By that time, it was common knowledge that Japan was suffering from a shortage of men and that fierce clashes with American troops had commenced in the South Pacific islands. My father explained, however, that there would probably not be any terrible battles in China. That Toshio would very likely return home safely.

As we had hoped, Toshio remained in China. He advanced from cadet to second lieutenant, and later we learned that he did participate in several small mop-up operations against guerrilla fighters, but fortunately he was never involved in a major conflict. We could tell that he seemed to be leading a life of leisure from the postcards that arrived once every few months, as though he had suddenly remembered to send one. Tokyo at that time was suffering from a string of air raids and food shortages, and his life seemed not only safer but like an enviable dream to us.

"Yesterday, we strangled a chicken, and some buddies and I made a pot of stewed chicken by the riverside." When such happy-go-lucky postcards arrived, we had to ask ourselves which of us was living on the true battlefield. Luckily, his family's home in Okayama was not damaged, but our house was destroyed by incendiary bombs and we had to live in a cottage provided by some relatives in a village called Tsurukawa.

You're probably wondering what any of this has to do with your initial question to me, Sensei. But if I don't first tell you, even in quick outline, about the past, I don't think you'll be able to understand what I shall relate hereafter. Please be patient just a bit longer.

Half a year after the war ended, Toshio was finally repatriated. Although he spent some time recuperating at his home, when he came to Tokyo he was still emaciated. His cheekbones bulged, and he wore the same baggy uniform I had seen him in as a new recruit. We could not believe that a man in his condition had actually been a second lieutenant. My heart throbbed, wondering how two years of military life had changed him. He told us he had been at great pains to locate us, carrying on his back a rucksack that seemed nearly as large as our temporary lodgings.

"I can't tell you how many times I read through the books you sent me in China. But some of them were lost when I was shipped back home, and others were confiscated," he told us apologetically. I had distinct memories of the joyous look on his face when we had given him that first volume.

He returned to school and studied like a man ravenous for learning. Perhaps because of his personality, he was a favorite of his teachers, and after he finished the graduate program, he was hired as a research assistant by the department. Shortly after that, he received a Fulbright grant and was able to study in the United States. At the time, I was attending a women's college.

Some time after he returned to Japan, Toshio was finally employed as a young lecturer by the Economics Department, and not long after that we were married. We could not even begin to make ends meet on his salary, so I spoke to a friend who worked at Hayamizu Publishing Company and got a job doing rough-draft translations of French mysteries by writers like Simenon. French was the one language to which I had really applied myself in school.

We rented a two-room apartment in a house that had survived the bombings at Meidai-mae. In those days, some new houses were beginning to sprout up on the charred earth around the station, but the house we lived in was one of the few old, dark Japanese-style houses still standing. A little marketplace had been opened in front of the station, but it wasn't safe for a woman to walk home alone after dark in the wintertime, so when I delivered a translation to the publisher, my husband would come to the station to meet me. Sometimes the two of us would talk over what we wanted to buy for dinner, and then we would stroll home hand in hand. I remember a large zelkova tree along the roadside, and in autumn flocks of starlings would cluster in its branches.

It is time to move on to the main topic. It is no doubt imprudent for me to write about such things as I am about to describe, but after my earlier conversation with you I have concluded that it cannot be avoided. I am not at all embarrassed about sexual matters. But I must ask you once again—please, once you have read this letter, please be sure to burn it.

I was a hopelessly late bloomer as a girl, and though I was certain I knew more about sex than most girls my age from the novels and books I read, it all felt very much as if I was peering through one eye at photographs of streets in foreign countries I had never visited. I really knew very little about my own body until I married Toshio.

He was a gentle man and, as I've indicated before, he was brought up pampered and sheltered from the world. Gentleness and willfulness, nervousness and sincerity dwelt side by side in him. There was something very self-seeking in his approach to sex. He seemed to crave it. For my part, on the day of my wedding my mother said to me, "You must do everything he wants you to do." I took her advice and put on a cheerful act that night, but, in all sincerity, as he embraced me I wondered how such an activity could bring joy to a person's life.

I didn't dislike Toshio making love to me, but I was often surprised by his insistence. He sought me out at different times, not just at night. Some Sundays he would grab me from behind as I worked in the kitchen. In the winter, as we sat under the coverlet, he would suddenly put his hands in my hair, push me to the floor, and climb on top of me. At first I thought of it as an expression of his fervent love for me. But as I looked up at his face hovering over me, I saw something I had never known in him before. Another face I had never seen before. It was utterly different from his usual face, the tender face that yet had its nervous shadows around the edges, the face that grew childlike when he smiled. It was a face with bloodshot eyes that flashed a look of cruelty. I even cried, "Who are you? Who—who are you?" I was overcome with worry—no, with fear. But his lust, though fierce, was also short-lived. When he had spent himself, the childlike smile returned to his face.

You could certainly call our life together happy. The only regret my parents had was that we produced no grand-child for them. We were examined by doctors, but they could find no clear cause. It was unfortunate, but at the time I felt neither regret nor sorrow. Toshio didn't dislike children, but some part of him feared the drastic change a child would bring to our lives, turning me into a mother who would devote every hour of the day to her infant. His excuse was that a child would interfere with his studies, and sometimes in all earnestness he would assert that this was the real reason.

I have many fond memories of those days, perhaps the most pleasant being the time when a book my husband wrote was recognized by the leading scholars in the field with the Sakitani Prize, and the trip the two of us took to Tōhoku.

The Sakitani Prize is awarded in two fields, science and literature, and the ceremony and reception for both are held simultaneously at the Tokyo Station Hotel. Toshio, wearing a bright-red artificial flower in his lapel, seemed rather dizzy that evening from all the excitement and the liquor he had drunk.

"Don't spill anything on your suit," I said, making a point of teasing him. "I want you to be able to wear the same suit when you receive your next prize."

As I circulated in a flush that evening among the throng at the reception, I saw someone there. It was you, Sensei. I suppose you were there as a friend of Mr. Kanō, who had received the literary award. That was the first time I ever saw you, and I never imagined I would one day be writing such a letter as this to you.

Midway through the reception, a man from a magazine who was acting as receptionist came up to me.

"Do you know a man by the name of Kawasaki? He says he wants to join the reception. I suppose it's impertinent of me to say this, but he really doesn't look as if he belongs here."

Toshio had never mentioned the name of Kawasaki to me, so I went out to the reception desk to find out what was going on. As the receptionist had said, a middle-aged man of questionable looks and dress was standing sullenly near the entrance.

"You're the wife, aren't you?" He was informal with me, probably drunk. "Please tell your husband that Kawasaki from his army days is here. I saw the announcement in the paper and came rushing over. This is really a happy day."

"Then you were one of my husband's wartime comrades?"

"A comrade . . . ? No, I think I'd say just one of his old chums." He gave me a pointed smile.

I went back into the hall and located my husband. He was surrounded by newspaper people, but I walked up beside him and tugged at his elbow.

When he heard the name Kawasaki, his smiling face hardened for a moment. No one else may have noticed the change, but I was his wife, after all. He nonchalantly excused himself from the conversation and said to me, "Would you be good enough to pay our respects to the people here." He left the hall.

I knew that something strange was going on, and as I circled the hall, bowing and voicing words of thanks, I glanced over my shoulder from time to time. Before long my husband returned, looking the same as ever. Anyone would have thought he had gone out to the restroom.

That night, we returned home late, following a second round of celebration at a bar. As I brushed his one best suit, I asked, "Who is this Mr. Kawasaki?"

Again his face went almost imperceptibly rigid. That hardness made me wonder if some secret unknown to me was shared by Kawasaki and my husband. I was jealous.

Because I loved Toshio, I was anxious about his behavior after that night, and whenever Kawasaki phoned I passed the receiver to him and then tried to analyze his expressions and the answers he gave over the phone.

One day when I was cleaning, I discovered something strange. The multiple volumes of the Larousse dictionary arranged on the shelf were reduced to their slipcovers, and the volumes themselves were missing. When had my husband taken them out of the house? And he had done it in such a way that I would not notice. . . . Come to think of it, I had noticed a couple of weeks earlier that, when he went out of the house each day, he was carrying some square object wrapped in a *furoshiki*, along with his briefcase.

"Oh, those?" He feigned nonchalance at my question. "I took them to our office at school."

No place that claimed to be a university research office would be without a set of Webster's or Larousse dictionaries. Even if they didn't have them at hand, they would be accessible in a campus library. It was the first lie I had detected in my husband since our wedding. I was hurt and saddened.

I had the feeling he had sold the dictionaries and given the money to Kawasaki. In my imagination I even concocted the kind of episode that is often described in newspaper scandal columns—a conventional sort of incident in which Kawasaki had something on my husband and was blackmailing him. I could almost picture my husband—a man fond of learning but totally ignorant of everything else—being driven into a corner by Kawasaki's threats, and I wanted to protect him. But what sort of failings had a man like my husband manifested during his army days?

It was a Saturday afternoon. I was alone at home when Kawasaki phoned.

"I'm sorry, but he's gone out." It was at that moment that I decided to try to draw the secret out of him. "Did my husband give you the money?" An image of Kawasaki's drunken, red-eyed face flickered on my eyelids.

He said nothing for a few moments. "Money? What are you talking about?" He was playing innocent.

I took my courage in my hands and asserted confidently, "You mean he didn't give you the money?"

I mentally prepared an impromptu rationalization in case he insisted that he knew nothing. Something about my husband saying he had lent Kawasaki some money. But he had been swayed by my self-assurance and dropped all pretense.

"Yeah, he gave it to me." Then after another pause, "So you knew about it?"

"Yes."

"Is that so? I never thought he'd tell you about it, no matter how well the two of you get along. But that makes it easier for me to talk to you. When he gets home, would you tell him that we may need some more money for the Memorial Association."

"The Memorial Association, yes."

Toshio had never said a word to me about a Memorial Association. And I was caught up on what Kawasaki had said: "I never thought he'd tell you about it, no matter how well the two of you get along."

"About how much more money should I tell him you'll need?"

"Let's see. Say that I'll let him know after we get it all worked out. But I'm really glad you're so understanding about this whole business. It was wartime, after all, and we had no other choice. But after we came back to Japan and the years went by, I started feeling really guilty, you know. Because there were dozens of women and children who died there. To be frank, I'd like to be able to build some kind of commemorative tablet in the village, but since we're Japanese they won't let us into China yet."

Our conversation ended there. I tried to continue working on my translation, but the words I had just heard kept popping up at random in my mind, like scattered pieces of a puzzle.

I said nothing to Toshio when he returned home. As I studied his face, for some reason I was reminded of his blue-and-white kimono and the white-toothed smile he wore the first time my mother and I visited his dormitory. . . .

That night he made love to me. I buried my face against his arm and blurted out, "It must take a lot of money to support a Memorial Association."

My voice sounded so sweet and so innocent that even I was surprised. For a moment, all his strength seemed concentrated in his arms.

"Why didn't you tell me? I heard from Mr. Kawasaki."

Toshio did not reply.

In my own cunning way, I spoke with even greater tenderness: "Did you think I'd be worried? I'm your wife. If only you'd told me. . . . It makes no difference to me. It happened because of the war."

"What did Kawasaki tell you?"

Toshio pulled away from me and stared up at the ceiling.

"Everything. About the women and the children, too."

I was able to take the scattered verbal pieces of the puzzle and deftly insert them in exactly the right places.

To be perfectly honest, at that point I still had no idea what kind of shape would emerge once those words were all fitted together. I had a vague premonition that seemed to be warning me not to ask what I most feared.

"Then you don't hate me for what I did?"

In the light from the nightstand, I could see a smile on Toshio's face. It was that face—that other face I had seen as a newlywed when I looked up at him after he had clutched my hair and pushed me to the floor.

"Why would I? I told you—it was wartime, and you had no other choice." I smiled like a mother or an older sister, desperate not to let him see the frantic contortions of my mind. "Then do you feel guilty like Mr. Kawasaki?"

"No, I don't. For some reason I didn't feel particularly

guilty that first time, or the second time either. In fact, I was hypnotized by the beauty of the flames as they consumed the houses." He spoke slowly, his eyes riveted on the ceiling.

"The first time and the second time. . . . So it happened twice."

"Yes."

"The houses burned. . . . And the women and children were inside the houses?"

"Yes, they were. We'd driven them all inside their own houses."

"And then you set fire to the houses and killed all the people. . . . Were you ordered to?"

"The first time we were ordered to. We were told there were spies hiding out in the village. The soldiers were all worked up—two of our own men had been murdered. But the second time, our platoon decided to do it all on its own."

With his head resting on his hands, he closed his eyes. He seemed to be listening in the deepest region of his ears to the sound of the farmhouses burning, with the women and children barricaded inside. I knew that sound. The sound I had heard every night during the air raids, like a train whistling by. And now, once again, I heard that sound, along with my husband, in our bedroom at midnight.

I neither loathed nor feared him. A feeling of numbness suddenly swept over me. For the first time, I had become aware that within my husband, who behaved sometimes like a younger brother to me, lay the silhouette of a totally different man, and the realization that these two contradictory aspects had fashioned the man I married was both startling and thrilling to me.

I suddenly rolled on top of him, and for the first time

I aggressively kissed his lips, buried my face in his chest, and passionately sought his body. As though he had been waiting for this, he roughly entered me.

"Talk to me," I shouted. "Tell me, tell me how you started the fires."

"We surrounded the houses. So they couldn't escape. . . . We used oil to start the fires."

"Could you hear their voices? Tell me! What did they sound like?"

"We heard them. Some of the children came running outside. We shot them."

We panted and thrashed about on the bed.

"Tell me. What happened to the women when you shot them?"

Suddenly it was all over. He withered, and without saying another word got up and left the bedroom. I lay there prone, bathed in sweat. When he came back to bed, he closed his eyes as though nothing had just happened between us.

We never again mentioned that experience to one another. He remained the same man, the husband in whom resided gentleness and petulance, purity and nervousness side by side. Occasionally I worried that old war crimes would be resurrected, but nothing of the kind ever happened. Had every witness been killed in the fires? Had no one ever filed any charges? That part of it still seems strange to me even now.

But neither was the scorching memory of that night ever erased from our relationship. Indeed, it became a never-ending means of kindling my feelings toward him. We never touched on the taboo subject, but for me it became a sacred secret in our marriage.

I will be perfectly honest.

After that night, whenever I slept with him I always imagined the same thing as I saw his face illuminated by the light of the nightstand. It is a tiny village I have never seen. He posts his men at the entrance and exit to the village. The women and children are herded into a squalid thatched hut with mud walls. Kawasaki scurries around the house, dousing it with oil. Meanwhile my husband waits, staring at his watch. When Kawasaki's work is finished, the fires are lit. The flames and smoke flare up with a flash and envelop the house. The burning straw of the roof swirls into the sky with the blackish smoke. Then, from inside the house, screams and weeping soar into the heavens with the flames. Children engulfed in flames and women clutching babies come running from the house. Along with his men, my husband shoots them, one after another.

He shot them. My husband. The man stretched out on my bed right now, sipping his whiskey and reading his book—he shot those mothers and children. Suddenly, an indescribable surge of excitement would shoot from my toes to my head, and many times I would start to say something to him. But Toshio seemed not to notice, and he would ask, "Something wrong? Can't you get to sleep? I can't put this detective story down now that I've started reading it."

That smile was the one I had known for many years. The face of a teacher popular with the students who came to visit us.

Whenever my husband made love to me, I imagined that scene in my head. By doing so I heightened my own unspeakable pleasure and the love I felt for him. The duality, the complexity that resided within him, strengthened my attachment to him. No, I never once had the slightest urge to criticize or scorn him. I never thought of him as repulsive. If I had been a man and been sent off to war as he was, I'm sure I would have done the same thing. And I would have gone on living as he had, exchanging looks of innocence with his associates. I don't have any idea whether he was tormented over that incident in his heart of hearts. I do know that he never betrayed the slightest hint of anguish to me as his wife.

Nor did I ever feel any self-hatred for using his experience as a stimulus for my own passions.

We were married for twenty-three years. He lived a happy life until he was fifty-five, when he was killed in a traffic accident on his way home from the university. We never discussed his war experiences again, but they smoldered within my heart, and whenever I chose to fan the flames they burned fiercely, providing intense stimulation to our bodies. Kawasaki never came around again. My husband achieved great fame as a scholar, and when he died the entire university mourned.

With my husband dead, I struggled against an unfathomable hollowness. I can't begin to tell you how much I regretted not bearing him a child. I had never felt the maternal instincts I thought I lacked as strongly as I did then.

In an attempt to fill the void, I took the advice of a friend and enrolled in a course for hospital volunteers. The class was established to help foster volunteer work in a country relatively new to the idea, and after a year of training I began working at a hospital in the city.

The hospital to which I was assigned after that year of instruction is the hospital where you visited me, Sensei. When I was asked which section I would like to work in, I applied for the pediatrics ward. I can remember even now the first time the head nurse took me in. I fed a bottle to a premature baby who was kept in a tiny glass case, and the tips of my own untried breasts throbbed. Children with leukemia, who had clung to me and badgered me for stories, after a certain number of months would begin to lose their strength. When I saw them being given transfusions and anti-cancer drugs as they lapsed into comas, I begged God from the bottom of my heart to be allowed to die in their place. I am telling you the truth. In all sincerity and earnestness, I pleaded for that to happen.

And still I have not forgotten what my husband did. When I finish my volunteer work and return home I have dinner, and then his picture hanging on the wall in my room revives those memories. A burst of flames engulfs the farmhouse, sparks of fire and clouds of black smoke swirl into the air, and as cries of agony spew from within, mothers and children come running out . . . my husband slaughters the children . . . no, laughing along with my husband, I shoot them, too. This memory, coupled with the face of my husband, summons forth an impulse I cannot suppress. I want to know from what part of my heart this impulse arises. Where is it leading me? This black portion of my heart that cannot be restrained by common sense or logic.

By chance, I happened to meet a young woman. She possessed the same irrepressible, abhorrent element inside her. I won't mince my words—I am speaking of Itoi Motoko, the one who painted your portrait, Sensei.

Motoko's obsessions take a different form, but she has enabled me to experience through separate means the same kind of pleasure my husband taught me. When she reaches the peak of her violent ecstasy, she cries out, "I want to die!" "Go ahead, die!" I say to her. Sensei, people will die for love or beauty, but they can also die through their

133

descent into ugliness and emptiness. I have that feeling when I look at Motoko. This is what I want you to understand.

The morning after I spend the night with Motoko, I go to the hospital with a cheery face, I hug the children, and I assist the nurses. But at night . . . When I was young my husband told me about the storeroom in the human heart. In that storeroom someone has placed a doll with large eyes that stare out at you, and at night she begins to move and dance. She dances in my heart, too. You might want to ask, which of these two is the real Mariko? All I can say is that both of them are me. You might ask, don't the contradictions between the two cause you any torment? Yes, sometimes when I think about those contradictions, I horrify myself. I am repelled by myself. But there are also times when I am not, and there is nothing I can do about it. Having written this much, I . . .

When Suguro returned home from his office, the brightly lit dining table was decorated with flowers and set with the soup bowls they had bought in Milan. They brought these bowls out only on evenings when there was some special occasion for the two of them to celebrate.

"What day is this?" he asked.

"Good heavens, it's our anniversary!" his wife replied in disbelief.

"Oh? Is it?"

His head was filled with the letter. Three days had passed since he had read it, but astonishment and a curiosity that burgeoned with each passing day churned inside him. In one sense she seemed a frightening woman, but the writer in him could not bear to spurn her. As he carried the spoon to his mouth, he mechanically asked his wife about the events of the day, and listened as she told him about going to the doctor and getting an injection of steroid hormones for her swollen knee joints, and about visiting an exhibition of new electric heaters on her way home.

These conversations were a form of ritual, or perhaps etiquette, between them, and Suguro always responded to his wife's comments with a smile or a nod.

"It seems as if new and handy appliances come out every year."

"With that kind of attitude, you'll end up never buying anything."

"Winter will be over before long."

Suguro had not told her anything about Kobari's visit, or of his own experiences at Château Rouge, and of course not a word about Madame Naruse's letter. Such things were unconnected to the world they had created together, matters that must not be discussed with his wife.

"I wrote Mitsu a letter and asked how she was doing, but she hasn't written back," said his wife.

"Young people these days aren't good at writing, I suppose."

"If you happen to run into her . . . while you're out walking . . . "

"I don't imagine I will. Listen, would you buy a little trowel for me? I've got to plant those bulbs pretty soon."

Deflecting any discussion of Mitsu, he sent the conversation back on its rambling path, peering, as he did so, at his wife's wrinkled face and the flecks of white in her hair. He stole a glance at her mouth as she chewed her food. Her manner of eating was totally different from Madame Naruse's, and utterly lacking in eroticism. . . . Suguro recalled the foreign short story and thought about what Madame Naruse had said in her letter. Did his wife, too, possess the same conflicting urges, and were there secrets lurking inside her that one would never imagine from looking at her? Was it possible that even his own wife had fabricated this surface image in order to stay in tune with him? Just having such thoughts seemed to him a profanation of his wife. But one passage from Madame Naruse's letter caught in his throat like a foreign object in his soup spoon: "You might want to ask, which of these two is the real Mariko? . . . Sometimes . . . I horrify myself. I am repelled by myself."

CHAPTER
FIVE

HE AWOKE in the middle of the night to the ringing of the telephone. The sound reverberated from the hallway at the bottom of the stairs, clanging penetratingly. The illuminated clock on his nightstand read 2 A.M.

"It's the phone." His wife shuffled in the next bed.

"Let it ring."

"Are you sure? I wonder if it's a crank call."

Suguro listened to the ringing of the telephone. His wife, too, seemed to be listening anxiously in the darkness. The sound impressed him as being like a groan from the depths of a human heart. The fathomless pit yawning at the bottom of that heart. The echo of a wind coursing through that pit. Something he had not yet described in any of his novels.

*　　　　*　　　　*

Like the dressing room at the television station, this waiting room was surrounded with mirrors on each of its four walls. It depressed Suguro to see so many images of himself projected there. As he drank the tea that a woman had brought in to him, there was a knock on the door and Kurimoto came in.

"The auditorium's already eighty percent full. It seems to attract a lot of housewives when it's announced that you and Professor Tōno are going to give a lecture."

His staid editor had never mentioned their walk down that disreputable street in Kabuki-chō. It was patently clear that he considered mention of such a subject an affront to Suguro.

"What is Mr. Tōno talking about today?"

"His title is 'On Hallucinations.' "

Once a month, the publishing company where Kurimoto worked sponsored a lecture and invited two speakers for the enlightenment of their readers. Tōno, who had accepted the speaking assignment with Suguro, was a Freudian psychologist. Suguro had run into him two or three times at various parties. He assumed that the psychologist's discussion tonight would afford a Freudian perspective on the hallucinations that are engendered by our libidos, but beyond that he had no idea what the psychologist would say.

Kurimoto went out again, and just as Suguro finished drinking his tea the portly Tōno entered. He appeared to have come directly from the university. He placed a brand-new attaché case on top of the makeup table, and in a shrill voice that seemed out of harmony with his enormous body he announced, "No tea for me. I've brought my own stimulants." Then, like some magician, he produced a small flask. "I have to have a good swig of this before I give a lecture."

"Does a drink give you energy?"

"Yes, a phony sort of energy. It makes everyone in the audience look like stones."

"That sounds like a hallucination well in keeping with your topic today," Suguro observed. "I have the feeling that hallucinations can be just as useful as reality."

Kurimoto returned to report that the six hundred seats in the auditorium were now all filled. Perhaps by chance, Madame Naruse was in one of those seats. Suguro had sent an unsigned postcard announcing the lecture to her, in care of the hospital. Somewhere inside he was hoping she would come.

Tōno glanced at the clock on the wall. "We've got twenty more minutes. I guess I arrived a little too early."

"No." Suguro shook his head. "It's a great comfort for a minor performer like me to have the star here already. While we're waiting, would you mind if I asked you a couple of questions?"

"Go right ahead. What is it?"

As he gulped his whiskey, Tōno fidgeted in his chair, looking cramped. Virtually any chair would have looked too small for his massive physique.

"Those of you who work in psychoanalysis . . . how do you explain sadists and masochists?"

"Sadists? Masochists?"

"That's right."

"Hmm. I didn't know you were interested in such things, Mr. Suguro." Tōno smiled gleefully. "You're a Christian, aren't you?"

"Yes, but I'm also a writer interested in every aspect of human experience."

"Of course. Forgive me. I didn't mean that at all. What I wanted to say was that I thought you were a writer with rather strong biophilous tendencies."

"Could you put that in simpler terms? I'm no good with jargon."

"The psychoanalyst Fromm has divided mankind into two types. There are, for instance, writers who essentially prefer harmony in their lives, a well-constructed unity. Someone like Mushanokōji, for example. Yamamoto Yūzō would be included in that group also. Abroad, you have someone like Goethe. Fromm would classify this type of writer as bio-philous, one who loves life. Wouldn't you say that you belong to the biophilous category, Mr. Suguro?"

"Oh, I certainly couldn't judge something like that."

"But there is another type of writer, one with suicidal tendencies who is more absorbed with darkness and the past than with a neatly ordered future. I think Dazai Osamu would fit into that class. Such individuals are classified as necro-philous."

"In our literary vocabulary we'd call them self-destructive writers. But what's that got to do with masochism?"

"Forgive me. The necrophilous type is definitely what you might call self-destructive. They tend toward self-immolation, degeneracy, and decadence. Sometimes when those tenden-cies are especially pronounced, they manifest a strong urge to revert to an inanimate or inorganic state."

"What do you mean by an 'inanimate state'?"

"Freud has an interesting explanation of this phenomenon. He says that the entire history of the human species, from its origins millions of years ago and through its development over the centuries, is preserved within our unconscious minds. In other words, before we received life, we existed in a state of inanimacy. Mankind is still drawn toward that primordial existence, and may even feel a nostalgia for it. As proof of this, when the tensions in our daily lives begin to mount, we wish we could return to an inanimate state. Some even attempt suicide to achieve that end. Others try to smother all emotion. It is our tendency as human beings to want to return to the state of matter before prehistoric life had begun to stir."

"Does everyone have these tendencies?" Suguro glanced at the wall clock and concluded that he still had ten minutes to question Tōno.

"Yes, we all do. But I think the tendency is particularly strong among masochists."

Tōno explained the whole thing with such marvelous clarity that it left even more uncertainty in Suguro's mind. That trance-like look on the face of the woman in the videotape, her hair caked with wax—had that expression come solely from a desire to return to her inorganic origins? Was there no motive more raw, more terrible, concealed in that look? Tōno's rational analysis of the phenomenon could not begin to account for the contradictory personas that Madame Naruse had described, a paradox that she herself considered uncanny.

Seeing the look of dissatisfaction on Suguro's face, Tōno snorted discontentedly, and once again his voice went shrill.

"Is there something wrong with my explanation?"

"No, that's not it."

"Then how about this idea. Before we were born, we slept in our mother's womb. Correct?"

"Yes."

"The fetus lives inertly within the amniotic fluid, hearing only the sound of its mother's heartbeat. The amniotic fluid is a murky white color, but it provides precisely the right environmental temperature for the embryo. It lives there spontaneously, breathing branchially like a fish, but then one day it is suddenly cast out of its garden paradise."

"Cast out?"

"Yes, it is ejected from the womb into the outside world.

We adults refer to this as birth, but for the fetus it is a forced eviction into an unknown, frightening world where it must learn to breathe in the air rather than under water. This is the first experience we humans have with death and rebirth. And thus the first cry that issues from a newborn's mouth is not the shout of joy at being born that we have imagined it to be—it is, rather, a shriek of fear."

"This is the first time I've heard such an idea."

"I'm sure it is. In any case, the fear that a child experiences when it leaves the uterus is extreme, and it lingers in the depths of the child's heart. That fear is never extinguished. Even after he grows to maturity, it remains a part of his unconscious mind. It is linked to the fear of death and, conversely, is also transferred into a profound longing to revert to the fetal state, to live once again within the amniotic fluids. Masochism just might be a deformation of this urge to subsist within the uterine waters."

"Is that Freud's notion?"

"Oh no." Tōno smiled wryly, but then with a touch of pride he added, "It's my personal theory."

"Then what about sadism?"

Tōno was about to launch into another dissertation when the door opened and Kurimoto poked his head in to announce that it was time to begin. Suguro thanked Tōno, stepped out into the hall, and climbed the stairs leading to the stage.

When he approached the podium, the stage lights beat down mercilessly on his entire body. From the lectern, he nodded his head to the members of the packed audience. Two-thirds of the crowd seated in the gently sloping auditorium consisted, as Kurimoto had said, of housewives, young women, and students, but he could not make out any individual faces. All he knew was that he was being scrutinized by the assembly.

He pretended to adjust the microphone as he tried to settle his nerves. He considered himself rather seasoned to these public lectures, but if he bungled the opening there would be no hope of recovery. He took a breath, drawing the attention of all the listeners to himself, and slowly launched into a discussion of his own writings.

It's going well.

It was not something visible to the naked eye, but he could feel throughout his body a positive responsiveness from the audience. He began to have a tactile sense of what sort of talk these housewives and young women and students expected of him. In fact, it was likely that the majority of his fans already had a fair idea what he would say before they even arrived in this auditorium.

As he established the proper rhythm for his remarks, the audience started to react with interest and nod their heads. Eventually he was able to relax, and as he did so he began to be able to distinguish individual faces that had previously been a blur. He searched for Madame Naruse's face.

"A young man once came to see me. He complained bitterly that he was a terrible conversationalist, and as a result he couldn't make any friends. In the past, I would have recommended a book on the art of conversation or suggested some other method to improve his speaking ability. But at this point in my life, now that I have concluded that there are assets lurking within every liability, I would tell him to make the most of his slowness of speech. Now what do I mean by making the most of it?"

Suguro paused and looked around the overcrowded auditorium. It was crucial to take a breath and pause here for effect.

"What I mean is that he should become a good listener. If he isn't good at conversation, all he has to do is keep his eyes focused on the other person's face as he talks to him, and to nod his head. That will make the speaker feel good. Just the way that all of you are making me feel good while I'm talking to you."

A ripple of laughter skittered through the hall. Suguro was elated as he glanced toward the doorway at the center of the auditorium. Then suddenly he blinked his eyes furiously.

He was there. The face identical to Suguro's own was poised near the doorway, looking toward Suguro with its mocking smile. It was the same experience he had had on the night of the awards ceremony.

"The asset of being a good listener . . . is built into the liability of being a poor speaker. This isn't just limited to conversational ability. None of the deficiencies we have as human beings is absolute. Every weakness contains within itself a strength. Even sin carries certain virtues in its make-up. The human hunger for rebirth lies within each sin we commit. That is what I have repeated to myself over the years as I have written my novels."

He felt a chill and blinked his eyes again. But this time the man did not vanish as he had before. The derisive smile. A smile that taunted Suguro. That obscene smile—yes, it was the expression in the portrait at the exhibition.

The friendly atmosphere of the auditorium abruptly collapsed. The harmonious chords he had sounded were interrupted by convulsive, discordant noises. Suguro lost the thread of what he was saying as well as his composure. He had been talking about sin not being meaningless in our lives, that it had significance in the process of salvation. But suddenly he had no idea how to develop that thought, and in confusion he fell silent. The more he struggled to recover himself, the deeper he was immersed in mire. In his ears rang the words Tōno had spoken in the waiting room: "Everyone has the desire to return to the womb, or to darkness or silence or the absence of feeling. It's a desire to repudiate self-improvement and plunge wholly into oblivion. . . ."

A red-etched maelstrom swirled before his eyes. As it picked up speed, Suguro felt himself about to be sucked into its center. "The most important thing is to write about humanity." His mouth intoned the words as if they had been memorized. "That is the first aim of any writer. To probe into the uttermost reaches of mankind—that, I think, is his ultimate duty. That aim and that duty do not change, whether he is a leftist writer or an ineffectual Christian such as myself. At the very least, I have never tried to idealize the humanity of my characters for the sake of my own religion. I have looked upon hideous things in all their hideousness. . . ."

The man slowly rose from his seat. He stood up, looking toward Suguro, stepped out into the aisle, and once again turned toward the speaker. It was brutally evident from his movements and his manner that he had only contempt for Suguro's remarks.

He stopped at the doorway, and once again the scornful smile appeared on his face.

You're a liar, you bastard. Suguro was almost certain he could hear the man's voice heckling him. *Do you really think you've looked at the hideous face of mankind? All you've done is put your craven little words on paper in order to maintain the image your readers have of you. It's the same way you've treated your wife.*

That's not true. I've tried in my own way to dirty my hands in the foul, dark corners of human experience.

All right, I'll grant that you've written about sins that yield to salvation, as all of your beloved Christian writers have done. But you've avoided writing about that other realm.

What other realm?

Evil. Sin and evil aren't the same thing. It's evil that you've ignored.

During Suguro's long silence, several members of the audience had begun to whisper among themselves. Suguro could feel the perspiration trickling down his forehead. He heard Kurimoto's footsteps as the editor hurried to his side.

"Is something wrong?"

The man had vanished, as though he had been obliterated with a rubber eraser. The perspiration dribbled onto his eyelids.

"I'm very sorry. Suguro Sensei has suddenly become ill, and we will have to cancel his lecture for now."

Through the microphone, Kurimoto apologized to the audience. "But we shall proceed straight into Professor Tōno's lecture, so please remain in your seats."

Tepid applause sounded at Suguro's back as he reached the wings.

"Should I call a doctor?"

"No. I'm sorry. Let me just lie down in the waiting room." His head still ached, and he could feel the sweat running down his back and forehead.

Tōno, who was waiting in the wings, reached for Suguro's wrist and measured his pulse. "Your pulse is normal," he mumbled. "I think this is probably just a case of nervous tension. You'll be fine if you get some rest."

On the sofa in the waiting room, Suguro loosened his necktie, undid some of the buttons on his shirt, and stretched out. When he closed his eyes, the face that had surfaced in the crowded hall and stared in his direction reappeared. *All right, I'll grant that you've written about sins that yield to salvation. . . .* Why had these unexpected words resounded in his ears? How had he been able to see the cynical smile all the way from the lectern on the distant stage? Then it had been

146

an illusion. Or, no—had it been the impostor? Had he come to the lecture? Very likely the shock of seeing a face that so closely resembled his own had induced an auditory hallucination.

He tried to persuade himself that it had been a hallucination. There was no other way to explain such an extraordinary, illogical phenomenon occurring in the life of a sixty-five-year-old man.

> In the middle of the journey of our life,
> I found myself within the forest dark
> For the straightforward pathway had been lost.

He had read the opening passage of the *Divine Comedy* many years ago. The only difference between its protagonist and himself was their respective ages; he himself had already advanced well into the late autumn of his life. And there he had lost his way, and wandered now in a dark forest, his path strewn with fallen leaves. . . .

He woke up to someone pounding on the door. He took a deep breath, as though he had just surfaced from the bottom of the ocean.

"How are you feeling?"

How much time had passed? Tōno, his lecture completed, was peering through the doorway.

"I'm all right. I'll get up now." He quickly sat up. When he reached for the jacket he had removed earlier, he felt a bit dizzy, but it didn't seem of any consequence.

"Probably a touch of cerebral anemia," Tōno commented shrilly, as he studied Suguro's complexion. "Are you sure you don't feel exhausted?"

"I think I must be."

"Would you like a little stimulant?" He took the flask of

whiskey from his case and held it up, but Suguro shook his head.

"I think I'd better get back home."

"Kurimoto will be down in a minute, so wait for him. He's making arrangements for a car right now."

Suguro sat motionless for a few moments.

"I hate to do this, but could I ask you a question? . . . This may be my only chance to talk with a psychologist."

"Well, certainly. . . . Anything at all. What is it this time?"

"Do you know of anyone who has claimed to see a person who looks exactly like himself?"

"Exactly like him———? Ah, that's called a *doppelgänger*, or a ghost double. It's not all that frequent, but there've been two or three reports of the phenomenon at medical conferences. One patient, who was suffering from tympanitis, became neurotic and began to experience auditory hallucinations. He saw himself lying down in front of his own eyes. It was his own corpse lying before him, as I understand it. He reported clearly remembering that the corpse was dressed exactly like him, even down to the gray trousers."

"Are the patients who see these *doppelgängers* always suffering from neuroses?"

"Usually they are. They seem to be accompanied by fairly extended spells of insomnia, abnormal body temperature, body-image agnosia, and loss of mental faculties. . . . But . . . why are you interested in this sort of thing?"

"Oh, I was . . . just thinking of using the experience in a novel."

"Ah, I see." Tōno showed no suspicion. "If it's for a novel, I seem to remember that Dostoevsky wrote about something like this."

"Does this *doppelgänger* condition occur other than in instances of neurosis?"

"It seems to. According to the documentation, a woman who taught at an elementary school in Iwate Prefecture had the *doppelgänger* experience without any of the other subjective symptoms. She was discharged from the school on three different occasions because of it."

"When did this happen?"

"In the Taishō period. The strange thing is that it wasn't she herself who saw the ghost double, it was the girls she taught. While they were gathered in the sewing room being instructed by their teacher, they looked outside the classroom window and saw someone who looked exactly like her standing in the flower garden. The whole class observed the apparition."

"Is that so?" Suguro could feel his kneecaps quivering faintly. An inexplicable discomfort, mingled with fear, had risen like a lump in his gut. "It wasn't the woman's twin or some kind of criminal plot?"

"Apparently it wasn't anything of that sort." Tōno tilted his head. "That's what's so unusual about it. Psychologists have various theories to explain it, but none of them has any compelling evidence in its favor."

Knowing nothing of the reasons behind this inquiry, Tōno lifted the flask of whiskey to his mouth with a massive hand. "Don't you think you could use this story about the teacher in a novel?"

"It sounds as though I could."

"One characteristic of this *doppelgänger* phenomenon is that it seems to happen mostly at night."

"In conclusion, then, would you say that this experience is the product of the patient's hallucinations?"

Suguro wanted Tōno to label it a hallucination. There was something not quite reliable about this psychologist who did not for a moment doubt that the chaotic nadir of the human heart could be explained in the distinctest of terms. But at this juncture, Suguro wanted to hear the words "Yes, it's a hallucination" from Tōno's mouth and be able to depend upon them.

But Tōno cocked his head innocently and said, "I'd like to be able to say it's a hallucination. But judging from the case of the teacher in Iwate, it can't be written off as a hallucination that only the patient observes."

Suguro went back to his office, buried his head in his arms on his desk, and reflected on each of Tōno's comments. There was one conclusion that could be drawn from Tōno's speculations. The figure he had seen from the lectern could have been a hallucination. If not a hallucination, then a vile prank perpetrated by the impostor. It had to be one or the other of these two options. If it was a hallucination, was it the product of a mild depression brought on by his advancing age? Suguro tried to nudge himself toward that conclusion, recalling the times in the past when his physical condition had deteriorated each time he completed a major piece of work. But such a thought made him feel unbearably glum.

The telephone rang. His body twitched in surprise. He listened to the ringing for a few moments, then made up his mind and went into the living room.

"I'm sorry. Were you asleep?" The politely apologetic woman's voice emerged from a background of clamoring voices.

"Who is this?"

"It's Mrs. Naruse. I was at your lecture today. When you got ill in the middle . . ." She seemed to be looking for the appropriate words. "I'm sorry to bother you."

"No, not at all. . . . I'm sorry for the scene I made." He did not want her to go away. "Where are you?"

"At Harajuku Station. One of the children I look after at the hospital is going to have heart surgery soon. . . . His tests are scheduled for today. He'll be frightened if I'm not there with him. He'll quiet down if I just stay there beside him."

Suguro thought of her letter and felt puzzled. This woman, so concerned now about a child scheduled for surgery, in another moment could become a woman who was the personification of cruelty. . . . His authorial mind kicked into operation, and he yearned to peer into her secrets, her darkest corners.

"Could I come right over to Harajuku to see you? I'd like to talk about your letter."

"His tests are starting in another thirty minutes. I promised Shige-chan—that's his name—that I'd be there without fail."

She was impatient. There seemed to be no room in her mind for anything but Shige-chan.

"I saw the film." Kobari unexpectedly brought up the subject as he listened to the gushing sound of the hot water that the maid was running into the tub. Earlier, as he and Motoko had drunk together in a back street in Shinjuku, he had been itching to ask her about the videotape, but he had restrained himself. Once they were both considerably intoxicated, he had let matters run their course, and they had ended up standing at the entrance to this hotel. As though they had arranged this in advance, Motoko offered no objection.

A white thermos flask and a plate of bean-jam wafers wrapped in paper had been set on a table with peeling varnish. The paper wrappers bore a suggestive verse that began: "The taste of bean-jam wafers/When two eat them together . . ." Through the sliding door they could see the edge of a red futon coverlet in the next room.

"I saw the film . . . the one at Château Rouge."

He assumed she would blanch, but Motoko simply said, "Oh really," as she languidly crushed a cigarette in the ashtray. *Is she dull-witted*, Kobari wondered; *maybe a little lacking upstairs?*

"Did Suguro Sensei come to the party shown in the video?"

"Hmm. Was he there? I can't remember very well."

"Then what about that other woman?"

"What other woman?"

Kobari equivocated. "Suguro Sensei told me about her. Let's see, what was her name? The really elegant lady with the large eyes."

"Oh, Madame N."

"That's right. Madame N. Why just 'N'?"

"Because that's what we call her," Motoko said artlessly. "Yes, she was there. She's my partner, after all."

"She's your partner? So the two of you are lesbians, is that it?"

Motoko cradled her teacup in both hands and slowly drank the watery tea.

"You are, aren't you?"

"You don't understand anything," she said ruefully. "You have to put everybody into your infantile categories of homos and lesbians."

"In the film you had your fun from wax being poured in your hair and being strangled. Is your partner into that stuff, too?"

"She doesn't dislike it. She wasn't that way at first. I taught her a little bit at a time. Eventually she started getting interested in it on her own, and she taught me other things and talked to me."

"Talked to you about what?"

Motoko drained her teacup and narrowed her eyes like a severely nearsighted woman and peered at Kobari. In the dim fluorescent lighting, her common face suddenly appeared strangely seductive, like a beautiful simpleton, and Kobari felt his lust aroused.

"Have you ever heard anything about a noblewoman from Hungary named Bátholy?"

"Who the hell's that?"

"Madame N knows all about her. She can read English and French, too. This Marquise Bátholy lived in the sixteenth century, and after her husband died she brought young girls from her domain into her castle or her house in Vienna and tortured them to death. They say she murdered six hundred."

"What's that got to do with anything?"

"Madame N and I did a lot of pretending that we were the Marquise. Or, I should say, she played the Marquise and I played her victims." Motoko narrowed her eyes even more, as though she were remembering the pleasure of those encounters. "As we played, we got seriously into it. She told me that when she traveled to Europe, she went searching for the remains of the Marquise's mansion in Vienna. When she found it, it had been turned into a record store. They were playing Andy Williams mood music, and young customers flocked there without knowing anything about the place. She said it had made her unbearably angry. . . ."

"Why would she get angry?" Kobari looked puzzled. "It's odd of her to feel angry."

"Do you think so? These people are listening to mood music and don't have any idea that three hundred years ago the place was filled with the cries of young women being tortured and killed. Madame N said it was hypocrisy. Hypocrites who close their eyes to the darkest depths of the human heart and try to cover it up."

"Ridiculous." Kobari stuffed a jam wafer into his mouth. "That's really twisted."

"You don't understand anything."

"Thanks for the compliment."

"Madame N often says that there's magma inside people's hearts. Do you know what magma is?"

"I'm not a complete idiot. It's the fires at the center of the earth."

"That's right. You can't see it on the surface, but suddenly the magma will erupt. There's magma buried inside every person at the time they're born. It's in every child."

"What are you trying to say?"

"Even a child has fun tearing the wings or legs off a dragonfly. These days, even elementary-school kids will gang up on a helpless child and beat him up. They do that . . . because it's fun. Because there's magma in their hearts." She drank some more tea and went on. "When the magma erupts in the form of sex, it comes out as sadism or masochism. But the difference between the two isn't important. Madame N and I are like two whirlpools that collide, sending up a tall column of spray, thundering like the pounding of a drum, then dragged deeper and deeper toward the bottom of the ocean. It's like a bottomless pit. I can't tell you how many times I've wanted to die at that point. I've really wanted to die in the middle of that ecstasy."

With a vague sense of revulsion, Kobari looked at Motoko's slightly parted lips. This was the face. The face he had seen on the videotape, the hair daubed with wax and the tongue flailing like a caterpillar. This woman is insane.

"When that happens, common sense goes right out the window. I can't control myself even if I try."

"That's enough!" Kobari shook Motoko by her shoulders, certain that she had begun to rave. Her mouth was rippling like a goldfish's.

"You don't understand. You don't understand! The two waves crash together, the water sprays out . . ."

154

Kobari instinctively slapped Motoko's cheek with the palm of his hand. The biting sound echoed through the room. His knee bumped against the table, overturning their cups and spilling tea across the top of the table.

"Hit me! Again!" Motoko shouted deliriously, feverishly. "Hit me again!"

"Stop it! Stop it!"

Kobari struck her again. A numb sensation coursed through his arm, filling him with an intense pleasure he had never before experienced. He clutched Motoko's shoulders and shook her again. She rocked back and forth like a helpless toy doll and collapsed onto her back. Her skirt rode up, exposing her thighs covered in pantyhose. She had short, thick legs.

"Fine. If you want so much to be hit, I'll knock the shit out of you!"

"Yes!"

"I'll beat the filth out of your soul," he shouted. "I'll turn you into a real human being!"

CHAPTER
SIX

As it approached landing, the airplane made a slow dip toward the surface of the ocean, which sparkled like a carpet of needles. Suguro's wife turned toward her husband.

"How many years has it been since we last went on a vacation together?"

"How many, I wonder. I suppose it hasn't been since I took you to Jerusalem when I was writing my *Life of Christ.*"

As the stewardess started walking down the aisle to check seat belts, they caught a glimpse of the islands and fishing boats in the harbor. Soon they felt a gentle lurch, and the airport runway darted across the windows on both sides of the aircraft.

Unfastening his seat belt, Suguro proudly explained to his wife, "We'll first go from Isahaya to Obama. From there we go on to Kuchinotsu and Kazusa."

The taxi they hired at the airport drove for some distance along the edge of the luminous bay at Ōmura. Suguro remembered every mountain that rose dimly in the distance and every row of houses they skirted past. He was gripped with nostalgia. He wanted to ask every landscape how it had fared over the many years. Twenty years before, he had shuttled back and forth along this road more times than he could count, nourishing the images and sketching out plans for the novel he eventually produced. He had been in his forties then, inspired by the novelist's zeal and spurred by enthusiasm to walk at full tilt down this road without once casting a sidelong glance. As he peered at the road ahead, walled in by old houses with low roofs and stone walls beside thick groves of camphor trees, he could almost picture himself as he had been then, a man possessed by some formless passion.

"It's been twenty years," he muttered to his wife. "But the road and the houses haven't changed at all."

"Nature is remarkable, it never changes," his wife concurred.

"You're right. We're the ones who've aged. We've deviated."

As he spoke the word *deviated*, he realized that it included another meaning he had not anticipated.

He had not told his wife about seeing a man at the lecture who resembled himself in every respect. He hadn't mentioned his sudden illness either, or that he had been to dinner with Madame Naruse. Those were incidents he did not need to relate to her, experiences he must not tell her about. Ever since their wedding, he had kept silent about any episode that might disturb the order they had established between them. This reticence was perhaps akin to that of a father who could never bring himself to tell his own daughter the facts of life.

He had made up his mind to go on vacation with his wife in Nagasaki before the onset of spring not so much because he had promised her, but because of the fear that had invaded his heart. The experiences that had pressed in on him this winter had progressively aggravated his anxieties. To escape them he wanted to be alone with his wife and spend several days together with her in some quiet corner of the countryside.

It was remarkably warm for winter, and as they passed through Isahaya the slope of Unzen appeared at the fringes of the vacant sky like a clump of cloud.

"That's Unzen," he genially instructed his wife, pointing to the map that lay open on his knees. "Three hundred years ago, Christians were cast into the boiling waters in the mouth of the volcano there."

"Can you still see the place where it happened?"

"It's called the Valley of Hell. But nowadays it's overrun with tourists and school outings."

He could feel a warm contentment radiating from within and spreading throughout his body. A husband and wife approaching the end of their lives are enjoying three days and two nights of uninterrupted companionship. Comprehended in this journey was one element that had not been part of their honeymoon: a profound sense of unity and trust that could be shared only by those who had passed through extended trials together. Suguro felt anew the satisfaction of having taken this woman as his life's companion.

They skirted the base of Unzen and came to the hot springs resort town of Obama. Beneath them stretched the waters of the bay, while white clouds of water vapor swirled over the streets of the village.

"The Christians in those days were forced to walk from here by foot to the top of the mountain. That was how they were taken to the Valley of Hell."

"This must have been a desolate little village at that time."

From Obama they followed the coastline along a narrow road. The road was unpaved, as it was when Suguro had first come here twenty years ago. The oncoming cars kicked up clouds of dust, and his taxi patiently stopped on the shoulder of the road to allow the approaching traffic to pass by.

"That's Dangō Island out there, and beyond that, the island that looks as if it's stretched out asleep is Amakusa."

"That's Amakusa?"

"Yes. This harbor is the place where the Christian missionaries from Portugal and Spain landed three centuries ago, after a journey of two years. The scenery must have been just the same when they arrived."

As he talked, Suguro could feel a warm revival of the same emotions that had boiled inside him twenty years before. He experienced a fresh resurgence of the concepts and images that had slowly formulated in his head as he had previously walked this land.

They got out of the taxi and went to look at a Christian grave site that had been discovered among the trees planted as a windbreak along the edge of the sea. The grave resembled a discarded gray boulder, and the only engravings they could make out were a cross and a few characters that appeared to be in Latin.

"Here in Kazusa is the first place where a printing press was used in Japan. You remember in the Tenshō period a famous group of young emissaries went to Rome and had an audience with the Pope. On their return journey, they stopped off in Goa and got hold of a printing press, which they brought back to Japan. As a result, religious books and some of the classics of Japanese literature were first printed here."

His wife listened intently, more for the benefit of her enthusiastic husband than for the content of his remarks.

"Seminaries were built in Kazusa and in the neighboring village of Kuchinotsu, as well as in Arie. The students learned Latin and Portuguese and studied the organ and harpsichord and painting, too. Not a single history book in Japan has recorded it, but right here where we're standing is the place where the Japanese people first learned about the West."

Suguro remembered that not far away there was a beautiful stretch of beach. Twenty years ago, when he had tired of walking, he lay down on this amber beach and fell asleep watching the gentle waves wash in. He had been in his prime then, and still had energy in his body.

They ate at a small restaurant in Kuchinotsu, after which they left their hired driver in the tiny village and walked together to the beach.

"This is where I fell asleep. While I was looking at the ocean."

"The water's so clear. You can see the seaweed swaying."

"See where it juts out there like a promontory? That's Hara Castle, where the Shimabara rebellion took place. Thirty thousand men and women were slaughtered there."

The word *slaughtered* tasted bitter in his mouth. This trip with his wife was a journey to experience life. It was not supposed to make them sink into the darkness. It was an excursion to escape from the world of Madame Naruse and Itoi Motoko.

"Look how pretty this shell is."

As he lay on the sand, his wife came up to show him a shell she had picked up at the water's edge. Cradled in her white palm, the pink shell looked like an ornament of some sort.

"Are you having a good time?"

"Well, of course. It's been so long since we've been away like this. I wish Tatsunosuke and Masako could have come with us."

"When I look out at this ocean, I realize how fortunate we've been to live as long as we have. First the war, and then the agonizing years after the defeat. But we've finally been able to struggle to this point in our lives."

"I always feel grateful for it when I go to Mass. When I die I feel that I'll be able to say 'thank you' to God."

No matter what, Suguro did not want to show his wife that other world, that world of wax-coated hair, of tongues writhing like caterpillars in Motoko's half-opened mouth as men's hands closed around her throat, of flames engulfing the farmhouse, the screams of women and children, the slaughter of thirty thousand men, women, and children at Hara Castle not so far from here.

He let a sigh escape. "Things are so good for you. I envy you."

"Why, for heaven's sake?"

"Because . . . unlike me as a writer . . . you don't have to look at things that are just as well left unseen."

The sense that his wife was close by gradually evolved into a feeling of security. It was in every sense identical to the feeling he had had as a child sleeping next to his mother. Why did he have to keep trying to leave this place of repose? The desire to view humanity. The yearning to know all there was to know about the human animal. To see to the very bottom of the pit. He had been a writer for more than thirty years, and now that desire had turned into something very near to an instinct.

The waves coursed in gently and regularly and then retreated. As Suguro listened to each distinct sound, scenes from his memory surged forth one frame at a time. That day in autumn after they had become engaged, when they had strolled the plains of Yamato. Those days when they had bought their first house in Komaba. His wife coming in every day without fail to care for him during his long convalescence in the hospital. The smile on her face that he had seen when he awakened dull-eyed from the anesthetic. Seated now beside her silent husband, she, too, said nothing. Perhaps her head was filled with identical memories as she listened to the quiet flow of the waves.

"Tomorrow's Sunday. Let's go to church together," she suddenly proposed. "I've always wanted to attend Mass here where your novels are set."

"Why?"

She smiled. "Well, it's the only way I can be a part of your novels. There's no room for me to be a part of your work."

She was quite right. From the beginning of their marriage, he had asked her to set up distinct borders between his vocation and his family life. She was never to have a say in his work. She was never to interfere in the content of his fiction. It was both a request and an expression of his thoughtfulness.

"I haven't been to Mass in a long time." He spoke quickly and looked away from her.

It's not that I didn't want to go, he thought, *but that I couldn't go*.

"I know a little quiet church on the outskirts of Nagasaki," he said. "Let's go there for Mass tomorrow. I'll call from the hotel and find out the times."

He vigorously brushed the sand from his trousers to signal the end of the conversation.

Several times during the Mass, Suguro and his wife heard the crow of a dull-witted rooster outside the sunlit church. Like the peasants of this village, the rooster was cared for by the foreign priest of the parish. Outside the window a huge camphor tree spread its gnarled branches, between which the ocean radiated. Small children walked past them down the aisles, their sun-baked mothers scurrying after them. An infant began to cry, and a woman tried to pacify it. The majority of the faithful who had gathered for the Mass were villagers who divided their livelihood between farming and fishing.

The previous night in their Nagasaki hotel, Suguro had remembered visiting this seaside village several years before, and he had told his wife about it.

"The brick church there is wonderful. Years ago the village was populated with *kakure* Christians,* and even now over half the town is Christian. The man who proselytized in this area was the famous Father De Rotz. The whole congregation labored and saved their money, fired their own bricks, and erected a handmade church to worship in."

His wife was captivated by the story.

"Then you'd like to go? It's about a forty-minute drive."

They took a taxi from the hotel at eight the next morning. Their route led them through two small tunnels, and when they caught sight of the inlet near the village, both were pleased that they had decided to come. The ocean glimmering in the sun welcomed them with its warm, friendly expression. Just as they arrived, a middle-school student sounded

---

*Kakure Christians: "Hidden" Christians who went underground to practice their faith during Japanese proscription of Christianity between 1637 and 1873. See Endo's story "Mothers" in *Stained Glass Elegies*.—TRANS.

the bell from the brick chapel on the hill beyond. Many families were proceeding up the slope to the church in single file, like a parade of ants.

They got out of the taxi and joined the procession. As they entered the chapel grounds, a white-haired foreign missionary, whom Suguro remembered from his data-gathering many years before, was greeting the worshippers. At intervals he would tease the children who swarmed around him and offer words of cordiality to the housewives of the congregation. When he saw Suguro, he seemed to remember him and joked, "The reserved seats are in the center."

The priest had served in this church for forty years now, and his beaming eyes seemed to take in not the dark side of humanity that Suguro perceived, but only the warm ocean, the camphors with their spreading branches, and the impish children who thronged about his legs.

When the Mass began, the foreigner delivered no sermon, but instead recited a passage from the Gospels in unison with the standing congregation. This appeared to be the custom each Sunday at this church, and the suntanned, pointed-cheeked parishioners all repeated the same words as their pastor.

"Come unto me, all ye that labour and are heavy laden, and I will give you rest."

Outside the chapel, the rooster's dull cackle echoed once again.

"Take my yoke upon you, and learn of me; for I am meek and lowly in heart: and ye shall find rest unto your souls."

Suguro and his wife joined the others to repeat, "You will find rest unto your souls." Those words were immediately followed in Suguro's mind by the passage from the *Divine Comedy*:

In the middle of the journey of our life,
I found myself within the forest dark,
For the straightforward pathway had been lost.

"Blessed are the meek."

The rhythm of the old priest's voice was as clumsy as that of the rooster.

In the middle of the journey of our life,
I found myself within the forest dark.

"Blessed are the meek." The voices of the faithful mingled with the cries of babies and the sniffling of noses.

"Blessed are they that mourn, for they shall be comforted."

"Blessed are they that mourn, for they shall be comforted."

When the Mass was over, Suguro and his wife, surrounded by children, threaded their way outside and climbed back into their hired car. The old priest tapped on the window and said, "Please come and visit us again."

The car drove alongside the friendly, gently radiant ocean, and Suguro's wife said, with a sigh, "Such a wonderful life they lead."

"Umm hmm."

I found myself within the forest dark, for the straightforward pathway had been lost. He glanced back. The chapel and the large camphor tree in the garden appeared to get smaller and smaller. *How old is that priest by now? I'm sixty-five, so he must be five or six years older than that. How much longer will he live? After he dies, he'll be buried at the foot of that tall camphor tree, and there he'll look out at the ocean. He'll watch the urchins running about, and he'll listen to the roosters crow.*

Not a trace of the world of Madame Naruse and Motoko could be found there.

*   *   *

The trip had lasted only three days, but Suguro felt as though he had been away from his office for a long time. When they arrived at Haneda Airport and saw the dark gray winter sky and the smoke rising from the factory chimneys, he felt as though he had been escorted back into the unclean domain of humankind.

A stack of mail was waiting on his desk. He changed his clothes and opened each envelope with a pair of scissors. His wife quietly looked in with a smile of gratitude for the trip.

"Thank you so much."

"Did you have a good time?"

"I really did. I want to hurry and write to Tatsunosuke all about it."

"We must take trips like that at least once a year," he offered considerately.

A smile like a burst of sunshine lit her mouth.

He gathered the letters and divided up the complimentary issues of magazines and books, then opened one of the accumulated newspapers. Japan had been tranquil over the past three days; not a single major incident was reported on the front page or in the society section. Suguro read over the monthly arts review and scanned the book-review column. Then, thinking of writing some thank-you notes for the several books that had been sent to him, he called to his wife, "Would you mind getting the postcards with the woodcuts on them that we bought in Kyushu? I need to write some thank-you notes."

His wife was peeling the skin from a persimmon as she watched television. Over her shoulder the screen flickered anemically. The square face of the middle-aged announcer for the afternoon news was on display.

"The body of a young female suicide was discovered today in Shinjuku. When the apartment manager, Mr. Shimizu Mitsuo, unlocked the apartment . . ."

"Did we buy these cards at the hotel?"

"No. It was on that street called Dōza or something. At a souvenir shop."

"The young victim was an artist by the name of Itoi Motoko. A cord was wrapped around her neck, and the police have determined that she used the leg of a desk to carry out the suicide. What appears to be a suicide note was found in her sketchbook. According to police . . ."

"Would you like a persimmon?"

Suguro stood up and walked toward the door of the apartment. The descriptions in Madame Naruse's letter had been neither lies nor exaggerations.

"What's the matter?"

Hearing his wife's startled voice behind him, he got a grip on himself. He returned his wife's wide-eyed stare with a glance calculated to assure her that nothing was wrong. The ocean shining between the branches of the camphor tree—that was all the world he wanted his wife to know.

"I'm going to go buy some envelopes," he lied. "I've decided a postcard is too informal."

He went out of the apartment building, stepped into a telephone booth and began to dial. He didn't know whether she would be at the hospital, but he had to try to reach her. The call was transferred to the nurses' station in the pediatric ward, but he was told Madame Naruse was not in today.

"But she will be here tomorrow morning. One of the children she looks after is having surgery then." The nurse, her voice sounding as young as a high-school girl's, politely volunteered the information.

*　　　*　　*

Suguro stepped off the elevator at around eleven the next morning, exiting onto the floor where the operation was to be performed. Two women were huddled like old nuns in chairs against the wall. One was the mother of the boy who was in surgery. The other was Madame Naruse, looking so weary he scarcely recognized her.

She walked over to him when she saw him. "What on earth are you doing here?"

"Has the operation already started?"

"Nearly three hours ago. The chief surgeon is a doctor from the Keiō cardiac unit, so I'm sure he'll be all right. But everything is so quiet it makes me nervous."

"Is it a difficult operation?"

"Yes, he has a tumor on a vessel near the heart. Surgery in that region is very delicate and risky. And when I think how much pain it must cause him . . ."

She shut her eyes. When her lids were closed he saw distinct shadows of age on her face that he had never noticed before. He was reminded, as though for the first time, of how old she really was.

"I've had major surgery myself, and during the operation you have no idea what's going on. I was in for six hours, but I felt like I only slept for five minutes."

"Yes, my head tells me he can't be in any pain while he's under the anesthetic. But when I think of the scalpel slicing into his little body, and then they'll open up his chest and the blood will pour out . . ."

Again she wearily closed her eyes. Her lips fluttered faintly, like those of a nun at Mass.

"Are you praying?" Suguro asked in disbelief.

"Yes, I can't help but pray. I'm an idiot, aren't I? He

169

isn't even my own child." Then, as though the thought had just occurred to her, "But how did you know I was here today?"

"I called the nurses' station yesterday."

"Oh . . ."

Suguro started to mention Motoko's death, but he swallowed the words. The woman in front of him now was not the same person who had chatted with him at the Chinese restaurant. She was a different woman while she labored as a volunteer, showering her maternal affections upon a fragile child.

He sat down beside the two women, but the boy's mother did not say a word. Her attention was riveted not on Suguro, but on the operating theater. Only the red lamp on that door was alive to her. The hallway was shrouded in silence.

Both women sat with their eyes closed. Madame Naruse's lips continued to quiver, but of course he could not hear the words of her prayer. This woman had used scenes of children barricaded with their mothers in tiny huts and burned to death as an erotic stimulus in her marriage. So, who was she praying to? Suguro felt his eyes begin to swim as he looked at her face.

"I have to go." He quietly got up from his chair.

She opened her eyes and nodded slightly.

It had grown dark before nightfall, the fault, perhaps, of the smog and mist. Such evenings were gloomy and forlorn even on the back streets of Kabuki-chō. The only sound was the mournful call of the man selling roasted sweet potatoes. The neon lights seemed blurred, and the blanket that covered her knees was damp. Ishiguro Hina glanced down and readjusted the tiny metal body warmer she had placed on her lap. At that moment, someone stopped in front of her.

"Do you want a pencil sketch or a watercolor?" she asked in a tired voice, glancing at the hem of her new client's raincoat and the tips of his worn-out shoes.

"Is this where you drew Suguro's picture?"

She lifted her head. The reporter she had met the night she was ejected from the reception was looking down at her contemptuously, his hands thrust in his pockets.

"What of it?"

"Don't give me any of your hard-headed answers. I'm not here for information. So don't worry."

"If you don't want a portrait, would you mind standing somewhere else? I have work to do."

"All right. Then do me a pencil sketch."

Hina wordlessly skidded her pencil across the drawing paper. Kobari looked down at her.

"Just listen to me for a minute. I believe you now, that you met Suguro here at Shinjuku. I really believe you."

"Hold still. I can't draw you if you move."

"I've been checking him out since I talked to you. I've learned a lot about him."

"It's got nothing to do with me."

"Then tell me just two things. What was the relationship between Motoko and Suguro? And there's an older woman who was very close to Motoko. Was she a friend of Suguro?"

The fingers holding the pencil stopped moving. He proceeded with his questions, but Hina maintained a stubborn silence.

Frustrated, Kobari stole a glance at the half-completed portrait and frowned.

"That's dreadful!"

"Why?"

"There's malice written all over that face. I'm not that hideous."

Hina looked at Kobari's sullen face and chuckled. "If you only want a superficial portrait, please go to another street artist. To us a portrait means drawing what the person is really like."

"Is this what I'm really like?"

"A person never knows his own true face. Everyone thinks that the phony, posed social mask he wears is his real face." She removed the blanket from her lap and stood up. The body warmer that had been nestled in the folds of the blanket fell to the ground.

"But this is too ghastly. Now that you mention it, though, there was a portrait of Suguro at your exhibition, wasn't there? It was a spitting image, I thought. There's an odious, murky something in his face. The portrait really caught that."

"Did you come to our exhibition?" Hina's expression thawed for the first time.

Kobari nodded. "Of course I did. You weren't there, but when I arrived, I saw Suguro talking with the older woman in a coffee shop right in front of the gallery. That's the woman—the one who was close to Motoko. Of course Motoko's dead now."

"How did you know that?"

"That Motoko's dead? It's been in all the papers."

"Motoko died just the way she wanted to, so I'm sure she must be happy. But how did you know about Madame N?"

Kobari decided it would be best to come clean with this woman. When he had finished his explanation, Hina still looked unconvinced.

"Why do you dislike Mr. Suguro so much?"

"Why? I really don't know," Kobari answered, half in jest. "For one thing, he strikes me as the epitome of the pseudo-literati in Japan. There's something untrustworthy about men of culture these days. No matter what grandiose, profound-sounding statements these genteel folk come out with, somehow I can't shake off the feeling that they're all a bunch of phonies. You know what I'm talking about. Maybe that's why I can't bring myself to like Suguro."

Hina taunted him. "Everybody's the same. You're the same kind of person yourself. You've sniffed out an image of yourself in Mr. Suguro, and you hate him for it."

"You're vicious," Kobari sneered. "Maybe you're right. But I'm not like him. I'm the pauper you see standing here, while he sits back smug with his thousands of readers, respected as a leading writer, saying things that only sound sincere with that sincere look on his face."

"You're jealous."

"Of course I am. But what makes him different from other writers is that he's a Christian. I even know somebody who became a Christian because of what Suguro has written. That's how ingenious he is."

"And so?"

"So if he's living a life completely different from the kinds of things he writes about and talks about, I think it's the duty of a journalist to expose that to the public."

"You're a real champion of virtue, aren't you? Truth and justice to a reporter these days means closing your eyes to your own shortcomings and judging everyone else."

Kobari ignored her sarcasm. "Anyway, there was a large painting at the exhibition titled *The Realm of the Unsightly*, wasn't there? Lots of naked men and women in it, along with snakes and toads and praying mantises. That one still sticks in my mind."

"Really? I painted that." She looked pleased, and her smiling face took on an unexpected cast of childlike innocence. "Do you know what I mean by an aesthetics of ugliness?

That's what we're promoting in our group—an aesthetic glorification of the ugly. Orthodox painters divide the world up into subjects that are beautiful and those that are ugly. They make a distinction between the objects that are materials fit for their work, and the ugly objects that aren't. But us, we believe that there's beauty in every ugly thing, and that the purpose of art is to reveal that kind of beauty. Do you understand?"

"But that's nothing more than the theories Suguro expounded to you at Shinjuku, isn't it? Anyway, you're right about one thing—there wasn't a shred of beauty in that portrait of Suguro. It really captured the essence of his dual personality."

"That? I didn't draw that one. Motoko did."

There was a bite to Hina's words that Kobari chose to overlook.

"It's the classic face of a schizophrenic. I believe that the shape and arrangement of the eyes is subtly different with a schizo. He has a separate personality inside him, and he may not even know it himself. There was a program about that on television some time ago. Did you see it?"

"No." In a huff because Kobari had not shown any interest in her views on the aesthetics of ugliness, Hina put the finishing touches on her sketch of the reporter. "Nobody could claim that there's nothing horrid about your face."

"This TV show was about a high-class woman who came to consult a psychiatrist. She complained of headaches and various other physical problems. He questioned her over the space of several days, and then one day, with no warning of any kind, she turned into a different woman right in front of the doctor's eyes. Her face and body didn't change, of course. But a woman who had been quiet and refined suddenly displayed a wanton, sluttish, coarse look on her face and laughed shrilly. She'd been transformed into a totally different person. The doctor was astonished, but before long the woman reverted to her normal self, as though she had awakened from a dream, and she had no memory of having changed into that other woman."

The story had caught Hina's attention, and she was listening intently.

"Then what?"

"Another woman was living inside her. A woman with a completely different personality. That's what schizophrenia is."

"I know. I . . . I can understand exactly how she felt."

"Why don't we go and have a drink?"

"Where?"

"On Golden Avenue."

"You want more information out of me, don't you? I'm not telling you anything else. I've got to go."

"Why?"

"Because I don't like the journalistic mind. How's that?"

"Ouch." Kobari reckoned that this woman had little more information to offer him.

"That'll be two thousand yen."

He grumbled at the price as he handed her two bills. He rolled up the paper, put it in his pocket, and walked away.

A glass of cheap saké with a lemon peel floating on top sat in front of Kobari in the Golden Avenue bar as he reflected on what Hina had said. He had enough to write a story now. He thought of the journalist whose stories had toppled the Japanese prime minister from his seat of power. The bomb he was about to plant did not have an equal degree of explosive power, but it would be enough to jolt the literati and their readership. And it would provide a solid means of making the name of Kobari known in the world of journalism. Offers of assignments would then start pouring in. And then he'd make enough money to break off the relationship with his current lover. One flight of fancy summoned up the next, and the drunker Kobari became the happier he felt.

In his elated state, Kobari summoned a taxi. "Nakano," he directed the driver, but suddenly he changed his destination. "No, take me to Yoyogi."

There was no reason for him to believe that Suguro would be at that hotel if he went there to inquire, but maybe he could get some information about the sex party from one of the hotel employees.

"This fog's unusual, isn't it?" the driver said cheerlessly, slowing down as he drove. "Sir, I'll have to stay on the main roads. If I get on a narrow street, I won't be able to see in front of me, and that can get scary."

"Fine."

Kobari got out in front of the hotel and pressed through the lapping clouds of fog as though he were elbowing his way ahead. Spurred on by his inherent audacity, he marched through the entrance where the lights were blurred by the fog. At the front desk, a young man in a formal black uniform and wearing glasses was nervously pecking at a typewriter.

"I don't want a room. I think you have a guest here named Mr. Suguro."

In response to Kobari's fabrication, the clerk pretended to be searching the guest register.

"I'm afraid we don't have anyone registered under the name of Suguro."

"That's strange. I heard there was going to be a party here tonight."

"Whose party, sir?" The young man responded with a somber face. He had evidently been trained in these procedures.

"Mr. Suguro's. That's why I . . ."

"I don't know of any party for a Mr. Suguro, sir." The young man looked inquiringly at Kobari. "Excuse me, sir, but we operate on a membership system here."

"Then there's no party, is that right?"

"I have not heard of any for this evening."

"Do you sometimes have parties for members only?"

"I really don't know, sir."

Kobari curled his lips in a contemptuous smile and walked away from the front desk. Then slowly and deliberately he surveyed the cramped lobby and the bar beyond before going outside. When he stepped from the loading zone into the street, a taxi came to a stop in front of the hotel. Through the fog, the man alighting from the cab looked like a slow-motion shadow picture. The shadow came walking toward Kobari and passed him by.

He felt as though he had received a hammer blow to his head.

It was Suguro. But it was not the Suguro he had seen at the awards ceremony or the Suguro who had spewed out his oh-so-moral messages in the lecture hall and on television. It was the Suguro whose face Motoko had captured in her portrait. As he walked past Kobari, ignorant of the reporter's existence, his profile exuded arrogance and cunning and profligacy. He continued toward the hotel, but then seemed to have a change of mind and set out directly down the wide road toward Shinjuku.

He saw me. He's on the lookout.

His exhilaration swelled. At last he had seized hold of the man's true nature. He felt the thrill of a hunter who gazes on his prey caught in a trap. Kobari was grateful for the thick fog. Suguro would not be able to tell that he was being followed.

But that was a miscalculation. Although Suguro had not noticed him, Kobari realized he was in danger of losing sight of his quarry. Knowing he might fall suspect if he drew too close, he picked up his gait, just the same. The enshrouded figure ahead walked for some distance along the main road, then suddenly ducked into a road on the right. When Kobari rounded the corner, Suguro had vanished, as though he had evaporated. He had disappeared without a trace. Incredulous, Kobari abandoned his fear of discovery and quickly ran to the top of the hill, looking left and right. Where had he gone? Where was he hiding? There was not a sound, not a single movement. At the top of the slope, the fog had enveloped the houses on either side of the road. The dampness seeping into the telephone poles and into his own clothing was ghastly. Kobari was assaulted by the uneasy feeling that his own eyes were playing tricks on him by suggesting that Suguro had simply disappeared. He clawed his way through the fog to the bottom of the hill, peering at every doorway through the milky stream that opened and closed around him. He paid special attention to the far sides of the telephone poles as he hurried back toward the main road.

Just then he heard a voice trailing through the fog from behind him. It seemed to be laughing, mocking his own confusion. When he turned around, he saw the shadow of a man midway up the slope looking toward him. The man laughed tauntingly. It was an oppressive sound. Then it changed into a prolonged, sobbing voice, and the man started up the hill, limping on one leg, and was swallowed up by the fog.

The telephone was jangling. It continued relentlessly, ceaselessly.

Suguro unlocked the door and stepped into his office. When he heard the telephone, his body stiffened. It was a night of dense mist and smog, and after he had returned from running an errand his coat was wet with moisture, though he made no move to brush it off.

From the mere sound of the ringing, he knew whom the call was from. Even if he picked up the receiver, he knew the caller would maintain his silence, never uttering a word.

The phone was jangling. It continued relentlessly, ceaselessly.

For some reason, a speech he had recently reread from *King Lear* popped into his head.

> *Pray, do not mock me.*
> *I am a very foolish fond old man,*
> *Fourscore and upward, not an hour more nor less;*
> *And, to deal plainly,*
> *I fear I am not in my perfect mind.*

Pray, do not mock me, he appealed to the caller. The ringing stopped.

His shoulders rising and falling as he breathed, Suguro removed his wet jacket, but his limbs felt heavy. He had already told his wife he would be sleeping at the office tonight, so, relieved of the long journey to his home in the suburbs, he sank into the sofa and closed his eyes, trying to plumb the depths of his weariness. It was evident to him that he had aged rapidly since the night of the awards ceremony in early winter. It was with a tangible sense of their meaning that he felt old age and death slowly drawing near.

Because he felt so languid, he put his hand to his forehead. It was hot. Perhaps a person who had undergone lung surgery in the past should not have been out walking in the fog. It was too much trouble to go to bed, so he lay back on the sofa, closed his eyes, and fell asleep.

He had a dream.

He was walking by himself through the fog. He had no clear idea why he had come out in the fog on a night like this. It reminded him of the times he had gone walking in the fog those winters he had been studying in Lyons. Many times then, still feeling exhilarated after seeing a play or a film, he had literally cut a path through the fog to return to his apartment. He had been young and full of hope then, convinced even that he was cutting a path through life for himself. But now, as he groped through a fog unusually thick for Tokyo, he did not even know in which direction he walked. He grew anxious, not knowing which way to turn if he decided to go back home. That anxiety gradually made it difficult for him to breathe.

In the midst of this trepidation, he heard footsteps approaching from the rear. He was being followed. The footsteps must belong either to the doctor who had swiveled on his squeaky chair and was coming to report his test results, or to that magazine reporter. One brought Suguro unrest about his physical health each month; the other troubled his mind. In either case, the footsteps, filled with rancor, tenaciously dogged his path whichever way he turned.

When he quickened his pace, the footsteps followed faster. Suguro remembered a turn up ahead, and relying on the heavy fog, he made a swift turn to the right and ran up the hill. He hid in the doorway of a house. He heard scurrying footsteps at the bottom of the slope; eventually they came to a halt in front of the doorway where Suguro stood. He could feel eyes peering through the fog. Had his pursuer heard his breathing, or was he trying to lure him into a trap?

"You've got cancer of the liver. No matter where you try to run, in your condition you'll never get away. I'm going to expose you for what you really are!" the voice shouted, but eventually the man appeared to give up and walk away.

Suguro felt a chill and realized that sweat was coursing down his back. *Pray, do not mock me.* He directed the words, like those of a prayer, toward the top of the hill.

Threescore and upward, not an hour more nor less.

I don't want to die in darkness any thicker than this. I want to bring some kind of resolution to my life.

Just then he noticed a faint light beginning to flicker through the fog. It did not emanate from the bleary house lamps. The source of the light seemed to be somewhere at the top of the hill, emitting a glow as if in response to Suguro's prayer. It shone through the stagnant fog and narrowed to a focus upon him. He had the distinct impression that some volitional force was trying to catch hold of him, but strangely he could discern no ill will or malice in that force. In fact, the moment his body was enveloped in the deep, soft light, he felt an indescribable peace within all his senses. The feeling far surpassed the repose he had achieved from sitting alone at the desk in his study. No longer did anything restrain him. The heavy weights that had burdened his mind were gone. He had been set free in an expansive field where he could breathe the fresh air. *Ah, this is death.* Suguro was steeped in an immense pool of joy as he wondered if this was what death was really like. He was amazed to find that death had a visage utterly unlike the fearsome aspect he had long dreaded. There was not a trace of menace or condemnation in the light that enfolded him in its arms. It was the incarnation of tenderness. "Come unto me . . . for I am meek and lowly in heart." The voice was like, and yet in some ways unlike, that of the old priest.

He woke up. It was the middle of the night. At the back of his eyelids the light that had appeared in his dream lingered as a vivid afterimage. He had never had such a dream. What did it mean? he wondered as he sat up on the sofa. It was cold; he had neglected to turn on the heater. He went into the bedroom and crawled into bed still in his clothes, not even bothering to change into the pajamas his wife had laid out for him.

Growing older means death looms closer—that must be the reason he had experienced such a dream. Being chased by someone in the fog—that must be a manifestation of his fear of being pursued by death. But what about the light? Is that his wish of how he would like things to be?

He was huddled completely under the blanket, but he still felt a bone-piercing chill from the base of his spine. The only certain thing was that something had changed inside him since that awards ceremony. A hand somewhere was trying to shake loose the tight grip on the world that he had built for himself. The hand was seeking to hurl him into a nightmarish world he had never before imagined. It was attempting to lead him into a world of women with flailing tongues and wax-caked hair.

Just what was that hand, that world, trying to show him? In his novels, Suguro had always asserted that not a single occurrence in human life is insignificant. If that view was not mistaken, what was the meaning of this experience, and where was it leading him? He felt as though he were wandering in a fog, knowing neither the direction he should take nor the path by which he should return.

Still feeling the chill, he closed his eyes tightly and tried to force himself to sleep. He wanted to experience again the bliss of the light he had seen and feel it envelop him. In a state of semiconsciousness, he realized that for many years he had relied on his knowledge and mental powers as a novelist, but that now suddenly he had been confronted by something he could not process with his mind, something that continued to expand around him. He did not even know what to call that "something."

He seemed to have a fever the next time he awoke; his mouth felt heavy and clammy. He did not have the energy to get up, and nursing a headache, he lay motionless throughout the morning hours.

The doorbell rang at about 3 P.M. He decided to let it go on ringing, but then he heard a key in the lock, and the apartment manager's voice called, "Is anyone home?"

"Yes." He sat up, his head still throbbing. "I'm here."

"Good. Mit-chan is here."

"Mit-chan?"

"The girl who used to clean for you."

"Send her in." He collapsed back onto the bed and closed his eyes. Even then his head felt as if it were spinning out of control.

The door to his bedroom opened a crack, and he heard Mitsu's nasal voice.

"Sensei . . ."

"I'm awfully tired. I went for a walk in the fog last night. I think I caught a cold."

"What can I do for you?" She gathered up the clothing and socks he had scattered around the room and placed her hand on his forehead. "You've got a fever. I'll call your wife."

"No, if I just rest today I'll be fine."

"I . . . I came to pay back the money."

"Money?"

She looked even more physically mature than he remembered her, and it depressed him to have her around. It felt as though her thriving vitality was bearing down on him even as his physical and mental powers withered.

"The money I borrowed here . . ."

Suguro remembered the conversation with his wife.

"Ah, that money." His head still ached from the fever, and he kicked the blanket off. "The money you gave to your friend . . ."

"Yes, but . . . I'm an idiot."

"It doesn't matter."

"What can I do for you? Can I get you anything?"

"Well, you could get a cold washcloth and put it on my forehead."

"Let me call your wife."

"No. On cold days like this her joints ache, and I don't want to worry her."

After Mitsu had brought him the cool cloth, she asked if he was hungry.

"No. Why don't you go on home."

She looked down at him with concern for a moment, then said, "I'll check up on you later."

He slept and awoke, awoke and slept. He continued to experience chills and a headache. When he took his temperature, it was 102.5 degrees.

That evening he had just about decided to phone his wife when she called him.

"Are you coming home tonight?"

"No, I can't. I've still got a lot of work."

"What about dinner?"

"The round table I'm scheduled to attend is at a restaurant."

"Good. My arthritis is bothering me today. It's rather painful."

"It's this piercing cold. Take care of yourself."

Once again he had lied to his wife. Just as he would not tell her about his dreams or his conversations with Madame Naruse, he did not tell her about his own illness. Knowing that it was through deception that he had been able to preserve their tranquil relationship over many years, he felt as though his entire life had been built on a foundation of mendacity.

He slept briefly. With clouded perception, he heard the bedroom door open, and through slit eyes he saw a blurred, peach blossom–like image of Mitsu's face.

"I'm sorry I woke you up, Sensei."

"Is that you?"

"Are you still uncomfortable?"

There was earnest concern in her voice. That's the kind of girl Mitsu is. A girl who frets, not knowing what she should do when someone else is experiencing even the slightest discomfort. There was something of the simpleton about her, but Suguro had always been attracted to such individuals. He had even written novels with such characters as heroes.

"I'm a little better."

"Are you sure I can't call your wife?"

"I'm sure. I talked to her on the phone a little while ago, and she's got bad arthritis from the cold."

Mitsu came over to him and put her hand on his forehead.

"You still have a fever."

Her breasts, shrouded in an inexpensive sweater, brushed against Suguro's head. The sweater had a musty smell. But this time he did not feel smothered by the vibrancy that flowed from her body.

"You're still really hot, Sensei."

"But I feel a bit better for having slept."

"I'll wring out another cold washcloth for you."

She picked up the cloth that had slipped down by his pillow and went into the bathroom. He relished the cool touch of

Mitsu's fingers on his face. He had no daughter of his own, but he wondered if a daughter would have nursed him as Mitsu was doing now. Unlike his wife, her ministrations were puerile and clumsy, but there was a painful assiduousness to them.

After making him comfortable in bed, Mitsu bustled about in the kitchen for a while, and eventually reappeared with a tray of rice porridge in an aluminum bowl, a cup of tea, and some pickled plums.

"Eat up."

"Did you make this?"

"Yes. I learned at the hospital where my friend's father was staying."

"Learned from whom?"

"An older lady who was looking after someone. I'm not a very good cook, though."

He had no appetite, though he hadn't eaten anything for nearly a day. But to avoid hurting Mitsu's feelings, he sat up in bed. Both the tea and the porridge that slithered down his throat were wretched, but the taste conveyed some of the young girl's devotion.

"Thank you," he managed to say after he had forced himself to eat. "I'm *happified*." He used one of the middle-school colloquialisms she had taught him.

"Really?" Mitsu grinned, accepting his gratitude at face value.

"You learned a lot at the hospital, didn't you? Did you go there often?"

"Just once in a while with my friend."

"There's a lady named Mrs. Naruse who works at that hospital as a volunteer. Do you know her?"

"No." Mitsu shook her head. "What's a volunteer?"

"A person who helps the patients. My wife's studying to be one. They aren't professional nurses."

"Is that what this lady does?"

"Yes, Mrs. Naruse is a volunteer at the hospital. She takes care of the sick children."

"I think maybe I've seen her. She's a pretty lady, isn't she?"

"Pretty? Well . . ."

Again his head ached, and he closed his eyes. Mitsu took the tray and went to the kitchen.

Another long night passed; he slept feverishly, and eventually woke up wet with perspiration. When he got up in the middle of the night to change his soaked clothes, his feet were unsteady, but he could tell that his temperature had dropped a bit. He wiped his body with a towel, put on a new pair of pajamas, and casually switched on the lights in the living room. There he found Mitsu propped up against the back of the sofa, asleep.

"What are you doing here? You didn't go home?"

Mitsu looked up at him with her customary grin. To him the look seemed a combination of a young girl playing the spoiled child for an adult and a woman flirting seductively with a man. Fear flickered inside him, persuading him to exercise restraint.

"There are blankets in the cupboard. And you know, we've got pillows, too."

She did not reply. He left her and went back to bed. Rubbing his chilled legs together like a fly, he again surrendered to his drowsiness. In his dreams he was rubbing his own unsightly cheek against Mitsu's. He was compelled by the hope that in so doing he could extend his own dwindling life by another year or two.

When he came to, Mitsu was pressing a cool, damp cloth on his head.

"Didn't you go back to sleep?" he asked in surprise.

"I couldn't. . . . . I thought you'd feel better if I held this here."

"How long have you been here?"

"Don't worry, Sensei. I'll take care of you."

She administered to him throughout the night, until daylight flickered at the window. He was certain that, like the old priest, this girl would have a place in the kingdom of God that seemed so distant now to himself.

"Good. I'm glad you came."

"Why?"

In one of the cafés squeezed onto Golden Avenue like a matchbox, the mama-san greeted Tōno and indicated with her eyes another of her customers. Tōno looked toward the man, who was leaning against the wall, sleeping unkempt beneath signs advertising boiled tofu and fried fish.

"Ever since he got here, he's been asking me over and over again whether Tōno Sensei would be coming tonight. I told him I didn't know, but he said he was going to wait here until you arrived."

"I don't recognize him." Tōno cocked his head.

"He's been saying all kinds of weird things. He kept asking whether there could be two of the same person, or something like that."

As she spoke, Kobari's eyes opened, and, still leaning against the wall, he bellowed, "What's weird about that? I saw it with my own eyes. A whole different Suguro."

"You're going to catch a cold," Tōno said shrilly.

"I'm . . . just fine. I'm no weakling, you know." Still battling with drowsiness, he yawned a gaping yawn. "You're Tōno Sensei, aren't you."

"Yes, but . . ."

"They told me over at the Swan up the street that you come here all the time. I've been waiting for you."

"What is it that you want?" Tōno took the chopsticks and dish that the mama-san held out to him.

"Water," Kobari ordered her. "I've got to sober up. This man here is Tōno Sensei. He's a famous psychiatrist."

"I know that. He's been a regular customer for many years."

Kobari gulped down the glass of water and shook his head two or three times, trying to crawl up out of the swamp of intoxication. "Sensei, I didn't say anything weird."

"I'm sure you didn't."

"You're *sure*? Sure about what? That's really irresponsible, Sensei. You're as bad as Suguro."

"Suguro?"

"Have you read any of his stuff—his novels?"

"Oh, you're talking about the writer Suguro? I lectured with him a while back."

"What do you think of him? Don't you think he's got a split personality?"

"Split personality." Tōno curled his lip. "That's quite an accusation. What do you have in mind?"

"Sensei, can there be two totally separate personalities inside one person?"

"Of course there can. Everybody has one face they wear in society and another they reserve only for themselves. You're no different."

"No, I'm not talking about that hackneyed old stuff. When a person has two personalities that are radically different from each other, you call that a dual personality, don't you? In Suguro's case, he shows his good face to the world while he writes his books, but on the sly he's involved in kinky activities with women." Then Kobari thrust his glass in front of the mama-san, demanding more water. "I've been collecting solid evidence. One day soon I'm going to tear his mask off. . . . But I'd like your opinion as an expert."

189

"Opinion on what?" Tōno appeared annoyed. "Tearing his mask off seems to be rather extreme."

"He's fooling a lot of readers. A man who wields a pen has to be accountable to society. After all, we're living at a time when even a prime minister can be censured for dereliction and booted out of office. What's your opinion of Suguro's split personality?"

"I don't know anything about Mr. Suguro having a split personality. I have no particular reason to believe that."

"Then what about split personalities in general?"

"In general? The point here is that people aren't nearly as simple as we think. There are a lot of different people living inside one individual. When you do the kind of work I do, you gradually come to realize that. I run into strange cases that someone like you wouldn't begin to believe."

"Strange cases, you say?"

"This was some time ago, of course. It happened when I was young, but a patient who was under hypnosis suddenly began speaking Chinese. He claimed that in a previous life he had been a Chinese merchant in Shanghai."

"That's ridiculous."

"No, it's true. In any case, his Chinese sounded like real Chinese, though I can't vouch for it myself. But while he was in a trance, this patient told me about his previous life in great detail."

"That was just a product of a wild imagination, I'm sure."

"I can't say for certain. There've been many such cases in foreign countries, and when you examine the details, it turns out that everything the patients said was true."

The mama-san put her knife down and joined Kobari in listening to Tōno.

"A housewife in Rome claimed there was a subterranean room from the remains of a medieval city beneath the spot where the Church of Mary now stands. While she was under hypnosis, she described the room in detail. Several years later—understand what I'm saying, several years later—the same underground room she had described was discovered exactly where she said it would be."

"I can't buy that," Kobari objected, sitting up in his chair. "It must have been some kind of play-acting put on to fool the doctor."

"It was no trick, and there was no play-acting." Tōno grinned broadly and took a drink of his saké. "The doctor's report is very precise."

"Can something like that really happen?" The mama-san sighed. "It's kind of eerie."

"Sensei, is it somehow possible for one person to be in two different places at the same time?" Kobari posed his unusual question without any warning.

"What does that have to do with anything?"

"Can one person appear in two separate locations simultaneously, at precisely the same time?"

"How does this relate to Mr. Suguro?"

"No . . . it's . . . What do you think?"

"I can't absolutely deny the possibility. That phenomenon is extremely rare, but it has happened. I was discussing this with someone recently. It's known as *doppelgänger*, and in the Taishō period a group of students at an elementary school in Iwate Prefecture saw their teacher in two different places at the same moment. Initially, the thirteen students saw a woman, the exact image of their teacher, standing next to her as she wrote on the blackboard. Later, when she was in the sewing room, they saw her ghost double standing outside the room in the flower garden. . . . The students actually saw this."

"Enough of these eerie stories, Sensei." The mama-san shuddered. "I won't be able to walk down the hall to the bathroom at night."

"It may be eerie, but it's true."

191

Tōno seemed to relish the shock his story had produced, and he took another sip of his drink as he studied the two wary faces before him.

"Exactly what was going on there?"

"Well, we don't know that. This is outside the province of psychology, but in psychospiritualism it's called astral projection. The only explanation we have as psychologists is that the students were under some form of group hypnosis. But there is no positive evidence to support that, either."

"That's absurd."

"Yes, it is. As for me, as I've worked in this profession, I've come to the conclusion that human beings can't be explained in purely logical terms. They are truly bizarre, full of contradictions, with levels so deep we can never hope to fathom them. . . . A totally unsolvable mystery. What I've just told you may seem like tales of the fantastic, but it's all true. Anything can happen with people. We scientists have finally come to this conclusion."

That evening Kobari had been disturbed by the conversation, but when he woke up the following morning the sky was so bright and clear he began to wonder if he had been taken in. He concluded that the uncanny episodes Tōno had related were intended as a grand joke on the mama-san and himself, or some subtle trick to which the doctors and witnesses had all been accessories.

After a full day's work, he stopped off at the hospital in Harajuku. The day he had followed the woman referred to by Motoko as "Madame N," she had paused at this hospital and chatted intimately with a woman who looked like a staff nurse. It seemed to him that he might pick up some clues at the hospital. The hallways in the late afternoon were nearly deserted.

"Excuse me," he inquired at the outpatients' desk. "I've forgotten her name, but there's an older nurse here. She must be about fifty."

The three women at the desk stopped chattering and examined him with suspicion.

"She's got buckteeth like this." With a straight face he parted his lips and mimed the bucktoothed face.

The women burst into laughter and said, "That's the head nurse in pediatrics." They directed him to the pediatric nurses' station on the fourth floor.

The air in a hospital blends many smells: the aroma of cresol; the rancid smell of the kitchen; the body odors of the patients. Kobari was indifferent to the scent of suffering that permeated the hallways.

At the nurses' station, a doctor was scribbling something on a piece of paper, and a young nurse held a telephone receiver to her ear. He caught sight of Madame N in an apron, carrying a patient's bedpan and heading for the incinerator. There could be no mistake, it was her. A liquid the color of coarse tea floated forlornly in the pan.

Soon she emerged again and went into a room at the farthest end of the corridor. Kobari stopped just outside the room.

The door was open. The afternoon sun trickled into the hallway. He could hear her voice but could not see her. The name on the door read *Uchiyama Shigeru*.

"The bronze statue of the Prince asked a favor of the Swallow." He could hear her voice through the curtain. " 'Faraway in this town there lives a poor woman with a little boy. She makes her living doing needlework. Her child has a fever and is begging her for oranges, but she doesn't have enough money to buy them for him. Will you take the ruby from the hilt of my sword and give it to her?' The Swallow was planning to return to his friends in his warm home in a distant land, so he took the ruby from the hilt of the sword in his beak and delivered it to the mother. With the money she made from selling the ruby, the boy became well again."

"Then what happened?" A boy's voice demanded more of the story.

"The next day, when the Swallow went to say good-bye to the statue, the Prince asked him to remain in the town for just one more night. 'There's a pitiful young man in the town. He is trying to finish a play for the theater to perform, but he can't buy any firewood to warm his cold, numb hands. Please deliver one of my eyes to this unfortunate young man. It is made from a rare sapphire.' The Swallow said he could not do anything so cruel, but the Prince said, 'Swallow, Swallow, little Swallow, do as I command.' So the Swallow plucked out one of the Prince's eyes and took it to the young man's room. The young man, knowing nothing of what had happened, was able to buy firewood and finish his play."

Laced between the words of her story came occasional questions and prods spoken in a pampered child's voice. The conversation that passed between the two was a disappointment to Kobari.

"The next day, the Prince asked the Swallow to stay just one more night. 'There's a miserable match-girl in the town. Please take my last remaining eye to her.' 'But, Prince, if I take that from you, you won't be able to see at all,' the Swallow protested. But the Prince said, 'Swallow, Swallow, little Swallow, do as I command.' So the Swallow took the Prince's other eye to the match-girl. Thanks to that gift, the little girl no longer had to stand on the cold street corners."

"Then what happened to the Swallow?"

"Although his friends were already in the warm country, this Swallow stayed behind. He couldn't abandon the Prince. One night there was a huge snowstorm. As the snow fell, the Swallow flapped his wings, struggling against the cold. He thought he would surely die. With his remaining strength he climbed onto the Prince's shoulders and whispered, 'Good-bye, dear Prince. Good-bye . . .' "

There her voice broke off for a moment, until she began tutoring the boy in his prayers.

"Shige-chan, repeat after me: 'Heavenly Father, help me to be a good boy.' "

"Heavenly Father, help me to be a good boy."

" 'Heavenly Father, please be kind to all the children like me. And I will be kind to them, too.' "

"Heavenly Father, please be kind to all the children like me. And I will be kind to them, too."

" 'Heavenly Father, help me to sleep peacefully tonight.' "

Chapter
Seven

His wife was practicing a *nagauta* as she plucked the samisen. She was so absorbed in the song that she did not even notice when her husband came into the room. *We've finally achieved a modest enough level of composure in our marriage that she can indulge in such a hobby*, Suguro thought.

"What's this song called?"

" 'Yokobue,' " she answered with uncharacteristic curtness, and began to sing again.

> *The robes of the villagers are intoxicatingly fragrant*
> *With the scent of blossoms;*
> *At Plum Harbor the spring winds are blowing.*

Snubbed, he went to the window and looked out at the garden. The new buds of the trees were still tightly closed even though it was March.

"It's been so long . . . winter this year," he muttered with genuine feeling.

The words were not particularly intended for his wife, but just as he spoke them she stopped playing to tune her instrument, and in response she said, "That's because we've gotten old. From now on every winter will seem long and take its toll on us."

"I suppose so. You're not going out today?"

"No, I went to my volunteer training group yesterday. Oh, that's right, I spoke to Mrs. Naruse for the first time."

The string of the samisen gave a sharp twang.

Startled, Suguro asked, "What did you talk about?"

He still had not told his wife that he had met Madame Naruse at the coffee shop, or that he had had dinner with her.

"About working as a volunteer. She was full of information."

He nodded in relief.

"Mrs. Naruse said there was a child in pediatrics she was caring for. He had just had an operation, and it was successful, she said. She was very happy about it. Apparently she goes every day to look after him."

Certainly Madame Naruse knew about Motoko's death, but how had she taken it? He had heard nothing from her since their last meeting, no doubt because she had been busy caring for Shige. Still, it had been too long since she had been in touch with him. Suguro realized with some surprise that he was looking forward to seeing her again.

He stole a glance at his wife, who had picked up the samisen to begin playing again. At once his writer's instinct impelled him, as always, to analyze why he felt as he did toward Madame Naruse. The answer was obvious. Never before had he met, or even written about, such a woman. A woman so shot through with contradictions. A woman who seemed so coldhearted, only to be transformed the next moment into a startlingly gentle and caring individual. He had never encountered such a woman before. And compared with her—and he realized that such a thought was a desecration of his wife and quickly stifled it—he felt a fleeting sense of oppression when he considered his unassailable spouse.

"I wanted to ask something about Mitsu," he called across his wife's shoulder. He was shifting the topic to Mitsu so that his wife would not read his emotions. But she did not seem to hear him over the samisen and continued to strum intently with her plectrum.

I shall not see Madame Naruse any more. . . . I should not see her.

He planted his elbows on his desk and repeated the words to himself. Even as he repeated the words in his mind, he recognized them as empty sounds, and knew that secretly he was looking forward to some contact with her.

A small parcel arrived. It was wrapped tightly in brown paper and bore no return address. Inside was a book. He knew at once it was from her. When he opened the cover he saw that a note had been placed inside.

> You'll excuse my presumptuousness, but I wanted to send you one of my favorite books. It's not available in the bookstores anymore, so you'll have to forgive me for sending my personal copy. This coming Wednesday, could you meet me at six o'clock at a restaurant called Shigeyoshi on Omote Sandō? I'd like to be able to repay you in some small way

for the dinner you treated me to. If that evening isn't con-
venient for you, please write to me at the address below. If
I don't hear from you, I'll assume that you'll meet me there.
The food is quite good. Please do try to come.

Suguro read the note over again and again, like a high-
school boy who has received his first love letter from a girl.
With the passage of time, a desire to avoid her and curiosity
about this unique woman had tangled and grappled inside
him. The moment he slit open this envelope, however, his
curiosity had emerged victorious.

The book was a biography of the medieval warrior, Gilles
de Rais, infamous for his crimes of infanticide. As Suguro
flipped through the pages, his eyes lit on passages Madame
Naruse had marked with a red pencil. At each red circle he
felt as though he could see Madame Naruse's profile and hear
her voice while she read and pondered what was written
there. Had she perhaps made these red notations and sent the
book to him out of frustration at not being able to make her
true feelings clear to him in person? Above one of the red-
marked passages she had written some words in the same
deft hand with which she had penned her letter. It seemed
as though, once Suguro had read to that point, she had opened
her spunky eyes to appeal to him for understanding.

How does this Rage burst forth? Why does Rage provide
such an intense experience of pleasure? As I read this book,
I felt that there is some fierce, hidden power that spurns
explanation, that defies every precept of morality.

Suguro finished reading the book in two days. Gilles de
Rais had been a comrade-in-arms of Joan of Arc, but, as the
biography explained, he had sought through acts of brutality

to attain the same heights of rapture that Joan had reached through religious ecstasy. An individual can reach the zenith of ecstasy only by becoming either a saint or a vile transgressor. Gilles de Rais had reached that conclusion as he had observed Joan of Arc.

Poe understood the Rage, as did Dostoevsky. The Rage is a seizure that can overtake even children. . . . It seized the children in T. F. Powys's story "The Hunted Beast," who gouged out the eyes of a rabbit they had taken on the English downs; and it gripped Mr. Gidden, the kindly, peace-loving vicar who came upon them and who, seeing what they had done, grew dizzy with voluptuous despair. He chased the children but

> . . .the boys escaped his hands and ran off. But the girl wasn't so fortunate. . . .
>
> Mr. Gidden threw himself upon her. He tore at her clothes. . . . He struck her, lay upon her in his fury, and held her throat. . . .
>
> During the struggle Mr. Gidden had wished to do the very worst a man could do. He had wished to violate her.

Poe has given us a near portrait of the Rage in his story "The Black Cat." There, Poe's narrator describes the Rage as a reflex against moral law. He called it

> . . . the spirit of PERVERSENESS. . . . I am not more sure that my soul lives than I am that perverseness is one of the primitive impulses of the human heart, one of the indivisible primary faculties, or sentiments, which give direction to the character of Man. Who has not a hundred times found himself committing a vile or a stupid action, for no other reason than because he knows he should *not*? Have we not a perpetual inclination, in the teeth of our

best judgment, to violate that which is *Law*, merely because
we understand it to be such: This spirit of perverseness, I
say, came to my final overthrow. It was this unfathomable
longing of the soul *to vex itself*—to offer violence to its own
nature—to do wrong for the wrong's sake only—that urged
me on.

His desk clock persisted in its regulated ticking, and the
soft light from his lamp shone upon him and upon the book
as he bent over it. There were several small framed photographs and inscriptions on the wall. One of them bore the
words that Mother Teresa, who had visited Japan recently,
had written specifically for this Japanese Christian novelist:
"The Lord will bless you through the things that you write."

As he stared at the inscription, with its sentiments as polite
and sincere as those of a college girl, Suguro felt as though
he had strayed too far afield to merit any blessings. *I'm a
novelist. A novelist who has to dirty his hands in the deepest recesses
of the human heart. I have to thrust my hands in, even if I find
something there that God could never bless.* Before him lay a
book that described the life of one man. A man named Gilles
de Rais. . . .

With one hand, he had erected churches to the glory of
God and paid his respects to the priests; with the other, he
had lured scores of children into his castle and killed them
one by one. His first victim had been a young singer in his
own castle choir. He had embraced the young boy, fondled
him, and doted upon him, but in the course of these attentions
his fondling had turned into a bloodthirsty rage.

There is the story of the beggar boy who stood in one of
the two lines of begging children before the castle gate at
Machecoul. When it came his turn to receive alms, he was
invited into the château on the kindly premise that the child

had failed to get any meat in the first distribution of food.
And he was not seen again. And there is the story of the
thirteen-year-old who had been taken into the castle to be
made a page. He came home one day, glowing with news
for his mother: He had been allowed to clean the great Sire
de Rais's room and had been rewarded with one of the
round loaves of bread that had been baked for the baron,
which—see—the boy had brought home. Then the lad
went back, "and that was the last they had seen of their
son."

Previously he would have read such words with loathing,
but he scoured them attentively now, hearing Madame Naruse's appeal emerging from between each line.

How does this Rage burst forth? Why does Rage provide
such an intense experience of pleasure? . . . I felt that there
is some hidden power that spurns explanation, that defies
every precept of morality.

On the designated evening, Suguro pushed open the glass
door at the entrance to Shigeyoshi. Apparently, he had arrived early: there were only two executive-looking gentlemen seated at the counter, slowly sipping their saké. But the
owner, who was chopping ingredients with a knife, said that
Madame Naruse had told him Suguro was coming, and he
escorted the writer to a table at the back of the restaurant.

At about five minutes after six she came in, wearing a
beige-colored coat and what appeared to be an Italian scarf.
They sat across from one another, drinking the tea that the
waitress had brought, glancing over the menu, and exchanging trivial conversation. They did not mention either the
book or Motoko's death. As they conversed, four or five

regulars came into the restaurant. They nodded to Madame Naruse, perhaps recognizing her face, and one of them gave a startled look of recognition when he saw Suguro.

When they had finished ordering dinner, Suguro said, "Well, then."

"Well, then," she rejoined with her customary smile.

The exchange was like a signal that it was time to launch into the topic they both knew had to be discussed.

Suguro poured some saké into her cup. "I received the book and the letter."

"Yes." She closed her eyes as though she were a patient receiving an injection in her arm.

"You knew that Motoko has died."

"Yes."

"Did the police come to see you?"

"No. Why?"

"Oh, I thought maybe they wanted to talk to you."

"It was suicide. She left a note."

"Yes, that's what they said on the television news."

Bright laughter was exchanged between the owner and his customers at the counter, and a waitress turned to the kitchen and called, "Three bottles of saké." Not one of them was paying attention to the conversation between Suguro and Madame Naruse.

"Aren't you having anything to drink, Sensei?"

"I can't. My doctor won't allow it. But don't let me inhibit you. It doesn't bother me at all."

The waitress brought a blue plate with finely chopped dried mullet roe.

"They make this roe here," she explained. "My husband was very fond of it."

"Did your husband come here, too?"

"He knew the owner before he even opened this restaurant."

"Did you know beforehand"—he decided he would try to trip her up—"that Motoko was going to commit suicide?"

"Yes, I knew."

Gracefully she reached out with her chopsticks, trapped some of the roe, and brought it to her mouth. She was thoroughly unruffled.

"And you didn't stop her?"

"I didn't stop her."

"Why not?"

There was more laughter from the counter. None of them had any idea of the kind of discussion that was taking place between the two people at the table at the back. Their own conversation was laced with words like "handy" and "the competition."

"Is that the power of Rage, then?" Suguro asked casually, as though he were discussing a game of golf. "Is that the dolls you talked about, the ones that start dancing in the middle of the night?"

"Yes."

"Can you explain this to me in a little more detail?"

"I'd be glad to."

She reached out once again with her chopsticks. The movement of her chopsticks toward her mouth, the lips that slowly, delectably savored the food—Suguro felt his eyes beginning to swim. She began to talk.

"She often said that was how she wanted to die. She expressed that desire to other friends, too. At first I thought it was just a joke. I understand that many people babble the same thing while they're in the middle of lovemaking. But several times she warned me. She said that next year she was going to die for real. I told her, 'Fine, go ahead.' On New Year's Day I met her at a hotel, and I asked her if she really intended to die this year."

Madame Naruse spoke indifferently, as though she were

relaying a piece of gossip about a mutual friend. Suguro thought of the haggard look he had seen on her face at the hospital.

"Would you like me to tell you about that day? We spent New Year's Eve together at a hotel in Yoyogi. When the Red and White Song Competition finished up on television, we changed to a silly program on another channel. As it blared out from the television set, she shouted over and over again for me to kill her. I told her she had to die this winter, and she promised she would."

"Did you mean that seriously?"

"Yes, or half seriously anyway. But I did want to know what it would be like. I wrote about it in the letter I sent with the book. About a power in the heart that transcends rationality, a power that can change into rage or depravity. It's a ferocious power that moral principles can never hope to subdue, and it drags us down into the depths of the pit— but can it also hurl us toward death? If we truly abandon ourselves to that power, can death, too, be filled with pleasure? I wanted to . . . observe that in Motoko."

"And that's why you didn't stop her."

"Yes."

When the waitress brought over two small bowls, they stopped talking until she had left. Madame Naruse brought the thinly sliced blowfish to her mouth. She parted her lips slightly, and the slender strip of fish disappeared inside like an insect being sucked into the petals of a flower. The movement of her cheeks transmitted to Suguro the unhurried enjoyment she derived from its taste.

"I hate drinking alone." She drained her cup. "Are you sure you won't have some? It's just as I thought from reading your books—you are a coward, aren't you?"

Perhaps she was drunk. She had renounced her normally courteous tone of voice and came on as the aggressor.

"It's my doctor."

"Who cares about your doctor? What difference does it make?"

Helpless, Suguro picked up his cup. "All right, I'll have a drink, if you'll tell me the rest. Motoko didn't contact you before she died?"

"She contacted me." She smiled, as though she had been expecting that question. "Three nights before I called you, I talked to her on the phone for a long time. She asked me, if after she died and was able to be reborn, whether we could meet again in the next life. We talked far into the night about transmigration and reincarnation. I told her about Shige's operation, and I asked her if she was going to die to see to it that Shige could live in her place. When we were about to hang up, she told me she was going to die the following evening."

"Then you even knew the day she was going to die."

"Yes."

"And you didn't try to stop her," Suguro repeated. "You let her go ahead with it."

"It brought her happiness. The insignificant activities of each day, the waiting on street corners for customers to sketch—none of that gave any meaning to her life. It was only when she surrendered herself to her passions that she felt as if her life was worthwhile. If plunging into the maelstrom and dying was her only source of happiness and meaning, how could I stop her? Although that evening I did go very near her apartment."

"You did? Why?"

"I couldn't resist the temptation. Very soon Motoko was going to die. Being aware of that, I wanted to be near her and share the experience. I sat in a little coffee shop next to her apartment, with a cup of black tea in front of me, and I waited there for, I don't know, maybe two hours. Three factory workers there were playing some kind of game. A small truck came by selling vegetables, and housewives from the neighborhood clustered outside the window. The winter sky peeked out from between the buildings. You see how well I remember everything? Over and over again I looked at my watch—already four o'clock, already four-thirty, already five . . . she's doing it right now, I imagined, right this very minute. And for the first time in a long while, I saw a little hut swathed in flames. I could hear the shouts of the women and children. I actually smelled the smoke and the charred ruins. When I came to my senses, it had turned to night outside. I stood up and left the coffee shop. As I walked out, I knew for certain that Motoko had kept her promise and had died in the throes of ecstasy."

Her story broke off and she sat in silence. Suguro, too, said nothing; he just stared at the chopsticks on his plate. There were no words, he sensed, that could describe what was passing through her mind—or, rather, through a gruesome chamber that lay much deeper within her soul. That gruesome something, the ghastliness that resides in every heart. Even as a creative writer, he had no idea how to define or interpret it—his only recourse was to lapse into silence. All that could be said was that the story he had just heard was a tale of evil. Not an account of sin like those he had written over the years, but a tale of evil.

"The next dish is fish milt," the waitress came to announce.

"Do you like milt, Sensei?"

"I . . ." Exhausted, Suguro shook his head. He was truly drained. "I don't want any."

He wanted to go home to his wife. Even though he sometimes felt stifled there, he wanted to go home.

"Oh, one more thing. The portrait of you—she gave it to me. As a keepsake."

"That portrait is not of me."

"Oh, that's right. Your impostor." She nodded and smiled, and ordered dessert from the waitress. "Would you be interested in meeting your double?"

"What?" In his surprise he spoke unexpectedly loud. "Why do you say that?"

"Motoko introduced me to him. I didn't tell you about it."

"What kind of man is he?"

"You ought to ask him yourself. You always just sit back and listen to what people say, Sensei, you never act on your own. You don't even drink. Even when you write, you don't go all the way to the very end. You never hurt anybody . . . you just run away."

She was smiling, but Suguro felt a defiance in her bold gaze that he had never seen before.

"Will you help me meet this man?" he asked hoarsely.

"Do you have some time next Friday?"

"Next Friday—is that the thirteenth?"

"Oh, that's right. That's an unlucky day for you people, isn't it? For Christians it's supposed to be the day Jesus died."

"That's what they say."

"Can you come to this address on that day? You just might be able to meet him then." She opened her handbag, took out a silver ballpoint pen, and drew a map on a coaster. "We'll be waiting for you."

CHAPTER
EIGHT

KANŌ ASKED SUGURO to wait for him on the second floor of
Tokyo Hall after the meeting of the executive committee of
the PEN Club. In a parlor on that floor, tea and coffee were
served. Beyond the window, the moat of the Imperial Palace
was visible, and rain was falling. As he peered at the moat,
obscured in the rain, Suguro thought of the day in early
winter when he had received the literary prize. On that day,
too, the stone walls of the Palace had been damp with rain.
That day the impostor had first appeared, and now . . . at
long last the day when he could confront the man was at
hand. Kanō had concluded some sort of conversation and
approached Suguro with a tired, bloated face. He was knead-
ing one shoulder with his right hand.

"Ah, damn, damn. I guess there's no way of pushing back the waves of old age that come rolling in." He seemed to be muttering to himself. "I wanted to talk to you about the PEN Club doing something for Yamagishi's funeral."

They discussed the forthcoming services for the elder critic, who had died just two days before. Although they regarded him as an "elder," Yamagishi had been only five years older than Kanō and Suguro.

"It's our turn next," Kanō said morosely. "I remember Kobayashi Hideo once asking me if I had made my preparations for death. But I still haven't written anything that would let me die in peace, knowing I had bequeathed one adequate work to the world."

"That's . . . that's how we all feel. Just one masterwork —I keep thinking it'll be the next thing I write, and then the next one after that . . ."

"But you're different from me. You've built up a solid literary framework that's all your own. Someone at the publisher's said there's a group of ten thousand readers that will go out and buy any novel you produce."

"There can't be that many."

"Yes, there are. So you have to be careful to protect the image your readers have of you. If, for some perverse reason, you decided to topple that framework . . ." Kanō spoke softly, then suddenly shifted his eyes to the window. "You're sure you're not frequenting any odd places?"

So that's what he wanted to talk about, Suguro realized.

"Is this the same old warning? I'm not going to any of those places."

"You're sure."

"I'm sure."

"I believe you, then. But it's also true that there's a rumor going around that you came out of a hotel at Akasaka in the middle of the night with a woman. If a magazine like *Focus* or *Emma* publishes a photograph of you in that kind of place . . ."

"I have never been there. But . . ." He tried to swallow back the word even as it came out of his mouth.

"But . . . what?"

"It's nothing."

"Watch out for the reporter who came to see me. He's tenacious."

Kanō stared for a few moments into the cup of tea in front of him, then reached for the bill. Suguro snatched it away, at which Kanō nodded, stood up, and left. As he walked away, he looked far more tired than he ever had before.

It was an unusually warm day, so Suguro and his wife, who had come to clean the office, went out for their first walk in some time. They had not taken a walk together for a while because the frigid weather bothered her joints. Suguro walked slowly, slowly down the slope, as though he were protecting his wife.

"I'm so out of breath from not walking for a while." She collapsed onto a bench, her shoulders heaving.

"It's just a question of getting used to it. Nobody dies of arthritis. Once it warms up, you'll feel a lot better."

He knew which of the two of them would die first. He was the one who had had chronic problems with his liver for many years. He was the one with a single lung. Every month after the doctor drew blood from his arm, he warned Suguro not to overdo things.

"I really enjoyed the trip to Kyushu." She had been staring abstractedly into the distant sky before she spoke. Then, as if she had suddenly remembered, "I wonder how that priest is doing?"

He knew that his wife had been reliving their vacation to Nagasaki over and over since their return. It was one of the happy memories shared by this aged couple.

"I sometimes think about him before I fall asleep at night," she said. "From the life he has led, I think he must be one of the truly poor in spirit."

"In some ways, you're one of the poor in spirit, too."

"Is that sarcasm?"

"Not at all. Unlike you . . ." Once again he tried to swallow the words, as he had with Kanō the night before. *Unlike you, I can never become one of the poor in spirit. I'm not the man you think I am. I have secrets I haven't told you. There's a man who looks exactly like me, and I may be meeting him soon. A man who is foul and ugly.*

"Dear . . . is there by chance something you want to tell me?" She turned toward him unexpectedly. There was anxiety in her face.

"Why do you ask? Of course there isn't."

As he studied her wrinkled eyelids, he thought, *I don't want to bring tears to these eyes. We have so little time left together.*

"Don't worry." He spoke like a priest in the confessional. Quickly he changed the subject. "About Mitsu . . . Since she's paid the money back, what would you think about having her work here at the office again?"

"I was thinking the same thing. So I phoned her, but she said she'd already found another part-time job."

"Is it a good job?"

"It's . . . Mrs. Naruse got to know her at the hospital, and she asked her to come help her twice a week. I think it will be very good for Mitsu. Mrs. Naruse can teach her a lot."

"Has Mitsu already agreed to it?" His voice came out louder than he had anticipated.

"She said she had. Is something wrong?"

"No. . . . But it's too bad. I'd really gotten to like her."

He had not forgotten the way she had pressed the washcloth on his feverish head, or the musty smell of her sweater, and her genuinely affable grin.

He tried not to let it bother him, but the appointment with Madame Naruse kept surfacing in his heart like bubbles of methane gas. "You'll be able to meet your double." That opportunity was only three days away.

As the days passed, the feeling that he must confront his double gradually changed into revulsion and a wish that he could forestall the meeting. Suppose he pressed the man for answers. His double would probably just flash his derisive smile and blurt out some excuse or equivocation. At the very least, he had to extract a promise that the man would stop using his name, but he had no power to proscribe his actions. Then how was he to prove that he was not the person making the rounds of all the disreputable neighborhoods?

And why had this man suddenly made his appearance this winter? Where had he been lurking until then? After his arrival on the scene, a crack had appeared in the foundations supporting Suguro's literature. And it had affected more than just his writing—a fissure had cut through his personal life as well. It was as though the man had delivered some evil omen to Suguro's doorstep. He remembered that the old man in Thomas Mann's *Death in Venice* had lost everything as a result of his encounter with a handsome boy. How old had the character been—was he already past sixty-five, like Suguro?

Over the years, Suguro had come to realize that God acts without warning. But at his advanced age he had never thought that God would strike such a blow at the world he had erected for himself.

Night fell.

He sat motionless, hunched over in the chair in his study. The telephone rang in the living room. It jangled persistently, challenging his usual determination to let it go on ringing.

The ringing stopped. As he breathed a sigh of relief, it began to ring again. He remained in his chair. He continued with his work, but the telephone raised its insistent voice a third time. Unable to endure it any longer, he picked up the receiver.

"Hello?"

Through the receiver he heard Kurimoto's low voice.

"So you're there after all. You didn't answer for so long. . . . It's Mr. Kanō. He collapsed and was taken to the hospital." Kurimoto was unable to continue.

Suguro's first reaction was one of anger. He had had enough of these ridiculous practical jokes and he was angry. But Kurimoto was not the sort of man to engage in such pranks.

"It was so sudden, Miss Noriko was the only one with him when he died."

Miss Noriko was the woman who had cared for Kanō during the five years since his wife died. She ran a bar, but she was a fan of Kanō's writing, and a relationship had eventually developed between them. Still, Kanō did not like to talk about her with his old friends such as Suguro.

"He suffered chest pains for about half an hour. He died while the doctors were working on him."

"I'm on my way. Which hospital?"

"It's not far—the Ōmori Hospital. But they're taking the body to his home right away, so please go there."

He quickly got ready, telephoned for a taxicab, and gave the driver Kanō's address.

In his mind's eye he could see Kanō's tired figure as they had sat in the parlor after the PEN Club meeting just five days before. That night his face had been dark and sullen and puffy, unlike his usual expression of feigned joviality. Had it been some presage of his death? But what had he grown so weary of? He thought of the many solid relationships Kanō had established in the literary world. He had attended every meeting of the executive board without fail, and he was considered an unaffected writer by the young editors who went drinking with him late into the night. Yet a nervous, misanthropic side of Kanō oozed from his novels. Perhaps only his old friends had had a real awareness of that aspect of his character.

The night streets appeared through the taxi window. Nothing about the landscape had changed. The winter sky was leaden. At the intersections, trucks and cars stopped and started, started and stopped. Outside an electric appliance store, a young employee was hoisting cardboard boxes. Mandarin oranges glistened outside a fruit stand. Even though Kanō had died, in reality nothing had changed. Suguro felt the same anger as before. It irritated him that his mind had still not accepted the fact of Kanō's demise.

Outside Kanō's house, at the end of a narrow residential road, editors in black clothing had set up a reception table, where they chatted with literary figures such as Segi, who had come rushing over at the news. The electric lights glared so brightly because of their reflection on the unpolished wood of the coffin; the heaps of chrysanthemums at the back of the house had a luminescence all their own. Miss Noriko, her eyes red with weeping, whispered to Suguro to look at Kanō's face. The face of the corpse had blanched, as though it were formed of wax, and shadows of pain still lingered between the brows. Suguro stared intently at the face, wanting to carve into his own mind the face of his longtime friend who had at last completed his life.

. . .*I'll meet you . . . on the other side*, he muttered inwardly. *No matter what, you and I . . . we lived, and we wrote.*

The reality of Kanō's death suddenly struck him, and the tears streamed down. The number of mourners began to swell. In the next room, where food for the wake had been set out, Shiba, another of their literary friends from the old days, had arrived. Shiba had given up hopes of becoming a critic and was teaching at a women's college. He had become an utterly drab man, bereft of all his former vitality.

As he poured beer into a glass, Shiba said softly, "I thought we still had plenty of time left, but now that Kanō's gone, I suddenly feel as though death is standing right in front of us."

Suguro nodded. "It's true. Our ranks are going to dwindle one by one now."

Segi, who was sitting in front of them, muttered with a grim smile, "Next it will be . . . me, I suppose."

It was midnight by the time he had offered words of sympathy to Miss Noriko, taken one more look at Kanō's face, and left the house. The taxi he had hired was nowhere to be seen. He had never imagined he would feel so much pain at Kanō's death.

The squeak of the chair as the doctor turned from his examination charts upset Suguro more than usual.

"Your GPT is two hundred and five and the GOT has climbed to one hundred and eighty-eight. I personally would encourage you to check into the hospital. . . . If you do nothing about it at these levels, you could take a sudden turn for the worse."

Suguro looked at the long, slender examination chart that the doctor had placed on his desk. He was strangely unruffled by the doctor's report. The only feeling that surged through him was the realization that he was moving one step closer each day to the world where Kanō now resided. This is what old age means.

"Going to the hospital right now . . . would be difficult."

"But . . ."

"I'll do my best to take it easy. I'll consider going to the hospital after my next exam."

"You won't have any pain or discomfort in the liver until it's already beyond all hope. By the time you start having abdominal dropsy, you'll have cirrhosis. It has to be controlled before it reaches that point."

"I understand." He nodded, but he was firm in his opposition to hospitalization.

He sat in a corner seat of the subway on the way home. He folded his hands on his lap and glanced absentmindedly at the advertising posters that hung in the train. Along with the advertisements for wedding chapels and weekly magazines, there was a poster offering condominiums exclusively for senior citizens. The man and woman who appeared in the advertisement as an elderly couple were actors Suguro remembered from his youth. Above their cheerfully smiling faces, the words "The Beautiful Mellow Years" were printed in bold letters. Clumsily, he tried to let the four words roll along his tongue. But the old age Suguro had come to know since the awards ceremony was far from beautiful—it bore a vile, putrid smell. It was like a dark, gloomy dream. Old age was something hidden from view for many years, only showing itself when it was fanned by the winds that blow from the pit of death. Suguro closed his eyes.

When he returned to his office, his wife was there cleaning.

"How did it go?"

"The examination? He said everything was normal. There is nothing to worry about."

"Thank goodness." She seemed truly relieved. "I've been worried about you since early this morning."

Suguro held his breath for a moment, grateful that he had been able to deflect her anxiety.

The memorial service for Kanō was conducted at the Seiganji Temple at Chiba. Representing Kanō's friends, Suguro stood facing the large portrait of the deceased at the altar heaped with chrysanthemums and read his eulogy. He had spent two hours that morning composing his remarks. Recounting Kanō's friendship, which had been evident in the masterly way Kanō had described Suguro's fiction at the awards banquet in early winter, Suguro went on to say, "Our departed friend's life and his writing, if they can ultimately be described in a single phrase, would be a literature that never brooked compromise. In his works he never curried favor with his readers, never ingratiated himself with the times—his was self-willed literature that expressed what he felt had to be written. That self-will itself became a way of life for him."

When the service was over, he left the main hall of the temple. Men and women dressed in mourning were walking across the temple grounds. Suguro noticed in the distance a man leaning against a votive lantern and staring at him. It was Kobari.

The reporter approached and said, "Could I talk to you for a minute?" He pretended to take Suguro's silence as consent. "Do you remember a foggy night in Tokyo last month?"

"Foggy?"

"Yes. The newspapers said it was the worst fog in thirty years."

"What has that got to do with me?"

"Where did you go that night, Mr. Suguro?"

Suguro ignored the question and walked away, but Kobari strode along beside him.

"You ran into me in front of a hotel in Yoyogi, didn't you? And you ran away into a nearby side street."

Responding with only silent contempt, Suguro passed through the temple gate. The publishing firm that had taken care of the funeral arrangements had provided cars for the principal mourners. Kobari abandoned his pursuit.

As he stepped into the hired car that Kurimoto had provided for him, Suguro pondered what Kobari had said about a Yoyogi hotel, and suddenly he reached into his wallet and pulled out a small piece of paper. It was the edge of the coaster that Madame Naruse had given him over dinner at Shigeyoshi's. In her fluid hand the name *Yoyogi* stood out vividly.

Kobari claimed he had run into Suguro in front of that hotel on a foggy night. He had in fact gone out walking that evening. Not with any special purpose in mind. He had simply wanted to wander randomly through the park at a time when the fog was so thick he seemed sure to lose his way. As he walked, he had felt as though this outing was a mirror image of his own old age. He had almost reached the point of self-assurance at which he could have a clear, unobstructed view to the bottom of the pool that was his life, when suddenly a soiled hand reached in and churned up the waters, turning his declining years into a murky, fogbound swamp.

I've had enough. He could feel anger swelling inside him again. Kobari might be persistent, but his own impostor kept turning up with equal tenacity.

I've had enough. It's time to put an end to this business.

Tomorrow was Friday, the day of his appointment with Madame Naruse. He had been uncertain whether he ought to go, but now his mind was made up. He had to meet his double.

Friday.

The previous night, the television news had predicted the possibility of snow, and although the weather forecasts were invariably wrong, it had turned bitterly cold. It was the sort of day likely to bring pain to his wife's joints.

He awoke early that morning, having slept at his office. He closed his eyes and tried to go back to sleep, but it was futile.

Impatiently he got out of bed, and without washing his face he took refuge in his study. On top of his desk was a piece of paper he had scribbled on the day before. . . . *for there is nothing covered, that shall not be revealed; and hid, that shall not be known. . . . And if thy right hand offend thee, cut it off, and cast it from thee. . . .*

He went into the kitchen, poured hot water in the coffee-pot, and plugged it into the electric socket. Then he got ready, drank a cup of coffee, and telephoned his wife.

"Is your arthritis bothering you?"

"Yes, I've been careful to keep a hot compress on my joints. Since it's Friday, I'll be going to church later on."

"Don't worry about me. I'm having dinner with someone from a magazine."

Suguro hoped he would have a constant stream of visitors today. It would be ideal if editors filed in one after the other. That way he could avoid thinking about what would be happening later in the day. He looked at his schedule and saw that Kurimoto was due to stop by before noon.

Kurimoto came to ask Suguro to solidify plans for his next full-length novel. Suguro asked for a year to prepare it.

"Why a year?" There was a look of doubt in the poker-faced editor's eyes.

"You know how old I'm getting. And I don't want to go on writing the same kind of things I've always written. And then . . . there's something inside myself I want to shake up."

"What do you mean by 'shake up'?"

"I want to shake the foundations of the literature I have built up over the years, to find out whether the whole thing will collapse or not."

Kurimoto tilted his head.

"Before he died, Kanō told me there were rumors circulating about me again."

"I doubt it. Besides, your true fans will know you're not that kind of person."

"My true fans?"

"Like the young man you met, the one who works with the handicapped children. But what will you do if you start shaking and the whole thing does collapse?"

Suguro gave a pained smile, but he really wanted to say, "Then it collapses."

"Anyway, it's going to take me at least a year or two to write it. I'm going to call it *Scandal: An Old Man's Prayer*."

After Kurimoto left, Suguro went over to the window and

gazed at the buildings in Shibuya and the west end of Shinjuku. The city was dourly silent, and though it was already the middle of March, on an afternoon like this it would not have seemed peculiar if it began to snow.

To divert his thoughts, he opened up a novel by a foreign writer. But neither the words nor the images penetrated his brain. It was not the fault of the novel. Suguro was aware that his eyes were merely skirting along the top of the printed words.

It's worthless. I can't relate at all to a novel like this.

But he knew that this forced utterance was a lie, that his thoughts were all focused on the hotel where he was to meet Madame Naruse.

He felt his legs getting chilled. Beyond the curtain, which he had drawn across the window, darkness was already pressing in. In truth, he should be preparing to return home, where his wife was waiting. But he had already told her he was having dinner with someone from a magazine.

When he got out of the taxi, a flake of snow grazed his cheek and came to rest on the sleeve of his raincoat. As he hesitated for a few moments in front of the hotel, the snow began to beat down furiously around him.

A row of Himalayan cedars, arrayed in single file like a rank of soldiers, stretched blackly from the gate to the porch of the hotel. Light seeped from the lobby, casting a feeble glimmer on the entrance, across which the snow flickered. It seemed more like a large mansion than a hotel, but behind him the neon signs from cheaper inns flashed malignantly, reminding him exactly what kind of business was transacted in this quarter.

Oddly, he had the feeling he had seen this hotel before. He even had the sensation that he had been inside. It was an inexplicable experience of déjà vu, like standing before a totally new landscape and having the impression that you had viewed the identical scene once in the distant past. But Suguro had no idea why he should have any memory of this hotel.

When he stepped inside, he heard the violent clatter of a typewriter being pounded. A man of around thirty, wearing a black jacket, sat with his back to the entrance. Waiting until the man turned toward him, Suguro stared at the swirling snow that was coming down with even greater force. The snow danced in the lights at the doorway.

"Good evening, sir." The man noticed Suguro and stopped typing.

"A lady named Naruse"—Suguro tried to mask his embarrassment—"should be waiting for me."

"I was told to expect you, sir." By virtue of his training, perhaps, the man's face suddenly lost all expression, and in memorized tones he instructed, "Please take the elevator to the third floor. It's room 308. At the end of the corridor."

He passed through a space that in appearance served only as a reception room and got into the elevator. The man at the front desk, who was watching his movements, was suddenly transformed in Suguro's eyes into the young man at the school for handicapped children who claimed to be a fan of his novels.

The elevator climbed past the second floor and stopped at the third. His first sensation was the dusty smell of the carpet. He walked down the corridor.

It was silent.

He walked past 306 and 307, and tapped at the door of 308.

"It's open."

She was waiting for him. She was wearing a cashmere sweater and lay stretched out on a sofa, smoking a cigarette. A silver rhinestone broach gleamed on her sweater. It was the first time Suguro had seen her smoke.

"I knew you'd come." She put out her cigarette and stood up.

He decided he had better drum up some sort of response. "Yes. I'm here to meet my double," he managed to croak.

"Would you like to take a look in the next room?" She wasted no time telling him what he wanted to know. "This is a suite of rooms."

She raised a finger slightly and indicated the door to the neighboring room. Room 308 led into the bedroom.

The first thing he saw when he poked his head through the door was a large bed. A doll-like figure dressed in a sweater and jeans lay prone on the bed. Unwashed hair hung down over the girl's face, which still maintained its innocence. It was Mitsu who lay there deep asleep.

"What is this? Why is she here?" There was surprise in Suguro's voice. He felt as though he had fallen into a trap that Madame Naruse had set. "You said you'd introduce me to the impostor . . ."

"Yes. He should be here shortly."

"Send Mitsu home before he arrives. Please get her out of here."

She smiled, her eyes glued to him. The smile was a blend of sympathy and impishness, as if to tell the little child in front of her that he was talking nonsense.

"She had a little to drink here. She seemed to be drinking

226

with great relish, so she's hardly in any condition to go home at the moment."

"What have you done to her?"

"Not a thing. While we were waiting for you to come, we watched TV and sang some songs . . . and I told her stories of when I was a young girl."

"Why did you bring Mitsu here?" He spoke accusingly, knowing that his mounting anger made his voice thick. "Outwardly she looks like an adult, but she's still a child. She doesn't know anything. She has a really gentle disposition. Whenever someone has a problem, she'll help them out even if it gets her in trouble. That's the kind of girl she is. . . . That's why she wasn't suspicious of you."

"I know that." Madame Naruse smiled and nodded. "I often saw her at the hospital working her heart out to help an old man who was sick."

"When I had a fever she stayed up all night and looked after me."

He thought of her smile and the hand on his forehead that night.

"But . . ." This time her face was serious. "Is it only love we feel toward these lovable creatures? Is affection the only emotion we feel toward those who are naïveté personified? Since you're a writer, I'm sure you understand what I'm saying."

Abruptly, a look brimming with sorrow spread across her face. "I don't think the human heart is all that simple. . . . Sensei, were courtesy and compassion the only feelings you ever had toward Mitsu?"

She had struck a sore spot, and not certain how he should answer, Suguro retorted, "Is that why you asked me here, to get some evidence of that?"

227

"There are many women around who left their husbands because the men were too nice. Everyone has had the experience of wanting to hurt someone who is too good and too innocent." She was on the offensive now. "Could I ask you one thing?"

"I already know what it is you want to ask."

He purposely avoided the question, but she plunged ahead.

"This Jesus you believe in . . . I wonder if he was murdered because he was too innocent, too pure."

"What are you driving at?"

"As Jesus, bathed in blood, carried his cross to the execution ground, the crowds reviled him and threw stones at him. Don't you think they did that because of the pleasure it gave them, the pleasure I'm always trying to describe to you? A naïve, pure human being is suffering right before their eyes. Can't we assume that it was the pleasure of heaping further indignities on such a person that consumed the mobs that day? Jesus was too blameless, too unblemished . . . so much so that we wanted to destroy him. . . . That feeling is shared by all of us. It inhabits the depths of our hearts. But no one wants to stare it in the face. That's how you've felt for many years, Sensei. Even in your novels . . . in reality all you've written about are men who have betrayed Jesus but then weep tears of regret after the cock crows three times. You've always avoided writing about the mob, intoxicated with pleasure as they hurled stones at him."

"There are things a novelist can't bring himself to write about."

"That's a neat evasion." She opened her dauntless eyes even wider. Then, contemptuous of Suguro: "Today just happens to be Friday the thirteenth, the day Jesus was executed. The day the mobs stoned Jesus. That's why I picked this day to invite you to this hotel." She smiled thinly. "I apologize. But I'm serious about this."

"And you tricked me into coming here by telling me I'd be able to meet the impostor."

"You'll be meeting him very soon," she said lightly.

"Where?"

"In the next room."

He started toward the door.

"You can't go in now." She stopped him. "He'll be angry if you go in without warning. In there . . ." She raised one hand and pointed to a door facing the bathroom. "There's a closet with clothes hanging in it. It has a peephole where you can see into the bedroom."

"A peephole?"

"Yes, they're all the rage at the sleaziest parlors in Shinjuku. Some of the members of this club have the same inclinations. . . . You can watch him through the peephole."

"What is he going to do to Mitsu?"

She answered softly. "I imagine he'll simply express the feelings you have toward her."

"Don't be ridiculous. I don't have any particular feelings for her."

"On the surface, perhaps. But in your unconscious."

"I don't have any improper desires toward . . ."

"Sensei, desires aren't just limited to sex. There are all kinds of desires."

"Then what kind of desire are you talking about?"

"If you watch," she said to spark his curiosity, "you'll see what I mean."

He was awash in his confused emotions. There was no question that a part of him wanted to get Mitsu out of there immediately. But he was also sorely tempted to steal a glimpse of what Madame Naruse had described as the urges in his unconscious that attracted him to this young woman.

"You need a drink," Madame Naruse suddenly muttered. She stood up and opened a cabinet at the far side of the room. Inside stood a small white refrigerator, and on the shelf above was a row of small bottles of foreign liquors. "I'll make you a cocktail."

"I won't drink it," he stated energetically. He had no further interest in responding to her enticements.

"Come now. You mustn't be afraid."

She had already chilled a glass and shaker in the refrigerator. She poured an amber-colored liquid into the glass and placed it in front of him.

"It isn't poison. I concocted it to help transport you to another realm."

He stared at the liquid. She left the room, perhaps to get something else. When he looked up, snow was gently falling outside. He stretched out his hand and brought the glass to his lips. An overpowering fragrance stung his nose. He coughed, having avoided strong drinks for a long while. But suddenly he was shaken by an urge to throw his life into utter disarray. The squeak of the doctor's chair, the voice proclaiming his levels of GOT and GPT. In anger, he gulped down all the liquid in the glass.

Heat fanned out from his throat and spread to his chest. The concoction coursed through his body, making him feel as though he had been infused with some element from a mysterious realm. The urge to take Mitsu away from this place was going numb within.

I'll take her home, he kept repeating to himself. *I'll take her home.*

230

To spur himself on he got up from the sofa and started walking toward the next room. His legs were trembling slightly. He should have been moving toward the door, but something stronger than his own volition was guiding him toward the closet.

"Just for a moment," he mumbled. "I'll only look for a moment. Once I'm satisfied, I'll take Mitsu home."

There were many hangers dangling from the pole in the closet, and the round hole in the wall was so tiny it was scarcely noticeable. He pushed the hangers aside and pressed his eye to the peephole. In that posture he became not only the author of *A Life of Christ* and *The Emissary* but the man who crouched in the same despicable hunch to indulge in the peepshows at Kabuki-chō.

A special lens had been fitted into the hole, and when he swiveled the black ring around the hole he was able to see the entire bedroom. He could make the bed itself appear larger, as though he had brought his face closer to it. There was even an earphone for a hidden listening device. Because he had not focused the lens, initially he had the impression that some white object had been placed on the bed, but when he adjusted the focus he recognized the object as Mitsu's supine body. At some point her dirty sweater and bleached jeans had been removed, along with her underwear, but she was still sleeping. Had she removed her own clothing, or had Madame Naruse done it for her?

Pale light from the nightstand shone on her childlike face. His chest ached as he looked at her. Her body was less attractive than he had imagined it in his dreams. Like other girls of her generation, she had well-developed thighs, but her legs were stumpy and ill-shaped. The light clearly illuminated the still not fully developed rise of her breasts and the chestnut-colored nipples that crowned them. Her breasts were not yet those of a woman—they seemed unripe, still hard at the core. There was no surplus flesh on her abdomen; her navel was a long, narrow slit like a faint indentation in the billowing rise of a sand dune. As he stared at her chestnut nipples and firm breasts, he sensed there the colors and smells of a grove of trees in early spring. It was the smell of a thicket still in bud, with no leaves yet on the branches. It was the aroma of life.

He detected no sense of "woman" or of sensuality in Mitsu's nude body. Still, her body was not that of a child. It was a body on the verge of maturation. In another six months, every part of her would take on the full-blown roundness and softness of a woman. Her dirty hair was splayed across her forehead, and her face, sleeping in utter innocence, was a child's, still bearing the marks of purity.

He kept his eye pressed against the peephole for a long while. Madame Naruse was nowhere to be seen, and there was no sign of his double. Perhaps Madame Naruse intended to let him devour Mitsu's body with his eyes until he was sated.

Studying the girl's nakedness reminded him of everything he had lost at his age. His internal organs were decrepit, their cogwheels worn smooth. The doctor had said his liver was beginning to harden. His face had become worm-eaten over the months and years. It would not be long before he left this world in the same way Kanō had. But there was hope for this innocently sleeping face and these swelling breasts that were not yet fully formed. If he pressed his face to the warm rise of her chest, he was sure it would smell like apples. That was an aroma he could never elicit from a woman whose breasts combined ripeness with the shadows of deterioration.

Suguro was impelled by an urge to inhale the aroma of Mitsu's breasts. If he could breathe it in, he felt as though strength, a new vitality, would be brought back into his decaying mind and body.

Music began to play from somewhere. It was a Mozart piano concerto. If he were granted another life to live, he wanted to savor such music again. It had never been repose, but the stench of death, that had flowed through the catacombs of his heart. For no reason, he suddenly thought of the sloping hills on the Shimabara peninsula, where he had traveled with his wife, and then of the winter sun glistening in the harbor, and finally of the gentle eyes and smile of the old priest. If that priest had been able to see Mitsu's body, he would not have felt this same envy. For the priest was fully confident that he would be passing on to a more abundant life.

Madame Naruse appeared from the bathroom in the next suite. He did not know whether she was conscious of his gaze through the peephole, but she seemed to ignore him as she sat down beside Mitsu on the bed and gently began to stroke her hair. Her fingers moved assiduously, like a mother combing her daughter's hair. Mitsu eventually woke up and looked sleepy-eyed at Madame Naruse, smiling when she recognized her. Her smile brimmed with the affability and simplicity that were Mitsu's special province. Madame Naruse said something, but Suguro could not hear it. He hurriedly plugged the earphone into his ear and turned up the volume.

"You got drunk, didn't you? You've slept an awfully long time." She showered Mitsu with a smile filled with affection, as though she were talking to one of the children at the hospital. "If you're still tired, you can sleep as long as you want."

Mitsu noticed that she was naked, and drew up her legs.

"I undressed you. It's more comfortable that way when you're drunk. It's all right, there's nothing to worry about. Relax and leave everything to me. . . . Think of me as your mother."

As she spoke, she continued her stroking movements, slowly, monotonously. While her supple fingers softly massaged Mitsu's head, the girl closed her eyes.

"That's right, close your eyes. . . . Little by little you'll start to relax. You'll relax, and you'll start to feel like you're sliding down a long, long, slippery slide. It feels so good to relax. You're falling down the slide, and it feels so good. . . ."

Suguro tensed and caught his breath. The way she spoke, repeating the same words over and over in the same tone of voice, was very much how you put someone under hypnosis.

In fact, Mitsu's tiny head was no longer moving. She lay there silent, like an insect that has struggled in a spider's web and finally exhausted all its strength.

As if to report that all preparations had been completed, Madame Naruse glanced toward the peephole. She seemed to be announcing to Suguro, "This is how we started everything with Motoko."

Suguro was still in a daze from the heady intoxication and the bizarre scene he was witnessing through the peephole.

Again he tensed up. As he wandered uncertainly between abstraction and daydream, Madame Naruse disappeared from the room, and from the rear he saw someone else hovering over Mitsu. It was a man's back, and below the left shoulder blade it bore the blackish line of a large, crescent-shaped scar. Suguro had had an operation on his chest many years before, and this was unquestionably his back.

It was the man. Just as Madame Naruse had said, he had come into the bedroom, and now he was gawking at Mitsu's body.

"Sensei." Mitsu opened her eyes a slit and spoke in a thick voice. "What's wrong, Sensei?"

Still not completely roused from her hypnotic state, she seemed not to understand why this man was looking down at her.

With the palms of his hands, the man stroked the conical swellings of her breasts over and over again. It was evident that he was slowly absorbing in his hands the softness and resiliency of her breasts. His palms journeyed back and forth between her breasts and the small gray evening shadows between her legs. Then he pressed his face lovingly into the tiny slit of her navel.

"Ahh." Suguro moaned involuntarily.

The sensations that the man was experiencing were communicated undiluted to Suguro. A face that was identical to his own in every respect was buried in the girl's abdomen. It was as if he were pressing his face into a futon that had dried in the sun—a smell of sand, the soft touch of her skin . . . He shut his eyes and listened carefully to the sound that emanated from her body. Was it the sound of blood coursing through her veins? The thump of her heartbeat? In a village once in early spring he had heard the same sound. It was not an actual sound, but the echo of every tree in the forest inhaling life from the universe, expanding, budding, and straining to send forth young red shoots. If life itself has a sound, it was reverberating now from this girl's fresh young body.

When he listened more carefully, he realized that a wealth of melodies were incorporated within that sound. Those melodies summoned forth reminiscences, memories, and images in Suguro's mind. He recalled his feelings of security as a child when he had walked with his mother along a path where the spirea had formed a tunnel overhead. The face of the young woman who had looked up at him to say "Yes" when he had asked, "Will you marry me?" The old priest who had intoned the words from the Bible: "Blessed are the meek." Mitsu's voice at his ear the night she had said, "Don't worry, Sensei. I'll take care of you." These were among the good and beautiful melodies he had sought out during his lifetime.

Suguro wanted to breathe in these sounds of life. He wanted to suck this life into his own body. At some point he became one with the man, and his own mouth was buried in Mitsu's abdomen. He sucked her belly, moved his mouth and sucked around her breasts, sucked her neck, and as Madame Naruse had done, he tried to transfer Mitsu's life into his own body, his old, wrinkled, stain-splotched body. A body devoid of life, blemished like a withered leaf that insects have gnawed upon. In an effort to save his body, he had become like a spider that seizes a butterfly in its web, and he sought to drain the vitality from Mitsu's body. His saliva gleamed like slug trails along her stomach and breasts. He wanted to taint her body even further. He felt the envy that one near death feels toward one in whom life burgeons. That jealousy flowed into plea-sure and burst into flames as his mouth roamed her body, and before he knew what was happening his hands had tightened around her throat. At that moment he heard inside himself a sound different from the one he had heard before.

*   *   *

It was ringing. A telephone, summoning him from the distance, was ringing. Again and again it rang, incessantly pursuing him, calling "The other you," "The other you," "The other you. You who set fire to the huts of women and children. You who cast stones at the frail, bloodied man who bore a cross. You who wrote the words 'Sensei, sometimes I horrify myself. I am repelled by myself.' "

"Sensei, you're hurting me!" Mitsu writhed, her eyes crinkled in pain. "Stop it, Sensei!"

It was the same voice that had whispered, "Don't worry, Sensei. I'll take care of you."

He came to his senses like one who comes to after being unconscious. Sweat had dripped from his forehead to his throat, a clear reminder of what he had just been trying to do. He had been trying to strangle a young woman with both his hands. He had been swept into an eddy of chaotic impulses far more complex than simple envy of her youthful body. The force of the swirling eddy had been intense, irresistible, and all too pleasurable. What had rescued him from that force?

The man stood up and looked behind him. He glanced back, and a condescending, mocking smile played on his lips. His cheeks were glazed with saliva, his sparse, white-flecked hair was in disarray, and he was bathed in sweat. This was the portrait of Suguro that Motoko had painted. He slipped out of the bedroom.

Exhaustion overtook his body, and Suguro leaned his head back against the wall. When he tried to leave the darkened space, his legs wobbled and his head bumped against the hangers, knocking a couple to the floor. His legs still heavy, he staggered into the bedroom.

Mitsu was stretched out on the bed like a corpse. Suguro averted his eyes, and like a criminal trying to cover up his misdeeds, he picked up a blanket from the floor and put it over her. Mitsu's sweater and bleached jeans were lying neatly folded on a chair. The careful manner in which her clothes had been folded reminded him of Madame Naruse, but she had not returned, and he had no idea where she was.

He stood by the drawn curtains of the window, not knowing what he should do. He was afraid to speak to Mitsu. Uncertain how she would react to him after what he had done to her, he waited in turmoil for her to make a move.

Eventually her eyes opened and she looked around absently, as though she had no idea what had occurred. When she caught a glimpse of Suguro, she seemed to recognize him, and she grinned.

"What's happened to me?"

He groped for a response, wondering if she was attempting to lead him on. But her expression was all too friendly.

"Don't you know? You had too much to drink."

"My head hurts. What happened to Mrs. Naruse?"

"I don't know. She may have left. That's why I came for you."

"Thank you, Sensei."

"No, not 'thank you.' You're supposed to be 'happified,' aren't you?"

Mitsu beamed. Her smile tormented him.

"Don't you remember . . . anything?"

"Nothing."

"Didn't you dream anything?"

"Maybe . . . I can't remember."

Suguro realized there was not a trace of saliva on her cheeks or her neck. But he was certain as he had watched through the peephole, thanks to the magnifying lens, that he had seen lines of saliva, like slug trails, glistening on her body.

Had it been an illusion? No, it couldn't have been. It was all too clear and vivid in his memory. He could no longer call it an illusion, as he had at the awards ceremony and in the lecture hall.

"I'm still groggy."

"Then sleep a little longer."

She fell back asleep almost at once. Suguro listened to the healthy sound of her breathing as she slept, the breath of young life, of one not tormented by the dark dreams he saw at night. One person moving into life, one into death. Suguro had never sensed the contrast as starkly as he did now, listening to her breathing.

He stepped over to the window and parted the curtains. Snow had accumulated on the sill, and the light from the room bounced off the innumerable dancing flakes.

Half an hour later he shook Mitsu again and told her to get dressed. When he turned his back, she put on her jeans and slipped her dirty sweater over her head.

They went out into the deserted corridor and got into the creaky elevator.

"It seems that I did have a dream," she muttered to herself as though she had just remembered. Suguro did not respond.

"I feel as if I saw your face over and over again in the dream. I wonder why."

The sound of typing continued to echo from behind the

front desk. The clerk intentionally did not turn to look at them as Suguro put his arm around the girl and escorted her outside. Suguro had wanted the man to call a taxi, but the wish faded as soon as he had a look at the back of the all-knowing clerk.

"We're close to the main road. We'll get a cab there." He tried to give her his muffler.

She shook her head. "I don't need it. I'm young. When a man your age catches cold, you become like you did a while back."

Snow was falling from the Himalayan cedars. They walked slowly, trying not to slip in the icy tire tracks. As they went out through the gate, a light flashed in their faces. It was not the headlights of a taxi.

"Sensei. Mr. Suguro!" Kobari was standing there, holding a camera in his hands. "What were you doing at this hotel?"

Suguro could not answer.

"Then you are . . . just what I thought you are. When this photo is developed, it'll reveal everything."

Suguro stared vacantly at the man, but he quickly came to his senses and, drawing his arm tighter around Mitsu's shoulders, walked away.

"Is this what you're doing on the sly? Even though you pass yourself off as a Christian writer?"

Kobari's piercing words struck the back of Suguro's head like stones. But he made no attempt to turn his head to explain or rectify the situation.

"Who's the girl? She looks pretty young!"

Not wanting Mitsu to hear Kobari's taunts, Suguro waved his hand at a taxi that was racing toward them. When the door opened, he pushed her inside, drew two or three bills from his wallet, and placed them on her lap.

"You go home by yourself. I want to talk to this man."

When the taxi sped off, he turned toward Harajuku and started walking.

"I'm going to write about you. About you and your scandal. You understand?"

Strangely the words summoned forth no uneasiness or fear from Suguro. *If he wants to regard this as a scandal, that's fine.* What Suguro had seen through the peephole had been no illusion, no nightmare. The impostor who had befouled Mitsu's body with saliva—that had been no stranger, no pretender. It had been Suguro himself. It had been another side of himself, a separate self altogether. He could no longer conceal that part of himself, no longer deny its existence.

"Aren't you embarrassed? You've . . ."

Kobari's shouts continued to echo through the snow, but the voice sounded now like a whistle blowing faintly through a distant fog.

The snow fluttered down. As he walked distractedly toward Sendagaya, the snow skittered across his thin hair and crinkled face, then vanished, melting as it touched him. Automobiles cast their lights upon him, then passed by, kicking up mud and snow. How was he to deal with everything he witnessed? How was he to consolidate the emotions that had overwhelmed him? His head was still a mass of confusion.

"Filth," he said aloud. "The very picture of filth."

The man's foul, dirty smile, and the way he had climbed like an animal on top of Mitsu, had been the epitome of filthiness. That man—no, "that man" was none other than Suguro himself. If the man was filthy, it was a filthiness hidden inside Suguro like a tumor. During his long writing career, Suguro had always felt that a token of salvation

could be discerned within every base act of man. He had
believed that a rejuvenating energy beat faintly within every
sin. It was for that reason that he had been able to believe,
however shakily, that he was a Christian. But after today
he had to accept this filthiness as a part of himself. He had
to begin searching for evidence of salvation even within this
filthiness.

But he had no idea how to go about it. He did not know
how to cope with his confusion. There could be no doubt
that a darkness he had never depicted in his fiction was concealed inside his own heart. Normally, that darkness remained dormant, but under certain conditions it suddenly
opened its eyes and began to move.

At this realization, he called out like a madman. From
behind, a taxi picked him up in its headlights and slowed
down briefly, but when he did not turn toward it the driver
raced off.

The streetlights caught the snowflakes that swirled like
dancing dwarfs. Suguro suddenly noticed someone walking
just as he was some fifty meters ahead of him. The slump
of the back looked familiar. He stopped walking for a moment and caught his breath when he realized it was his own
back. It was that man.

The man did not turn his way, but kept walking intently toward Sendagaya. A multitude of white flecks hit
by the streetlights whirled ahead of him. The thin flakes of
snow seemed to emit a profound light. The light was
filled with love and compassion, and with a maternal tenderness it seemed to envelop the figure of the man. His image
vanished.

Suguro felt a rush of vertigo. He peered into the space
where the man had disappeared. The light increased in intensity and began to wrap itself around Suguro. Within its

rays, the snowflakes sparkled silver as they brushed his face, stroked his cheeks, and melted on his shoulders.

"O Lord, have mercy." The words fell from his lips. "Have mercy on us whose minds are deranged."

It was a vaguely recollected verse by Baudelaire. He may have gotten the words wrong, but it didn't matter. This verse alone adequately described his feelings at that moment. "In the eyes of Thou who knowest why we exist and why were were created—are we monsters?"

CHAPTER
NINE

THE MUDDY SLUSH that had lingered in the shade until two days before had finally melted away in the bright sun. In the living room, with the sounds of his wife's vacuum cleaner humming in his ears, Suguro sorted through the mail that had just been delivered.

"I'm certainly a fickle one. On icy cold days, I get so depressed, wondering if the weather's going to stay like that forever. But when it turns warm like this, I completely forget that there's anything wrong with my knees."

"You don't have any real problems with your insides like I do. You'll live a long time."

"Will you be working here all day?"

"I've got a PEN Club meeting in the afternoon."

"The PEN Club." Her face clouded. "I can't help thinking of poor Kanō when you mention it."

"I know what you mean. The last time I saw him was right after the executive meeting."

His conversations with his wife were as unchanging as ever. The dialogues between husband and wife never varied. Suguro wondered how long the mascarade would continue. Just how would he explain things to his wife when Kobari peddled his photograph to some magazine and the whole affair was exposed to the public?

He had, of course, resigned himself to that eventuality. And he had the sentimental notion that his wife would forgive him in the end. But it grieved him deeply to think of the shock, the painful hurt, and the torment he would have to watch his wife endure. What words could he possibly utter to her then?

"The other day at my volunteer meeting I heard a strange story. It has to do with terminal-care patients."

He stiffened, but pretended to be looking through the mail. He was concerned that perhaps his wife had talked with Madame Naruse.

"The head nurse came to our meeting. She said there've been several people at the hospital who started to die and then came back to life."

"Is that possible?"

"She said all of them had been through very similar experiences. Just before death, they suffer severe pain, but suddenly they distinctly feel themselves being separated from their bodies. And they can see members of their family standing around their body weeping, and the doctor in the room listening for their heartbeat."

"I can't imagine it." He smiled, feeling rather foolish. He had heard such stories many times before. Most likely these patients had confused their actual experience with flights of imagination that had come to them after their return to life.

"After that, though, they said they were shrouded in an indescribable orange light. They could feel themselves being embraced by this light. They described it as a very gentle light."

He was silent. He thought of the light he had seen through the snow. An orange light. When it had surrounded him, he had felt an inexpressible sense of peace. But he could not bring himself to mention his own experience to his wife.

"One of the women who was restored to life said she knew for certain while she was within the light that she was deeply, deeply loved."

"By whom?"

"By God, who dwelt within the light."

"Did you run into Mrs. Naruse?"

"No. She hasn't come to the hospital for a long time."

He selected the important items from the mail and went into his study. The small clock ticked softly, and the pencils and ballpoint pens in their holder patiently awaited his arrival. He sat down in front of the desk. This was the only place where he could uncover the face he had shown to no other living soul.

He took out some stationery embossed with his name and address and began to write a letter to Madame Naruse.

> Since you slipped away that night without my noticing, I wasn't able to convey my impressions of the experience to you. That is why I'm writing this letter. In one sense, I want to try to collect my confused thoughts by committing them to paper. Most certainly you wanted me to . . .

He wrote briefly with his pen, read over the words, and tore up the paper. There was no way he could bring order to the chaos in his mind by writing a letter. He took out another piece of stationery and once again sank into reverie. He needed to disgorge these thoughts in one form or another.

Dear Kanō, (*In place of Madame Naruse's name, he penned in the name of his deceased friend.*)

I have no idea where you are now. But wherever it is, I will be joining you there soon. That's why I'm writing you this letter that can never be mailed.

I would never have guessed that growing old would be like this. When I was young, when we used to get together at Meguro to talk, and later in my prime, I had a kind of inner optimism, and I believed that when I got old I'd be standing on top of a hill at last, looking peacefully down at the plains gently lit by the afternoon sun. At the very least I assumed that I'd derive something very much like certitude from my own life and from my writing.

But this winter, as I've gradually begun to hear the footsteps of approaching death, I've found out for myself what it really means to grow old. Old age doesn't mean being free from perplexity as Confucius claimed; there's nothing serene or mellow about it. To me, at least, it has loomed up in ugly, nightmarish images. With death staring me in the face, I can no longer prevaricate, and there is nowhere to escape.

Growing old, I have come to see sides of myself I never knew existed start to expose themselves. That hidden self began to appear in my dreams, then in phantom visions, and finally as the impostor you worried so much about— but no, it was not an impostor; it began to live inside me as a separate part of myself. It was my living ghost, a creature so foul I could never mention him to my wife. It was a creature unworthy of the sumptuous praise you heaped upon me the night of the awards ceremony.

I read somewhere long ago that in our youth we live through our bodies; in our prime we live through our intellect; and in our old age we live through our minds as they prepare for the journey to the next life. And they say that the older we get, the more sensitive our minds grow to the shadows of that looming world. Does this mean that the filthy landscape that stretches before my eyes is part of my preparation, my rite of passage, into the life to come? What's the lesson that this realm of filth is trying to teach me? I don't have the faintest idea. My only feeble hope is that the light will embrace even that murky realm.

Just before you died, I saw extraordinary weariness in your back. Is it possible, even though you never confessed it to me, that you felt this same confusion, that you were thrust into this same pit of uncertainty and struggled there? At the wake I saw shadows of torment between your brows. What were they?

That afternoon he went to T Hall and attended the PEN Club executive meeting. Unlike Kanō, he had skipped many of these meetings, but now that his friend was dead he felt an obligation to attend on Kanō's behalf. The meeting had already started, and a foreign writer who had attended the international conference in Santiago was reporting on the details of the gathering. It was hard to believe that Kanō was no longer one of the directors listening to these reports.

"In the sectional meetings, the slaughter of blacks in Johannesburg became an issue. . . . The fact of the matter is, black people are being arrested."

As he listened to the foreign writer's remarks, Suguro wondered which publisher Kobari had taken his photograph to.

Christian Writer Lures Middle-School Girl to Hotel. He could almost see the headline. What sort of expression could he expect to see on the faces of the other PEN directors if such a story appeared next week? Would they feign ignorance, or would they urge him to resign from the committee?

"A resolution opposing the tortures and massacres was introduced. . . . We would very much like to have Japan's support for that resolution . . . "

Suguro thought of the lovemaking that had taken place between Madame Naruse and her husband. Was he any different from them and the murders in which they had participated? The same lusts lurked inside himself. Who was to say that he did not possess the same potential for slaughter? Even guileless children bore within their hearts the desire to taunt and torment the weak and the defenseless. In various parts of Japan, children lynched their frail classmates.

"Mr. Suguro, are you opposed to the motion?"

The question caught him unawares and he stammered in confusion. "Opposed to what?"

"If you're in favor, would you please raise your hand?"

"Certainly." He raised his hand, all the while muttering to himself, "Hypocrite. You're still trying to live by deceiving others and deceiving yourself." He stood up and left the room, making it appear that he was going to the rest room. In the lavatory he splashed water on his face. A gray, tired face stared back at him from the mirror.

"We haven't had any of those telephone calls lately."

His wife, dressed in a negligee, had crawled into bed and was stretching out her arm to turn off the lamp when she had a sudden thought and made the observation.

"What telephone calls?" he asked.

"The calls in the middle of the night."

Suguro closed his eyes. "They may start up again."

She did not reply, and in less than five minutes he heard the soft, regular breathing that meant she was asleep. Her breathing was like the rhythm of a world into which Suguro could not enter. When she died she would probably take her final breath as though she were lapsing into sleep.

As always he had considerable difficulty getting to sleep. White flecks danced against the back of his eyelids. Those white spots blurred and spread out to become a light. An orange light that enfolded the snow and took him into its embrace as well—what had it been? Had he hallucinated a glimmer of light that had been formed from the innumerable flakes of snow? He fell asleep.

In his dream, he was hunched over his desk doing his work in his dark study. The clock on the desk ticked regularly. This was his only refuge.

"It's true!" He could hear his wife's voice somewhere. "You like it there better than you like being with me!"

He stood up and tried to open the door, intending to contradict her remark. So she had known the secrets of his heart after all.

"Don't be ridiculous."

The door was tightly shut, and even though he pushed against it with all his weight, its sturdy thickness rebuffed him.

"You can stay in there. I'm not mad at you. No, it's true. After all, you're inside your mother's stomach. As long as you're in there, you can feel at ease."

Her words brought home to him the realization that this room was in fact his mother's womb. Perhaps he had always known that. What he had always thought was the tick of his clock turned out to be his own heartbeat; the room was dark

251

because he was inside her uterus, and the dampness was due to the amniotic fluid. He felt once again like a child bobbing in the ocean, drifting on his back in a life-preserver. And he remembered floating in the amniotic fluid and sleeping for a long, long while beneath the surface of the milky liquid. Basking with his entire body in these feelings of pleasure and protection, again he dropped off to sleep. He remained in that state for a while, until suddenly he heard his wife's voice again.

"Wake up! Please wake up!"

There was an uncharacteristic urgency in her voice, an intensity he had never heard before.

"You're going to be born now. You're going to be pushed into the outside world."

His body still felt exquisitely languid, and he did not want to budge. But the fluids in the sac were beginning to sweep across his body with a powerful force. The pressure of the surging fluid mounted, and an inexpressible fear of drowning overcame him.

"Wake up and head for the exit!" he heard his wife shout. "Come outside. If you stay in there, you'll be still-born."

He shivered with fear. He thrashed, he defecated, and, soiled with his own wastes, he desperately thrust his head toward the cervical opening. Even then he struggled between a desire to return to the deep sleep he had enjoyed in the womb and the will to fight off that seductive pull. Some power tugged at his leg, attempting to pull him back into his uterine sleep, while a separate force was trying to push him out.

"What's wrong?"

He opened his eyes.

"You're shouting. What's the matter?"

"It's nothing." His neck was soaked with perspiration. "So it was a dream?"

"You scared me. Would you like some water?"

"No. No, thank you."

The dream lingered vividly in his memory. The feelings of fear and floundering revived within him, and he almost thought he could see the light shining through the cervical opening.

Is that really what it's like being born into the world, just the way Tōno had described it? Do we really feel such dread in the womb? Maybe some of Tōno's remarks had colored the content of his dream.

The deep sleep within the amniotic fluid. A sleep that engenders incomparable feelings of peace and pleasure. Suguro could fully understand the desire to return there once one had been expelled. It explained why he had enjoyed such contentment as he labored each day in his dark study, listening to the ticking of the clock. Did the thirst to plunge back into that sleep, that pleasure, reside in the heart of every man?

Then, in a flash of revelation, he thought of the look on Motoko's face. Her mouth half-open, her tongue thrashing about. The look of utter rapture. That look expressed—no, epitomized—the yearning to return to the womb and drown in its muddied fluids. *Was that why she had wanted to be tainted by the drops of wax, the way she would have been polluted by the waters of the uterus? And knowing that death is stalking me, have I been reexperiencing the terrors of the womb? Did the struggle between the desire to stay peacefully somnambulent in the womb and my urge to leave it manifest itself in the way I tried to strangle Mitsu? First when we exit the womb, again when we grow old and leave this world—twice we taste death. . . .*

But the light he had seen, which seemed to welcome him

as he emerged from the womb—he linked it with the light that had enveloped the myriad flakes of snow and embraced him. Was it a light that emanated from the world that lay just one step beyond him?

His wife looked up from her knitting, studied his face, and finally spoke.

"Can I . . . ask you a question?"

"What is it?"

"Are you sure there isn't something you haven't told me about?"

"Of course there . . . isn't."

"You can tell me. At my age, nothing will surprise me."

"There isn't anything. Don't worry about it."

Her eyes remained fixed on him, as if to pierce through to the workings of his heart. Eventually, though, she gave up and smiled at him. Over the space of years, she had accepted the fact that her husband was a novelist. She knew just how far she could enter into that life and where the boundaries were that she could not cross. Though she could not have inferred anything concrete from his eyes, she seemed to have already determined that something had been tormenting him this winter.

Unexpectedly Suguro felt that his wife had been unhappy, truly unhappy. Like medicine, he swallowed the confession that rose involuntarily to his throat. Nothing could come of telling her what he had been through. It was a complicated situation that she could do nothing about, a thorny problem that had been thrust upon him to deal with, not only as a writer but as a human being. She would learn everything if that photograph was ever made public. In that eventuality, how would he explain it all to her? The thought cast dark shadows over his mind.

* * *

He had a call from Kurimoto.

"Are you free at all today?"

"Is it about my manuscript?"

"No." There was tension in Kurimoto's voice. "The president would like to meet with you right away. When would be convenient for you?"

"The president?" Intuitively he knew what the subject would be. "Any time today would be fine. I have an appointment in the area, so I'll drop by his office."

With thoughts of the president's massive body and broad face, he hung up the receiver. The current head of the publishing firm had been an assistant professor at a university medical school, but when his father-in-law, a mainstay of the publishing world, collapsed with a stroke, he had assumed a position of leadership in this unfamiliar industry. Kurimoto and the other young employees of the firm had considerable respect for the man.

Over the past two weeks, Suguro had steeled himself for such an encounter, and after he hung up the telephone his mind was strangely at peace. He changed his clothes and phoned for a taxi.

Apparently they had already been given their orders at the reception desk. A woman from the secretarial pool came out to meet him, bowed her head politely, and escorted him to the elevator. She deposited him in a spacious room, again bowed her head, and withdrew.

Suguro sat down on the sofa and gazed at the large Rouault painting on the wall. It was perhaps some village in biblical times, or possibly a rural scene in France. Three or four peasant women, their heads veiled with scarves, stood in a road that was flanked on either side by shabby huts with peeling stucco. It was a typical Rouault, with the evening sun setting on the horizon. At a glance, it was evident to Suguro that the women and their huts represented human life, and the sun symbolized the grace of God that poured down on them. *Blessed are the meek, for they* . . . Suguro saw the world of the old padre and his own wife in the painting, but it was far removed from the other world he had glimpsed through the peephole. The rays of the setting sun may have shone upon these humble peasant women, but upon Madame Naruse and himself?

There was a knock at the door, and the president came into the room along with Hoshii, a senior editor. The president gestured to prevent Suguro from getting up and sat down directly in front of him. Hoshii sat deferentially beside the president.

"I'm sorry to ask you to come here on such a cold day."

With a smile the president talked about the current publishing slump until a woman had brought in tea and left the room. When the three were finally alone, however, he launched into the discussion.

"To be candid, the reason I asked you to come . . . "

It was precisely as Suguro had imagined.

"This reporter brought a photograph of you, Sensei . . . and said he wanted to do a story. Hoshii here spoke to him first, but the situation being what it is, he came to talk it over with me."

He rested his thick, entwined hands on his lap and purposely looked down to avoid seeing Suguro's discomfort. But Suguro listened to his comments with an attitude of resignation similar to his feelings of many years earlier when he was informed that he needed massive surgery.

"Our firm has published quite a few of your books, and since such a photograph would reflect badly both on you and on us, I purchased the photograph and the negative at the price he demanded."

Not knowing how else to respond, Suguro simply nodded.

"I also extracted a promise from him that he would not take this story to any other publisher. Then Hoshii and I burned the photo and the negative."

There the president paused and rubbed his hands together. He seemed to be searching for his next remarks.

"I think that has settled the matter."

"Thank you."

"Aside from Hoshii and myself, no one else knows about this—not even Kurimoto."

"All right. I'm sorry . . . for all the trouble." He bowed his head deeply.

"Ridiculous rumors can stir up a hell of a mess," said the president, concluding that topic of conversation. After a couple of minutes of idle chat, he stood up and said, "Well then, let's forget this whole thing." With warm solicitude, he was doing everything he could to avoid causing Suguro any further embarrassment.

They walked with Suguro to the elevator, where Hoshii muttered, "Don't let any of this worry you."

It was cold outside. Although spring was at hand, the sky was dull and overcast. It was a lifeless, bone-chilling afternoon. He thought of how painful his wife's joints must be. Lines of automobiles spewing out exhaust fumes, trees along the promenade still holding back their buds, bargain sales for kerosene and electric heaters—everything was back to normal. He had not even imagined that matters would end in this fashion, and yet he did not feel in any sense that he had been rescued. The photograph and negative had been reduced to ashes. But that man had not been burned to death along with them. With his sneering smile, he continued to live inside Suguro.

The man had long since moved beyond the trivial "sins" that Suguro had spent his career writing about. There are limitations to sin and its concomitant potential for salvation. But there were no bounds to the impulses that Suguro, fused with that man, had experienced at the hotel. With a rage that had spilled out unrestrained, driving him toward an inexorable destination, he had defiled Mitsu's body and ultimately had even attempted to strangle her. The images were vivid in his memory.

As he passed a flower shop, clusters of spirea and forsythia, which heralded the approach of spring, adorned the interior and sent a sweet aroma out to the street. Through the large glass window of a tearoom next door, he saw a cheerful group of three or four young women seated around a table. One of them noticed Suguro and pointed him out to her neighbor, not even knowing he was a monster. Suguro smiled back at them.

Sunday.

As it was the Sunday after Easter, the church was more crowded than usual. Beyond the altar, the emaciated man spread his arms wide, and his head drooped. Powerless to resist and soaked in blood, he had dragged his weary legs toward the execution ground. Along the way, the crowds had jeered at him, hurled stones at him, and reveled in his torments. Suguro had not given any thought to that mob before. But he could not be at all certain that, had he been present, he would not have stoned the man and taken delight in his agony.

He went to his office in the afternoon, and then to Yoyogi Park to search for Mitsu. The same groups of young women in Korean skirts were gathered in circles and dancing. Young men in sunglasses, their hair bleached blond and teased into coxcombs, strutted up and down the street. The onlookers were so numerous that some had assembled on the pedestrian overpass to witness these bizarre gyrations. He walked through the crowd and threaded his way among the street stalls, but he could not find Mitsu anywhere.

It occurred to him that she might be at the hospital. Walking there seemed too much trouble, a factor of age, perhaps, and he picked up a taxi at the train station. They traveled a circuitous route, until Suguro finally got out near the hospital.

Because it was Sunday, there were no patients or visitors in front of the pharmacy or in the waiting room. He sat for a while in a chair, staring distractedly at the wintry sun. Somewhere he heard an infant cry. He thought perhaps the sound came from the pediatric ward, but it was on a different floor.

A middle-aged nurse wearing glasses came into the lobby and stopped, glancing inquiringly at Suguro.

"Aren't you Mr. Suguro?" she asked.

"Yes."

"Are you here to see someone? I'm the head nurse, Miss Fujita."

"Oh, how do you do?" he hurriedly responded. "My wife is in your volunteer class."

"She's very enthusiastic." The nurse smiled. "May I help you with something?"

"No. I was just wondering if a girl named Morita Mitsu might be here today.

"Oh, Mit-chan. I wonder if she's come in." The head nurse seemed to know a good deal about the girl. "I understand she worked for you for a while. Would you like me to check at the nurses' station over in Internal Medicine?"

"No, I'll go myself."

She punched the elevator button for him.

"This is a strange thing to ask you about." He tried to mask the awkwardness they felt as they rode together on the elevator. "The other day my wife said you'd told the class about some patients who had returned from the dead. Do people who have lost consciousness all have the same experience?"

"Oh, good heavens!" She smiled in embarrassment. "Did your wife really tell you about that? I was just making idle conversation with them."

The elevator came to a stop on the third floor. The creaking of the gears reminded him of the elevator in the hotel.

"Are the stories true?"

"You probably know more about it than I do, Sensei. But that's what the patients claim."

"That they were surrounded in light . . . is that true?"

"Well . . ." She seemed flustered. "I really don't know if it's true or not."

"How is Mrs. Naruse doing?"

"She hasn't been in at all lately."

She made inquiries of a young nurse at the desk, but Mitsu was not in that day.

With a word of thanks, he went downstairs again. He sat down in a chair in the waiting room and thought of Madame Naruse lovingly helping with the rehabilitation of a child on the fourth floor of this building, and telling the children fairy tales.

On the wall was a poster announcing training for potential nurses. When he saw it, Suguro thought how well suited Mitsu was to such work. He decided he would like to help her out if she was interested.

He made the suggestion to his wife that evening.

"I'm all for it," she responded from the next bed. "That's a wonderful idea. It's the perfect work for Mitsu's personality. But I wonder if Mrs. Naruse will agree."

"I don't suppose she'll object."

He turned out the lamp on the nightstand.

In the middle of the night, he awoke to the sound of a telephone ringing in the distance. It jangled insistently, summoning him. Her eyes wide open, his wife heard it, too.

ABOUT THE AUTHOR

Shusaku Endo was born in Tokyo in 1923. After his parents divorced, he and his mother converted to Roman Catholicism. He received a degree in French Literature from Keio University, then studied for several years in Lyons.

Widely regarded as the leading writer in Japan, Shusaku Endo has won a series of prestigious literary awards. Other books by Shusaku Endo include *The Sea and Poison*, *Wonderful Fool*, *Silence*, *Volcano*, *When I Whistle*, *The Samurai*, and *Stained Glass Elegies*. His works have been translated into more than twenty languages.

ABOUT THE TRANSLATOR

Van C. Gessel teaches modern Japanese literature at the University of California, Berkeley. *Scandal* is the fourth of Shusaku Endo's books he has translated.

VINTAGE INTERNATIONAL is a bold new line of trade paperback books
devoted to publishing the best writing of the twentieth century
from the world over. Offering both classic and contemporary
fiction and literary nonfiction, in stylishly elegant editions,
VINTAGE INTERNATIONAL aims to introduce to a new generation
of readers world-class writing that has stood the test of time
and essential works by the preeminent
international authors of today.